THE KING'S PRISONER

THE HENCHMEN CHRONICLES

BOOK THREE

CRAIG HALLORAN

The King's Prisoner

The Henchmen Chronicles Book #3

By Craig Halloran

Copyright © 2018 by Craig Halloran

Amazon Edition

TWO-TEN BOOK PRESS

P.O. Box 4215, Charleston, WV 25364

ISBN eBook: 978-1-946218-46-9

ISBN Paperback: 978-1-793081-33-9

www.craighalloran.com

Publisher's Note

This book is a work of fiction. Names, characters, places, and incidents either are the product of the author's imagination or are used fictitiously, and any resemblance to actual persons, living or dead, events, or locales is entirely coincidental.

✻ Created with Vellum

1

Abraham stood inside the captain's quarters of the pirate ship *Sea Talon*. He and the Henchmen had acquired it after he battled the terrifying Flamebeard, a notorious pirate of great repute. That was his first official sword fight—at least, for him. The same couldn't be said for the body that his mind currently occupied. Supposedly, Ruger Slade was one of the greatest swordsmen in the world called Titanuus. Now, Abraham was him.

Clasping his hands behind his back and rolling his thumbs over each other, he looked out his windows, which gave him a full view of the churning seas. The boat rocked and swayed, and the floorboards and walls groaned. The china on his small dining table rattled and bounced. Abraham's eyes were locked on another ship much like *Sea Talon*. The ship in pursuit had sails with black stripes crossing a field of maroon. It had given chase hours before, and two more ships sailed behind it. The Henchmen were in the enemy waters of Tiotan, headed north on a bold journey.

"I never figured myself for a navy guy," Abraham said.

His words were met with silence as he was the only person in the room. The captain's cabin was dim and wall to wall with dark polished wood. Most of the other hands were on deck, keeping a close eye on the closing enemy. The boat rocked, but Abraham's feet remained steady. His new body was no stranger to the seas. It didn't seem to be a stranger to anything. Ruger Slade's body was cold and as fearless as they came.

A hard knocking came at his cabin door.

"What?" he asked with irritation.

"Permission to enter, Captain?" a grizzly-voiced man said.

Abraham turned and faced the door. "Come in, Horace."

The door creaked open, and Horace entered. He was a bald-headed and thick-bearded bear of a man, wearing a sleeveless tunic that showed off his hairy, beefy arms that hid iron muscle underneath. The buttons of his leather tunic strained to keep his belly in one place. "Captain, Lewis and Leodor are having a tantrum on deck. They have everyone confused on who they should be listening to. He's tossing his heritage around."

Abraham's nostrils flared as he breathed in deeply. Lewis and Leodor were proving to be nothing but a royal pain in his back-side. They were newly branded Henchmen, but the headstrong men had been nothing but obstinate since their sea quest began over a day before.

"Why don't you throw them overboard?" Abraham suggested.

Horace tilted his head toward Abraham and said, "Captain?"

"You know, have them walk the plank. Feed them to the sharks. Put chains on their legs and drop them to the bottom of the sea."

"Er... Aye, Captain." Horace turned around to exit the room.

"No, stop. I'll handle it." Abraham grabbed his sword belt, looped around the headboard post, and buckled it on. He ran his fingers over the leather grip of Black Bane like a gunslinger before an old western standoff.

Over one week before, zillon dragon riders from the territory of Hancha had flown across the Bay of Elders and tried to assassinate King Hector. They did it using a modern assault rifle that unleashed a dangerous hail of bullets. He managed to save the king's life. The old man was indebted, but he was determined to learn more about his enemies and their strange artifacts. He peppered Abraham with questions.

In a private group, he met with Queen Clarann, Pratt, Leodor, and Lewis. For two days, Abraham talked at length about his world. That seemed strange, but it brought him some comfort. With his help, they tried to get a handle on what they were up against. Arcayis the Underlord had made a bold move against King Hector. At least, that was where Hector laid the blame, and Abraham agreed with him. After all, Arcayis had made the threat. He followed up on it too.

King Hector vowed vengeance. He hatched a new plan: kill the Underlord. The froward viceroy, Leodor, let out a doubting laugh that drew the king's ire. King Hector busted the man across the jaw, and Leodor collapsed like a tent. Lewis laughed, but his chortling was quickly cut off by the king's glare. Abraham inwardly grinned at it all, but nothing delighted him more than the king's plan. The king wanted the head of the snake, and that line of thinking was right up Abraham's alley. It awakened the dominating spirit in him, lighting a fire under Jenkins the Jet.

Now, the original mission was askew. Originally, the king had wanted the stones from the crown found. He wanted the Crown of Stones restored. But now, he wanted his biggest threat dead: the Underlord. And the Henchmen had been sent to do it.

Abraham followed Horace up the stairs, which groaned under the weight of the hardy men. The ship pitched left, and Horace leaned into the wall of the shallow stairwell. Abraham didn't. At the top, the chill winds of the sea breeze bristled Horace's beard and Abraham's hair. Lewis and Leodor were waiting. So was

Sticks, dressed the same as always, tight leather breeches, a loose white cotton jerkin, and a bandolier of knives across her shoulder. Her short dark hair and cute expressionless face made her fetching, in simple garb and gear.

Lewis faced Abraham. He was tapping his foot and still wore the same cap and the black leather armor under his clothing. The wind kept his hair in his eyes, though he kept sweeping it away. "What is your plan, Ruger? Those Tiotan warships are gaining on us. And in case you didn't notice, there are three of them and only one of us. You need to make a decision."

"And you need to shut up," Abraham said. "And you better stop ordering my men around. The only reason they are gaining is because we're losing wind 'cause your mouth is open."

Lewis's jaws clenched, and his eyes narrowed. His fingers drummed on the handle of his sword. "You should watch your tongue."

Abraham stepped toward Lewis. They were almost the same height, but Ruger was taller and thicker in frame.

"Are you going to draw that steel or stand there tickling the handle?" Abraham asked.

2

LEWIS CAME NOSE TO NOSE WITH ABRAHAM AND SAID, "IF IT weren't for this ridiculous branding, I'd carve you up like a turkey."

"If it weren't for the brand, you'd be dead. Your own father would have hanged you," Abraham replied.

With a deepening frown, Lewis leaned back. He took his hand from the handle of his sword and said, "Someone had to take charge while you were stewing in your quarters."

"And that someone would be Horace."

Abraham brushed the hair from his eyes to take a head count of the Henchmen. The day at sea was sunny, and the scruffy fighters Apollo and Prospero were above in the crow's nest. At the front of the ship, on the foredeck, was the ebony sprite of a woman, Dominga, dressed in snug leathers. Vern was with her, geared up in his tunic and chain mail. The rest of the crew was dressed in a sailing outfit or some sort of pirate's garb.

The brothers, smoky-eyed Tark and Cudgel, searched the seas on the starboard side. The broad-faced and fierce-looking

Bearclaw worked with the new Red Tunics, brothers, Skitts and Zann, who mopped the decks. Skitts was a well-built young man with a farmer's rugged frame. Zann was lean and moved slow, smooth, and easy. Also, a few holdover pirates from Flame Beard's crew had stayed with *Sea Talon*. All the men and women stayed busy. The sweet, pie-faced mystic, Iris, was prepping meals in the galley below.

Solomon Paige, the troglin, was on board but nowhere to be found. He hadn't come on deck since they'd departed.

Abraham moved up to the poop deck and gazed at the trailing ships. Horace, Sticks, Lewis, and Leodor climbed up the steps from behind him. He set his foot on the back rail and leaned forward.

In his strong voice, he spoke over the winds. "This is what we are going to do. We'll let them catch up with us."

"Are you insane?" the flummoxed Lewis asked. "If they don't butcher us, they'll enslave us! This is how you operate? With blatant stupidity?"

"No, that's how you operate," Abraham said as he turned. "There is a reason we stripped down this ship and put merchant's sails on it. All the markings of Flame Beard are gone. It's called preparation. We knew this would happen. That's why we disguised ourselves."

No one looked much different than they normally did, but nobody else would know that.

"This is what Henchmen do." Abraham looked at Lewis and Leodor. "You should know that. After all, you are the one that put a spy in our camp."

Leodor swallowed and pulled his billowing robes closer around his frail body.

Lewis shook his head. "You'll get us all killed before we even make it past the Left Arm. We should outrun them."

"And look guilty? It only makes sense that *you* would think that way. No, if anything, we should slow down a little."

"What if one of them recognizes me?" Lewis whined. "I'm the prince, a valuable prisoner."

"Ah, that's perfect. We can use you to barter for our release if need be." Abraham nodded with enthusiasm. "I never realized that advantage until now." He laid a hand on Lewis's shoulder. "Thanks for pointing that out."

Lewis slapped Abraham's hand aside. "I hate you." He departed with Leodor.

As Horace watched the two men go, he said, "I agree with your earlier sentiment. We should toss them overboard."

Sticks nodded. "I wonder if the brand will allow us to do that. Can one Henchman turn against another?"

Abraham shrugged. He didn't have time to worry about Lewis's hurt feelings or whatever troubles the man might cause. He had three warships to worry about. "Horace, go ahead and peel back on our speed, but not too much. We'll just have to wait and see what happens."

"Aye, Captain." Horace headed off the poop deck and barked new orders to the crew.

Sticks looked at Abraham with a straight face, as hard to read as ever.

"What's on your mind?" he asked.

"Nothing."

"It doesn't look like nothing... even though it's hard to tell. Do you disagree with my plan?"

"No," she said. "We've done similar things in the past. Sometimes it works, and sometimes it doesn't."

"Do you think this won't work?"

"I don't know, but we can't outrun them."

"Thanks for nothing."

She tilted her head. "You asked."

"Just make sure that everyone is ready. Tell them to stay calm. Me and Horace will do the talking."

Sticks turned and walked away. He couldn't help but notice her walk in those tight leather breeches. Sticks had something he'd always liked, though putting his finger on it was hard. As soon as she went down the steps, Iris came hurrying up. The curvy mystic's eyes were wide and her robes disheveled.

"What's wrong?" he asked.

Iris brushed away her wavy brown locks, which had blown into her face, and said, "We have stowaways!"

3

"WHAT SORT OF STOWAWAYS?" ABRAHAM ASKED. THE LAST THINGS he wanted to see were the Frights. The strange albino, reddish-pink-eyed witches came to mind.

"I don't know. I was in the supply deck, gathering goods for cooking," Iris said as she led the way down the steps into the ship's hold. "I scooted aside some chests and barrels. That's when I saw a set of eyes looking right back at me." She stopped midway down the steps and grabbed Abraham's hand to place it right over her bosom. "Can you feel that? My heart jumps. It races." She smiled at him. "It's still racing."

"Yeah, I bet it is," he said as he pulled his hand away. "Are you sure you saw someone?"

"What I didn't see, I smelled. There are people in the hold. A bit fragrant at that, like perfume." She scuttered to the bottom of the steps and into the supply rooms, poorly lit by the ship's portals. She sniffed the air. "Do you smell that?"

Abraham's nostrils twitched, but it wasn't by any desire of his own. It was more of a reflex of Ruger's. He narrowed his eyes. The storeroom was loaded with crates and barrels. "Where?" he asked Iris.

Iris pointed toward the back of the storage room. A wall of barrels was stacked there, one upon another, and tied down with rope. Wooden crates sat waist-high on the floor.

She fastened her fingers in Abraham's pants and pressed her body behind his. "Protect me."

He couldn't tell whether she was fooling around or not. Perhaps this was a ploy to get him alone. She'd been close to Horace but always flirted with Abraham. With her tied to his rear end, he made his approach toward the back. The boat pitched hard, and some dry goods stored in the rafters fell from their perch in a storage net behind the barrels. A gasp escaped from behind the barrels.

Abraham pulled his sword. "All right. We know you are in there." He shook his head, realizing he'd used a line spoken in countless shows and movies. "Come on out. I'm serious." *I know that smell.*

No one said a word or moved. Iris's fingers started working their way across his abdomen and feeling his hard muscles. He ignored her.

"Listen, I heard your voice, and I can smell your perfume. If you won't come out, then I'll uncage the rats, the big ones that eat toes and fingers for breakfast."

A figure rose from behind the barrels. She had beautiful eyes and a rounded teardrop face. She wasn't very tall but was young and full-figured. It was Princess Clarice.

"What in the world are you doing here?" Abraham sheathed his sword.

"I'm a Henchman. I belong here." Clarice stepped out from behind the barrels, followed by two more women, taller than her, cloaked, and very pretty. "And now, I'm here."

"Are you out of your mind? Your father, King Hector, was very clear. You stay at the castle. He didn't want you going on this mission." Abraham wanted to grab the young woman and shake some sense into her. He had enough to deal with as things were. "And who are they?"

"These are my guardian maidens, Hazel and Swan." The women were attractive, in their thirties or possibly forties, stern looking with their hair pulled back tightly. They wore well-crafted, curve-enhancing breastplate armor with tight leather leggings

"Guardian maidens? Wow. They sound like a real big help." He rolled his eyes and pulled Iris's hands away from his waist. "There's your stowaways. I wish you never even found them, but you can have them. Your father must be having a fit trying to find you. Your timing couldn't be worse."

"No, I told my maidens to let them know what I did long after I'm gone. He'll have to understand. We only hid down here until you got far enough away that you couldn't turn around."

"Clever." He pointed in her face. "Don't think for one minute that I won't turn this boat around."

One of the guardian maidens sliced a dagger at his fingers, and he jerked his hand away in the nick of time. The two tall women formed a shield in front of Clarice, brandishing daggers.

"You insult the princess, dog," one of them said in a husky voice. Her hair was stone white, where the other's was pitch-black. "You must pay."

Quicker than the blink of an eye, Abraham yanked the daggers out of both of their hands and tossed them to the floor. "I'm in charge. You're trespassing."

The gaping women's hands went for their belts.

"Don't do it. I'm not in the mood."

The women dropped their hands to their sides.

"It's fine, Hazel and Swan," Clarice said as she stepped through the two guardian women. "Ruger is the Captain of the Henchmen. I'm under his orders, and you're under mine. Do whatever it is that he says. And Ruger, don't worry about my father or mother. My maidens will notify them of my whereabouts when the proper time comes."

"He'll come after you. All you are doing is putting Kingsland in jeopardy. What you did is a very selfish and stupid thing to do."

"It shouldn't surprise you, Ruger. The hierarchy rarely plays by its own rules," someone said in a chill but cocky voice that hadn't been a part of the original conversation.

Abraham found himself looking at a smallish man crammed casually on a storage shelf. The man had a strange mark on his cheek, like a star tattoo or brand. His body was wrapped up in a cloak, and a hood shielded his eyes. He bit into a small green apple, and juice squirted down the short tawny hairs on his chin.

"Who in the hell are you?" Abraham asked.

4

"Shades!" Iris exclaimed. She grabbed a potato out of a barrel and threw it at him.

The man snatched the vegetable out of the air in a fluid motion. "It's good to see you too, Iris."

"You know this guy?" Abraham asked Iris.

Her eyes were hot as flames.

"Of course she does. The curious thing is that you don't, Ruger," Shades said as he started to exit his perch.

Abraham put the tip of his dagger on the man's throat. "Be still if you don't want to start leaking." He studied the man's face. It was familiar. A lot of things were, but he didn't recall the man. Ruger probably did. "Iris, refresh my memory."

"Shades was one of us. A Henchman. You banished him from the group. He was the one that we suspected caused all of the problems," Iris said with a frown.

"What's he doing here?" he asked.

Shades opened his mouth, only to shut it again as Abraham put more pressure on his neck.

"He's with us," Clarice interjected. "Shades snuck us on the ship. He's our guide of sorts."

Abraham put his dagger away and faced Clarice. "You're full of surprises, aren't you? Now I have four stowaways. How'd your paths cross, anyway? He doesn't look like the sort of fella that you would spend time with in the castle."

"My maidens hired him. I don't know him personally. If I'd known he was a Henchman, I'd not have done it," Clarice said unapologetically.

"He's not a Henchman," Iris stated. "And he was one of the king's prisoners in Baracha." She walked up to Shades and punched him in the thigh. "That's where he tried to have us killed. All of us!"

"When did this happen?" Abraham asked.

"After we docked at Seaport. We were held in Baracha while you met with the king." Iris's fingertips started glowing. "Shades tried to make us brides to those barbaric savages, the Gond."

"I can explain all of that," Shades said.

"Sure you can, rat dung!" Iris said.

Lewis and Leodor waltzed into the storage room. Lewis had his arms crossed over his chest and said, "I saw you rush off. I wanted to see what you were..." His voice trailed off as his widening eyes landed on his half sister. "You! What are you doing here? Ruger, what treachery is this?"

"Lighten up, Lewis," Abraham said. "Your sister is a stowaway. Apparently, she misses you."

"I do not!" Clarice said like a child.

"You little brat. You snuck onto this ship for what purpose?" Lewis asked. "To continue to be a thorn in my side. It's bad enough I had to rescue you once, but now I have to take you back again. Ruger, turn the ship around."

"I'm not turning anything around," Abraham said, realizing at that moment that he was beginning to respond more easily to the name *Ruger*. "In case you have forgotten, we have three warships that we have to deal with. We'll sort this out after that."

The long-faced Leodor stepped forward, his hands hidden in his sleeves. "Ruger, I would suggest that the princess be returned immediately. She and Lewis are valued by the enemy. They'll only use them for leverage against the crown."

With the butt of his palm bouncing on the pommel of Black Bane, he said, "This mission would have been a whole lot easier if neither one of them would have come."

"Ruger, my maidens want to become Henchmen, like me," Clarice said. "Can you brand them? That way, you'll know that we all have to be loyal to the king."

"It doesn't work like that," he said. "You're supposed to earn the brand. You have to prove yourself. You"—he pointed his finger at the princess—"and these two sandbags"—he pointed at Lewis and Leodor—"didn't earn it. The brand was used to save their necks. You were given it because you have a big heart, but you're hard-headed and spoiled. The three of you are nothing but baggage on this mission. We have to work as one. None of you seems to get it." He looked down at Clarice. "Let me make this clear, little sister. No one gets branded by me until they earn it."

"What if you had a brand and lost it?" Shades said.

"Iris, what is this clown talking about?"

The mystic reached up into Shades's hood, grabbed him by the ear, and pulled him off the shelf. He landed easily on his feet. He wasn't very tall for a man.

She reached into his clothing and felt his chest and said, "His brand is gone."

"Yes, my chest started smoking suddenly, and to be frank, it scared the skin right off of me. It took some investigating on my part, but I was able to put together what happened. Apparently, my freedom was granted, but no one stopped by Baracha to tell me."

"There would be a good reason for that." Iris tried to punch him in the crotch, but Shades turned his hips and blocked her effort. "I might not get you, but once the others find out you're here, they'll handle it for me."

"I can explain," Shades said.

"I don't care," the mystic replied.

"Who is the tiny man?" Lewis asked.

"That's your baby sister's guide," Abraham said.

"Don't call me that!" Clarice said.

"Yes, please don't call her my sister," Lewis requested. "Even though I do find *baby* to be perfectly fitting."

Horace's booming voice carried throughout the galley. "Captain! The warships are coming alongside. They are signaling for us to drop anchor. What do you want us to do?"

"Just wait. I'll be up."

Horace shouted back, "They don't look like they want to wait. They look like they want a fight."

5

BEFORE ABRAHAM RUSHED TOPSIDE LIKE A CHICKEN WITH ITS HEAD cut off, he searched the lower holds for Solomon. The troglin had alluded to being very adept at hiding, and inside the bowels of a tightly quartered ship, that proved to be true.

"Solomon! Solomon! Where are you?"

"Never too far away. Never too near," the troglin said.

Abraham spun around. Solomon was squatting behind him with his neck bent over. The hairy old bigfoot, who normally stood eight feet tall, filled the narrow corridor between the storage areas.

"Are you all right?" Abraham asked.

"I have no idea. Would you be all right if you were a troglin?"

"Listen, I don't have time to discuss what you're going through. But I might need you topside. Tiotan warships are knocking at the door."

Solomon sighed as he used his long fingers to play with the long hairs underneath his chin. "I might look like a monster, but

I'm not an apt fighter. Actually, I'm more or less a coward. You know how we hippies can be. We are peaceful. Abhor violence."

"I know, and you abstain from meat. Look, no disrespect, but you're a Henchman now. The sooner you learn to let those hairy knuckles of yours get bloody, the better. It's going to be a fight if we want to get back home."

"Anything is better than this," Solomon said as he gazed upon the naked palms of his hands. "Anything."

"The triplets didn't seem to mind your company, right?"

Solomon showed some teeth. "That's true." He scratched his head. "Huh."

"Now quit moping. Just make yourself available if I call." He put a hand on Solomon's big shoulder. "We'll get through this."

"If you say so. Just give me a shout," the troglin said.

Abraham tried to pass Solomon, which made for an awkward moment as he couldn't squeeze by. "We're gonna have to have this dance later. You need to back it up."

Solomon silently maneuvered his way backward and vanished into the blackness of one of the storage rooms.

Without a second glance, Abraham headed back up on deck. His brows rose. Two warships had flanked *Sea Talon*. They cut through the waves less than a stone's throw away. Soldiers were lined up along the railing, numbering in the dozens. They wore metal skullcaps with nose guards, and the spears they carried pointed toward the sky. Their leather armor was dyed a rich maroon and trimmed in black clothing underneath the supple gear.

Sticks slid alongside and said, "So glad you could join us. What are your orders? Perhaps we add more of them to your crew, along with the others." Her eyes were on Clarice and her maidens, standing by the mainmast.

There was no sign of Shades.

"One thing at a time," Abraham said. His crew was manning their stations, not a nervous look among them, except for Lewis and Leodor, who stood near the guardian maidens.

Abraham sought out Horace, standing at the helm, and shouted up to him, "Lower the sails and drop anchor!"

Lewis marched right up to him. "We'll be dead men if they attack us."

"No, you'll be a dead man. I'm confident the rest of the Henchmen can handle it."

Lewis turned his nose and walked away.

The crew of *Sea Talon* lowered the sails, and the ship slowed. The anchor was dropped. The Tiotan warships managed to close in within a few dozen feet. Their sailors tossed the grapples across the sea and hooked *Sea Talon*'s rails. Hand over hand, the sailors pulled the warships alongside *Sea Talon*. The boat rocked when they hit. The Tiotan soldiers stood almost eye to eye with Abraham's crew. None of the men or women blinked.

"Ahoy!" a man shouted from the helm of the warship's quarterdeck on the starboard side.

From the same deck on the other warship, on the port side of *Sea Talon*, another man shouted, "Ahoy!"

Abraham sized up the two ship captains. They wore grand maroon hats, like those of old eighteenth-century admirals. Their maroon uniform shirts had many large brass buttons. The decorative shirts had black shoulder pads with tassels. Their tall black leather boots shone. The men were rangy but deep chested, with angular features, and clean shaven. They carried curved sabers on their hips. As best as Abraham could tell, they were twins.

The Tiotan captain on the starboard side spoke with strong, confident, military authority. "Who is our ship's captain?"

Abraham took his place center stage on the main deck, where

both of the brothers could clearly see him. "That would be me. I'm Captain, er, Slade."

"I am Captain Rafael Alphonso, of Tiotan, and those are my brothers, Captain Donello Alphonso on your port side, and Captain Sloven Alphonso in the ship behind your rear."

Abraham hadn't even paid attention to the third ship behind him. He couldn't see the other brother.

Captain Alphonso said, "Permission to come aboard? We need to execute an inspection. There are many smugglers and spies traversing the waters these days, and we make a quick account of them."

"Uh, yes, permission granted," Abraham said.

Captain Rafael Alphonso made his way down the steps and politely said, "Please have your ship's manifest ready as we cross. Tell your sailors to keep their distance. I'll have my soldiers gore them if they get too close."

"Yes, yes, absolutely," Abraham said. "Clear Captain Alphonso a path." He looked at the ship on his port side. The other brother was coming down his steps. "For both of them."

The *Sea Talon*'s crew made a path to Abraham wide enough to drive a wagon through. Captains Rafael and Donello Alphonso quickly made their way on board. They marched right up to Abraham. With their hats on, they stood a little taller than him.

Awkwardly, he said, "Welcome aboard."

"Spare me the pleasantries. I'm a quick judge of character, and your ship has stink all over it," Captain Rafael Alphonso said as he and his brother looked about, searching the faces of *Sea Talon*'s crew. The nostrils of his triangular nose widened. "Yes, stink all over it. Where is your manifest?"

6

Sticks handed a rolled-up manifest to Abraham. Before they departed on their seafaring journey, they'd prepped plenty of documents that matched the supplies they carried. Captain Rafael Alphonso looked down his nose at Sticks. "Is this your first mate, Captain Slade?"

Abraham gave Sticks a sideways glance and said, "Yes."

"Interesting choice. A young boy instead of a seasoned man," Captain Rafael Alphonso said.

"I'm not a boy," Sticks retorted. "I'm a—"

Abraham shoved her away. "Give Captain Alphonso some space, will you? He's very busy."

"Unbridled tongues. No discipline," the other brother, Captain Donello Alphonso, said. "A sure sign of treachery. The boy should be whipped."

Sticks opened her mouth.

Abraham gave her the eye. "I'll see to it unless you'd be interested."

"Not our crew member, but outbursts like that are not tolerated in the ranks of Tiotan. I can assure you of that," Rafael said as he looked over the manifest. "Sugar, meal, grain, rolls of fine silk, pepper, spices, and potatoes. Hmm..." He kept reading the list and muttered, "Hmm... hmm... hmm. We need to verify all of it. This manifest might look authentic, but it smells of forgery. I know. I've destroyed my fair share of pirates posing as merchants. Have you ever heard of Flame Beard?"

"Er... yes," Abraham said.

"We are the reason that he doesn't traverse the Sea of Troubles anymore," Rafael said with pride. "We caught him and his crew smuggling from that wretch of a king, Hector. We slaughtered every last one of his crew." He patted his sword handle, which rattled in the sheath. "And him. My brother and I took Flame Beard down personally. Oh, he was formidable for a large man but no match for our speed."

Abraham wanted to say, "You lying sack of donkey dung. Punk." He held his tongue.

Horace, who stood behind the brother captains, stiffened as his meaty fingers clenched. Abraham didn't take it lightly either. That had been his kill. If anyone was going to boast about it, it should have been him.

"An impressive feat," Abraham said. "I crossed paths with Flame Beard once myself."

Rafael's eyes lifted.

"Let's just say, I'm glad to be here. So, he was smuggling for King Hector, you say?"

"Elders, yes," Donello piped in. He adjusted his large hat. "That's what pirates do. They play both sides, but they are only on their own side. But we caught him harboring the king's spies and killed them. King Hector. His very name makes me want to spit. What sort of man takes children for brides and slaughters innocent women that dare speak out against him?"

Lewis, who was leaning comfortably against the mainmast, shoved off with his shoulders. His handsome eyes narrowed, and the white scar on his lips tightened. Leodor's gentle hand pulled him back by the elbow.

Abraham didn't miss the entirety of the subtle event. Ruger's keen vision and senses never seemed to miss anything. *So, the young windbag still cares for the king. Maybe there is hope yet.* He decided to fan the flames. "From what I understand, ol' King Hector's days are numbered."

"You don't know the half of it," Rafael said as his gaze searched the manifest. "You and your crew better hope that you aren't on the wrong side of the storm that is coming. Kingsland, for all intents and purposes, is dead to the other five lands." He smirked as he rolled up the scroll. "Soon, it will be known as Southern Tiotan."

"Shall we begin the inspection?" Donello asked.

"Yes, brother, bring over the hatchet men." Rafael looked at Abraham. "Make sure that all of your men are on deck. If we cross any strangers, we'll kill them."

Donello waved a group of soldiers over from his ship. There were six of them. They carried hatchets. They saluted their captain and stood at attention.

"Go below. Open everything." Donello took the manifest from Rafael and handed it to the lead hatchet man. "Let us know if you find any surprises. We'll be waiting."

The hatchet men vanished down the steps leading into the bowels of the ship. Within seconds, the sound of wood being hacked into carried up on deck. Rafael and Donello had smug smiles on their faces. With their arms folded over their deep chests, they rocked on their heels.

Abraham fought the urge to bite his nails. Horace had given the order for all hands on deck, but Solomon had never appeared. Abraham popped his thumb knuckle with an index finger.

"Are you nervous, Captain Slade?" Rafael asked.

"No, but I don't like the sound of my cargo being busted open. I'm going to have to repackage all of that."

"If that is all that you have to do, consider yourself fortunate," Rafael said.

Abraham nodded. He scanned the faces of his crew. Horace's, Bearclaw's, and Vern's eyes were as hard as hammered iron. They looked like wildcats ready to spring from their cage. The rest of the crew that he could see were as still as stone, aside from the constant sea breeze stirring their hair. He was confident that the manifest and the cargo would match up, but something about the Captains Alphonso didn't seem right.

One of the hatchet-wielding soldiers hurried up the steps. His eyes were as big as moons. The captains turned to face the man.

Abraham's heartbeat spiked. *Holy baloney, here we go.*

"What is it, Corporal?" Donello asked.

"There is a troglin in the brig," the corporal said.

The brothers' bushy eyebrows almost jumped from their brows. "There's a troglin in the brig?" both men asked.

Rafael spun on the heel of one black leather boot and faced Abraham. "I didn't see any reference to a troglin on the manifest." He bared his teeth and drew his saber. "It's this sort of dishonesty that makes me have to kill people."

7

ABRAHAM LIFTED HIS HANDS PALMS OUT AND QUICKLY SAID, "THE troglin is not cargo. He's a prisoner."

Rafael rested the edge of his saber on the top of Abraham's chest. The curved tip of the blade pointed at the soft flesh underneath Abraham's neck. "I don't care if the troglin is a prisoner or cargo—only a fool would not mention a troglin was on board. Captain Slade, I am disappointed. You appeared to be a man with good sense. Instead, you will die like a fool."

Donello lifted a hand and waved his soldiers over. Three dozen men carrying spears climbed from their respective ships onto the deck of *Sea Talon*. They held every crew member at the tip of a spear.

Abraham lifted his hands as his company did the same. "Captain Rafael, Donello, if you please, I can explain."

"Do we look like men that take matters lightly?" Rafael asked. "I didn't become a top commander in Tiotan's navy by bending my ear to every liar that pleaded. I show no mercy to smugglers and especially sympathizers to Kingsland." He leaned forward until the bill of his hat touched Ruger's forehead. "But don't worry, Captain Slade. I'll let some of your sailors live so they can swab the ship's deck with your blood. Then I'll sink it and them with it."

Without batting an eye, Abraham said, "Before you kill us, could you do me one favor?"

"What is your request?"

Abraham didn't know what to say. All he wanted to do was buy time. Then, he came up with something quick. "Make sure that the Sect in Dorcha gets the troglin. That's all I know."

Captain Rafael looked him dead in the eye, pressed the tip of his saber deeper into Abraham's neck without breaking the skin, and said, "No."

Abraham was a split second away from slapping Rafael's blade away when a pleading man's voice cried out from below, in the hold. "No, no, no... apologies! Please don't hurt my men!"

Captain Rafael lowered his sword, and along with his brother, he turned to face the man who scrambled up the stairs.

The man speaking with a thick drunken accent was Shades. He wore lavish robes too big for his body. His tawny hair was messed up underneath a soft cotton nightcap. He stood on the deck and swayed. "I-I... apologize, good captains of Tiotan." He said it with a gusty slur and waddled over to the captains, both of whom towered over him. He hiccupped and reeked of strong wine. "I am Slarten Manliest. A merchant. And this is my ship." He hiccupped again. "Forgive my captain. He means well but is not known for making sound decisions. Only executing orders." He put his arms around both men's waists. "My *henchmen* are rather stupid, but thank the Elders that I am finally awake."

Rafael and Donello looked down their noses at Shades, shoved him aside, and said, "If you would have awakened sooner, perhaps this coming tragedy could have been averted. But it's too late now, little merchant. Join the others."

"Oh, but wait, I think there has been a misunderstanding." Shades's deft hands vanished into his robes and reappeared with two hefty leather pouches that filled his hands. He tossed them lightly up and down, and the bags clinked with the rich sound of coins. "I believe this is what you were looking for." He tossed the sacks to each man.

The brothers caught the bags in their chests. They tested the weight of the coins with short tosses of their own.

"You better pray that these are golden shards," Donella said. "Insult us with silver, and I'll slit your throat first." He peeked in his sack and gave his brother an approving glance. "It's the right color but still light."

"The exchange is not complete. I hoped that your brother would be coming aboard." Shades hiccuped again. "Sorry, my heavy indulgence has made me sloppy." He produced another bag of coins. He handed it to Rafael. "*Hic.* I hope that will do."

Rafael and Donella looked at one another and nodded.

Then Rafael said, "It will. Slarten Manliest, I suggest that you search for a more apt captain when you port." He raised his voice. "Sailors of Tiotan, return to ship."

Without another word, the captains departed along with their crew. The Tiotan crew unhooked their grappling hooks and pushed away. Within minutes, their warships were breaking away from *Sea Talon*. Their grand sails filled with wind again.

Abraham couldn't help but feel dumbfounded at the sudden turn of events. He could have sworn that tense situation would have become a fight to the end, but somehow, Shades had twisted it away.

"So, that was a shakedown. Sweet donuts. I didn't see that coming."

Shades slipped his nightcap off his head and said, "I'll take that as a thanks. Once again, it seems that it's up to me to do all of the quick thinking. *Shakedown.* That's an interesting way of putting it."

The Henchmen encircled Shades. The rogue appeared like a child among the towering men.

"What is this conniving wretch doing here?" Sticks asked in a heated tone.

"As I stated, I'm saving—*ulp.*"

Vern had whisked a dagger out of his belt and put it to Shades's throat. "I took one whale of a beating the last time we crossed in Baracha. Now, I can return the favor. Ruger, let me gut this fish."

"Ease off, Vern. I'm not disagreeing with you, but there's some sorting we need to do first," Abraham said. "The men of Tiotan are gone. We live without a scratch. There is something to be said for that."

"We could have killed them," Horace stated.

Abraham nodded. He didn't doubt his men anymore. "I know, but we need to get sailing. We have a mission to complete. Raise the sails. We'll talk later."

Vern jammed his dagger into his belt. His burning stare passed between Abraham and Shades. He looked the rogue dead in the eye and said, "I'll get you. No Gond to save you now."

Tark put a hand on Vern's shoulder and led him away. "You aren't alone, brother. We all want a piece of him. And we'll have it."

8

IN ORDER TO SETTLE THE UNEASE CARRYING THROUGH THE SHIP, Shades was put in the brig. He was kept under guard too, by Solomon, which left Shades's eyes wide and mouth gaping. This gave Abraham time to sort matters out. He had four stowaways on board: Clarice, Hazel, Swan, and Shades. One was a Henchman and another a former Henchman. He trusted the ones he knew, but he had two more bags of trouble whom he didn't trust: Lewis and Leodor. So he called a meeting.

In order to keep the peace, he summoned Sticks, Horace, Bearclaw, Vern, and Iris to the private meeting in his quarters. He had Tark and Cudgel stand guard at the door. If they listened, he didn't care. He only wanted to keep the other prickly new Henchmen away. He poured everyone a goblet of rum.

"Time to chat," he said. "Tell me about Shades. And forgive me for not knowing better. Was he a Henchman, as we are?"

Rubbing his beard, Horace said, "One of the original. He started with us not long after we were formed. After we deserted the king and were branded. He's one of the survivors. He lasted, unlike over a hundred others that didn't."

"He's a weasel. A snake," Vern said as he sipped his rum and grimaced. "Mmm... that's good. Black rum from Dorcha. Ol' Flame Beard carried the best. I could set Shades on fire with this concoction. Be happy to do it, too."

"You'd waste good rum on him," the stark warrior Bearclaw said. "Use oil. He's not worth a dram of rum."

"It sounds like all parties present are against him. If he was a Henchman, why was he in Baracha and not with us?" Abraham asked then took a stiff drink. The black rum burned all the way down his throat to his stomach. "It does leave a mark in you, doesn't it?"

"You put him in Baracha, Captain," Horace said. "And all of us agreed. After one of our missions, while you met with the king, we waited there, but you didn't pick him to come out."

"And why was that?" he asked.

The Henchmen in the room exchanged looks.

"All of us were convinced that he was the saboteur of our missions," Horace said. "Especially you. You would have had him dead if you could have. And no one faulted you for it. We were losing men like sheep in a slaughterhouse."

"But we've since learned that Twila—or Raschel—Leodor, and Lewis were behind those failed missions." Abraham tapped a finger on the rim of his goblet. "Shades would have been cleared the same as the rest of us."

Iris raised her voice and said, "We don't know for certain that he wasn't in on it. He fits the part. Besides, he tried to put us under in Baracha. He nearly pulled it off too."

"I still have sore ribs from it. Those Gond got ahold of me and shook my bones loose," Vern said as he rubbed his ribs. "Just give me ten minutes with the little worm alone."

The company rattled off a few more points. They didn't want anything to do with Shades and made it clear that they didn't trust him. But if he'd been a Henchman at one time, then at one time, he must have been trustworthy. Or at least he should have been. "Sticks, you haven't said a word. What is your feeling about Shades?"

Without showing any emotions in her creaseless face, she said, "Aside from what happened in Baracha, I never saw Shades betray us."

"Ah, by the foul wind of the Elders, you got along with him worse than any of us," Vern said. "Now you side with him?"

"I'm not siding with him. I know what I know, the same as you, but even when Ruger tossed him, I had my doubts. I went along. It was better off not seeing him," she said as she wound her fingers in one of her ponytails.

"Tell me, if he was a Henchman in Baracha, how was he able to assault you?" Abraham asked. "Certainly, there would have been repercussions of it. A sky demon. Tragic accident. Some ill must have befallen him."

Iris drained her goblet and said, "As a mystic, I think that actions of a branded must be directly linked to the branded, as opposed to indirectly. Shades didn't attack us, but his legion of thugs did. I still think that it would bring forth ill will, but I cannot say for sure. The power of the brand seems to work uniquely depending on the person. I hate to say it, but Leodor might know more about it than me."

"For the time being, he's locked up," Abraham said. "So let's not worry about that. We can always leave him on the coast."

"Or strand him on an island," Bearclaw suggested. "Remember, he's not branded now. I say we do as you suggested. Get rid of him the first chance that we get. We'll be better off for it."

"Remember, this isn't a 'majority rules' situation. I have to make that decision. I think leaving him on the coast is the best decision. We'll move on after that. I don't want anyone among us that isn't a Henchman. It's bad enough that Leodor and Lewis have it but don't deserve it."

"They didn't want it," Horace said. "All of us wanted it. It's an honor, as dark as it might seem. I revel in the purpose that it gives me. I like serving the king. People like them... They only serve themselves."

"Hearts can change," Iris muttered.

"What do you mean by that?" Vern asked.

Iris let Horace refill her goblet and said, "Well, the first time I saw Shades in the ship's hold, I wanted him dead. But now that I think about it, we put him in Baracha in error. And he said he could explain his actions. He did bail us out above decks too. He didn't have to do that."

"We didn't need bailed out," Horace growled. "It was under control. We would have killed them."

Iris gripped Horace's hand and said, "I know, but we have a bigger crew. Sailors. They wouldn't have made it. Or the new Red Tunics. I'm all for getting out of a bind without bloodshed, and all of Tiotan's ships might have come for us after victory. And before, even when Shades was in question, well, he delivered as well as any one of us."

"Well, why don't you give him a big fat kiss and an apology?" Vern said. "I'm through talking about this." He made his way to the door and flung it open.

After he pushed by Tark and Cudgel, Bearclaw and Horace followed after him.

Tark and Cudgel, the smoky-eyed athletes, peered into the room, and Cudgel said, "I'll stand by what you say, Captain, but I feel the same as them. What Shades did in that prison was low. He needs punished." He closed the door again.

The ship rocked hard left then right.

"Choppy waters," Abraham muttered. "I don't like them. I can't have the company divided. Once we take to land, I think it will be best for all parties to cut Shades loose." He wished he had a better memory of Shades and what he was like, but it was a blank. He didn't even recognize the man, even vaguely, as he did the others. "I don't suppose anyone is going to object. Should be simple enough."

Sticks lifted two fingers and said, "There is one thing you should consider."

"Oh, what's that?"

"We need him."

9

"HOW'S IT GOING?" ABRAHAM ASKED. HE WAS DOWN INSIDE THE ship's hold, at the rear, where the brig was located.

Solomon sat outside the cell barred with steel, his elbows on his knees. Shades was inside the cell, sitting on a lone bench, his back to the wall. He still wore the garish oversized robes from earlier, when he'd posed as a merchant.

"He likes to talk," Solomon said. "Too much."

"Yes, he has always had a big mouth," Sticks said, hanging back behind Abraham.

Nobody else was with them.

Shades showed an easy smile that hid his teeth. He spoke again in his silky voice. "Oh yes, the unflappable Sticks. The princess of personality. How delightful it is that you should join me." He wagged his finger. "I must say, though, that those pony-tails do little to make up for your boyish exterior. Perhaps if you let it all hang out, you would fare better as a woman."

Abraham slid his gaze between the two debaters and asked, "What's going on with the two of you?"

"Nothing," Sticks said. "He's all talk."

Shades stood up and grabbed the cell bars and said, "Now, Sticks, you know that there is much more to me than that. Much more."

"It doesn't look like it from where I'm standing," Abraham said. "But I'm used to runts with big mouths. It's how they protect themselves."

Shades lifted his eyes to Abraham and said, "You really aren't the same man as the last. You are someone different. Ha. Even I have to admit that this is fascinating, and very little fascinates me. Well, this troglin does too." He tapped a finger on the bars. "Tell me, what is your real name if it's not Ruger?"

"You're a smart fella. You tell me."

"Abraham. You can thank Clarice for filling me in. She's a young girl that likes to talk. But do not fret. I always figure everything out anyway." He licked his teeth. "So, you are the new otherworlder. I can only hope that you are better than the last one. He was quite the fool, trapped in Ruger's body."

Abraham exchanged a glance with Solomon.

Shades's light eyes brightened. "Ah! I'll be—the troglin is an otherworlder too. This gets better and better. Tell me, did you know one another from your world, or are you from different worlds completely? I say it's easy to pick up on because of the way that you talk. Your speech is very uncommon."

Abraham really wished he remembered more about Shades, who seemed to know more about Abraham than he knew about himself. He wasn't sure whether he liked him or not, but at least he had some personality. "So you're from Hancha?"

"I can't change where I was born. You should know that. But yes, I'll entertain your questions. I am from Hancha. It's a big part of my mysterious past. Why do you ask?" Shades sat back down. "Oh, wait. I know why. Princess Clarice blathered about everything. The zillon dragon riders attacked the king with a strange weapon that shot sling bullets. I assume it's another one of those crazy artifacts from your world or perhaps another. Who knows? Anyway, you need a guide through Hancha." He made a welcoming gesture with his hands. "And here I am, a man who has thoroughly leveraged himself to meet your needs. You can let me out now. Perhaps get me something to eat. Some of that Dorcha rum you've been drinking would be mighty fine."

"He's cocky," Solomon said. "I hate cocky."

"I'm an acquired taste. Just ask Sticks. She knows me more intimately than any," Shades said.

Abraham gave her a sideways look and said, "Tell me you're brother and sister or something."

She didn't say a word.

"Cousins?"

Shades popped up out of his seat and said, "I'll be happy to retell the story that you most certainly don't remember. It was years ago, when Sticks joined our ranks and quickly cozied up to me. She was so cute, trying to be so rugged and boyish, just to fit in, but it wasn't long before she proved to be all woman. Then there was some back and forth—awkwardness when you showed an interest. She seemed to be one that wanted to move up the ranks and stepped on me to get into the top tent."

The muscles in Sticks's jaw clenched. If her eyes could have shot poisoned arrows, she would have done so at Shades.

"Your gossip isn't very Henchmanlike," Abraham said. "It sounds more like the words of old chattering women. Sticks, do you really think that we need him to guide through Hancha?"

"I'm only saying that he knows it better than any of the rest of us. There were more Henchmen from Hancha, but they are all dead."

"Don't blame that on me," Shades said. "I wasn't responsible for any of what I was accused of."

"If that's the case, then why did you try to kill us in Baracha?" she asked, her voice cracking a little.

"Now that I have time to explain, I will explain." Shades poked his finger at Abraham and Sticks. "You abandoned me in Baracha. What was I supposed to do, lie down and die? In the past, we would wait as a group and be strong. But not this time. It was me. One on one." His jaw tightened. His small deft hands turned white knuckled on the bars. "So, I managed to join one of the gangs." He pulled up his sleeve, revealing white scars carved into his arm, making a crude image of a snake with fangs. "Over time, I proved my worth and overtook the gang called the Serpent's Tail. I recruited the Gond, which wasn't easy, and after that, we had the run of the prison yard. When you came, I had to prove who I was. It was only fighting. No one got killed. Sure, some broken bones and bloody noses, but the Henchmen can handle that."

"You came after the women. We know what they do with the women in Baracha," Sticks said in a tone that was almost a growl.

"Well, to be clear, all of the women except for you. Listen, it was for your protection. It might not sound that way, but there were other gangs bent on taking a fatal poke at the Henchmen," Shades said. "I know this because the Serpent's Tail was offered accommodation to bring about your demise. We were only one of the gangs involved, but I acted first." He pressed his face between the bars. "It... was... a... show."

Solomon clapped his hands together, making a loud pop. "I told you he was a talker. I tell you, if I could have woven my words like that back when I was young, I would have saved myself a heap of trouble."

"I agree," Abraham said.

"Sticks, you know better than any that I was never the trouble," Shades said. "I was a good Henchman. But I found out what was going on with Twila. But she got me first." He made an angry shake of his head. "Clever. So clever." He shook his head and frowned. "And I was onto the old Ruger too. He was letting her do that damage and put the blame on me. I should have acted quicker."

"Yeah, well, we have a long trip ahead. I'll decide tonight whether or not to cut you loose," Abraham said. "Solomon, do you want some relief?"

"No, I'll stay. I'm as comfortable here as anywhere."

"Good. Just holler if you change your mind. It's time to get back on track." Abraham pinched the bridge of his nose. A small headache was coming on. "I'll be in my quart—"

"Captain!" Horace called out from the main deck. "Trouble comes. All swords on deck! All swords on deck!"

10

TAKING THE STEPS THREE AT A TIME TO THE MAIN DECK, ABRAHAM quickly found himself in a scene of chaos. At first, he imagined that the warships from Tiotan had returned. Instead, he gaped at something completing unimaginable, at least by Earth's standards. Flying men circled the skies above. They had great heads like pterodactyls' with lengthy gray beaks, the arms and legs of men, and talons for toes and fingers. Their skin was blackened scales like fishes', but thicker like a great lizard's. They had lean, wiry muscles, skinny arms, and bellies that appeared as hard as iron hide.

Horace, Bearclaw, and Vern stood on the main deck, aiming crossbows at the creatures. They fired volley after volley. The creatures twisted through the sky. Apollo and Prospero manned the crow's nest, brandishing their swords at flying fiends circling them.

Abraham had snaked out his own sword without even realizing it. Energy coursed through his hand. "Holy sheetrock! What are those things?"

"Windreavers," a pirate cried out. He was one of Flamebeard's old crew. "They are hellions of the skies." He ducked underneath a windreaver that dove at his head. As it took a swipe at the pirate with its claws, a hunk of flesh in his shoulder went with it. "Gargh!" the pirate cried out.

Horace shot a crossbow bolt into the windreaver's neck. It flopped on the deck like a fish and died.

Abraham climbed his way up to the poop deck of the ship, where Dominga and Vern were locked in battle with a small flock of windreavers that had landed. The windreavers' great snapping jaws, filled with rows of tiny sharp teeth, made loud clacks. Vern buried his sword in a creature's chest. Blood spurted from the wound as it twisted away and dove off the ship.

Dominga fought with sword and dagger. She stuck a wind-reaver in the arm. It lashed out with its winged arm with claws that cut her across the face. She dropped down and lunged her short sword into its belly with her full force. The blade went into one side of its abdomen and out the other. Its mouth opened wide, and a horrifying birdlike shriek came out.

Black Bane flashed across the shrieking bird-thing's neck and took its head from the shoulders.

"I had it under control," Dominga said as she jerked her sword out of the windreaver's belly.

Abraham didn't slow. Two more windreavers landed on the deck, and more were landing. They were long armed and quick, and their biting beaks struck out like serpents. The ferocity of Abraham, Vern, and Dominga sent the windreavers diving over the edge of the ship's stern. The fiendish flyers vanished underneath the surface of the choppy waters.

Abraham tore his stare away from the water to the commotion in the crow's nest above. He pointed his sword. "There!"

Apollo and Prospero were in the fight of their lives. Wind-reavers hung to the rim of the crow's nest, biting and lashing out with their talons. Prospero locked his arms around one of the windreavers' beaks and started punching the strange birdman in the face.

A windreaver clamped down on Apollo's arm, and the man let out a fierce scream. He turned wild-eyed and bit the windreaver on its arm. Then his sword cut clean through the membrane of its wing and sliced fully through it. With a quick punch of a dagger, he gored its heart. The windreaver fell away and tangled up in the ratlines, twitching.

The windreavers, dozens in all, circled above, screeching and squawking harrowing sounds. Without any warning, they dove into the waters and vanished underneath the ship.

The ship's company looked overboard.

"Does anyone see them?" Horace asked as he joined the other onlookers leaning over the ship's railing. He'd dropped his crossbow and rearmed with a spear. "They fly like birds and swim like fish."

"Keep this ship moving," Lewis ordered. "Those things probably had all of the taste of steel that they could handle." He had the drab red blood of a windreaver dripping from the edge of his sword. "They might look frightening, but they fight like stupid animals."

"Animals that fight in packs can be deadly," said Clarice's guardian maiden Swan in her husky voice. "Be wary."

Lewis spat off the railing. "The only one that should be wary is the fool that crosses me and the king's steel. It cut their scaly skins like butter. They won't be back," he said as he swept his dark hair from his eyes. "Like pigeons, they scatter."

Abraham counted six windreavers lying dead on the deck. One lay dead near the mainmast, its blood oozing from a gaping wound onto the wooden planks. The windreavers were ugly, with no charm about them at all. Their pterodactyl heads were oddly long and looked too heavy for their bodies. Like animals, they looked the same alive as they did dead. Their large eyes were like polished onyx, and they stood over six feet tall.

"Seems strange that they attack for no reason." He fanned his nose. "Whew, they smell like rotting sardines. What agitated them?"

The pirate who had called out the names of the windreavers earlier limped over to Abraham. He wore a vest and was hairy chested and lazy eyed. He said, "They are scavengers. They feed on men for meat. Anything. They like it fresh. I've only seen them twice before. Once when we crossed a sinking ship after a battle we came on. They snatched the dying from the waters and flew away. The other time, they flew away. A sky dragon was giving chase. 'Twas a scary thing with a tail like a stick of fire. Humph, the Sea Elders must be with us since they fled beneath. A good sign."

"Sea Elders. Yes, of course. They are looking out for us." Lewis sheathed his sword. "I wonder, was the same sea elder looking after them?"

With her flowing hair billowing in the wind, Clarice said to her half brother, "Vermin like them don't pray. Vermin like you don't either."

"Ha ha," Lewis said as he adjusted his leather gloves. "I've made it this far without the Elders." He twisted his head around. "Where is Leodor? Old sour face, are you hiding? It's safe now!"

Abraham walked away and looked over the rail down into the waters. The ship moved at a brisk pace, cutting through the choppy waters like a knife. He squinted. Several feet below the surface it looked like something swam like a dolphin by the ship's hull. "Guys, look closer. I think those windreavers are swimming alongside. Take a look for you—"

Like a salmon swimming upstream and jumping the breaks, a

windreaver sailed up into the deck. They came all at once by the dozens from all directions. The windreavers let out fiendish earsplitting screeches as they launched themselves into the Henchmen and the crew.

Abraham split the nearest monster's face wide open with lethal blow of his sword. A woman screamed. It was Clarice. Two windreavers hooked her arms with their taloned fingertips. They launched themselves into the air and sped away in hasty flight. "Nooo!" Abraham yelled.

"Help meee!" Clarice screamed. "Help meee!"

11

"Once again, the Sea of Troubles lives up to its name," Bearclaw said. The axe-wielding warrior's eyes were searching over the sea. In the distance, the windreavers were carrying off part of the ship's crew.

"Dirty donuts!" Abraham said as he helplessly watched Clarice, Sticks, Horace, and the Red Tunic Skitts being carried off by the strange creatures.

The reptilian birdmen sped toward the horizon and disappeared over the sea.

He pounded his fist on the railing. "Where are those things going? They can't be flying that far away..." He searched the eyes of his crew. "Can they?"

The pirate who'd spoken to him earlier stood beside Abraham and said, "Those windreavers reside on Crown Island. It's a place of horrors. No ships can dock there. At least, no ships such as this. The beaches are cliffs of stone. Even Flame Beard avoided it."

"Well aren't you a cluster of good news?" Abraham told the pirate. "What is your name, anyway?"

"Jander. I was Flamebeard's top deckhand, at least until you slaughtered him." He stuck his chest out and gave a crisp salute. "It's an honor to serve Captain Ruger Slade. Even this sea dog's ears heard about you."

Abraham pushed past the man and said, "Horace... ah crap, Horace is gone. Who can drive this ship to that island?"

Bearclaw arched a brow and said, "Drive, Captain?"

"I mean sail! Someone set sail to that island." He was trying to find the right lingo. All he could think of was *Star Trek* episodes. "Why are all of you looking at me like that? Helmsman, set a course for Crown Island."

No one moved. Horace had manned the wheel before, and Abraham wasn't sure who backed him up.

"Well done," Lewis said. "You have a ship and no one left to sail it."

Abraham gave Lewis a dangerous look and said, "Well look at you, all broken up about your sister."

"Half sister, and I'm all ripped apart inside," Lewis said with casual smugness. "She's gone now. I don't think there is anything that can be done to save her unless sailing in circles will somehow bring her back."

Abraham locked his fingers around Lewis's throat and said, "If you weren't a Henchman, I'd kill you." He pushed the man away.

Red-faced, Lewis rubbed his throat. "You'll pay for that."

Abraham ignored him. He needed to pull it together. Four members of his crew had been snatched, and he had to get them back. "Listen up. I know we can sail this ship. Who backed up Horace?"

Cudgel stepped forward and said, "Tark and I did. We can handle it."

"Good. Get us on course," Abraham said.

Jander spoke up and added, "I can sail the ship with a skeleton crew if need be. I've been on the waters all my life. None knows them better than me."

"Good. See to it that they don't get off course."

"All right, Henchmen, let's fill those sails with gusty wind and get this sea cutter moving!" Cudgel said in a booming voice. "It can't sail itself!"

The ship's crew scrambled into action.

Abraham moved back to the railing. Without Sticks and Horace, he felt more lost than ever, as if a part of him were missing. Everything that could have gone wrong was going wrong. *Man, I can't believe this is happening.*

"Tough break," someone said.

Abraham noticed Shades standing on his left. "How did you get out?"

"You should know me better than that, *Ruger*. There isn't a lock that can hold me. Besides, your furry friend went to see what the commotion was all about." Shades made a quick scan of the deck. "But perhaps he is still hiding. Anyway, quite a dilemma. Quite a—"

"Bearclaw, stick this rodent back in his cell. Bind him up if you have to. And tape his mouth shut."

"Pardon?" Bearclaw said.

"Never mind. Just get him out of here."

Bearclaw took Shades by the scruff of his neck, lifted the grimacing man up on tiptoe, and said, "Gladly."

"Ahem."

Abraham turned.

Leodor was standing behind him with his hands tucked in his rustling robes. "Abraham, may I have a word with you?"

"I'm kinda busy," he said.

"It will only take a moment. As much as I would like to support

46

your efforts to save our comrades, I strongly caution against it," Leodor said.

"We don't leave Henchmen behind. Of course, you wouldn't understand that even though you are one," he said.

"If it was me, I would understand," Leodor calmly said. He rubbed his scrawny chest above his heart. "My life is the king's. I die in his honor. We serve the king and his glory. We don't serve ourselves, or rather, the Henchmen. We have a mission to complete. The quest is long. We need to move with haste in that direction."

Lewis popped up behind Leodor and said, "He's right. It might take weeks to find them. And then what? If we find their carcasses, we bury them? I know that I sound cold, but I speak truth, despite my lack of affection for my sister. We serve the king, not her."

Abraham rubbed his temples and said, "Good Lord, why couldn't have they just taken you two windbags? It would have made this a whole lot easier." He pinched the bridge of his nose and dropped his hands. "Even if the two of you were whisked away, I'd come. It's the right thing to do because we're a team, not a bunch of expendables even though, well, we are. But so long as I'm in charge, I'm going to keep the Henchmen together, hell or high water." He stepped up on Leodor, smashing the man between himself and Lewis and said, "Got it?"

Leodor nodded. Lewis shrugged, covered his mouth, and yawned.

"I respect your firm attitude about this," Leodor said as he squeezed out from between the two men. "But consider this. No one can serve the king if we all wind up dead."

"Yes, no one," Lewis scoffed.

Abraham's headache started to throb. He wanted to toss both men overboard. "Is that all? And before you say anything, know that I won't be changing my mind on this."

Leodor cleared his throat and added, "If you think your trek to the Spine was treacherous, I'll give you fair warning: based off of the histories I have studied deeply, for decades, I know that what lurks in Crown Island is infinitely more dangerous than what you've already seen."

12

DEALING WITH PROBLEMS WAS ONE THING. DEALING WITH PROBLEMS with a headache was another. Abraham had a bad one, so bad that he took to his quarters and lay facedown on the bed. He put a Do Not Disturb sign in front of the door. It was Bearclaw.

The loss of Horace, Sticks, and Clarice wasn't something he needed now. *Just another debacle I have to fix. Sticks and Horace? Why them?* He also felt bad for the young fellow, Skitts, too. He hardly knew the young man. He rolled over on his back and stared at the ceiling. "This sucks."

Lewis and Leodor continued to prod him at length even after he ended the conversation a half dozen times. The problem was that they made sound points. The first point they made caused Abraham to have many regrets. As they'd mapped out their mission to invade Hancha, find the zillon dragon riders, and kill Arcayis the Underlord, he chose to take the long route, including what would have otherwise been a short trip across the Bay of Elders.

He wasn't alone in his reasoning. They could have sailed the southern seas below the Bay of Elders and found a place to dock at Little Leg in Hancha. This was Lewis and Leodor's suggestion. Abraham was naturally inclined to go against it. King Hector and Queen Clarann agreed with him. They opted to take their time, sailing north along the western coast of Titanuus and over his head, and settle down on the coastline south of Titanuus's East Arm. The logic was simple. Their enemies wouldn't be looking for them from there. The enemy would expect a southern approach.

As things turned out, perhaps Lewis and Leodor were right. If they had sailed south, perhaps they'd still have the crew intact. Sadly, the arrival of Clarice, though she was a Henchman, only complicated things.

Abraham pushed his face out of his pillow, sat up on the edge of his bed, rubbed the back of his head, and asked, "What is with that kid? She's as hardheaded as a bull. I just hope those wind-reavers haven't turned her into lunch meat."

Jake's Pirates backpack caught his eye. It was hanging on the headboard post. Abraham scooted over the sheets, leaned over, and grabbed it. As he held it in his hands and stared down at it, guilt swelled in his chest. The past several days had been so hectic that he hadn't even thought about Jake and his dead wife, Jenny.

He ran his thumbs over the straps. "Sorry, Son. Sorry, hon." His eyes watered. "What am I doing here? I don't even know if this place is real. I know my life with you was, though, wasn't it?" He flicked the zipper with his finger. He remembered the day he'd given Jake the backpack. It was a birthday present right before the accident, not too far removed from when he'd signed his big baseball contract. He swallowed the lump in his throat. "Ah, man. I hope you guys understand. I'm sorry." He hung the backpack up on the post. "I have to save them. But I'll never forget about you."

Outside, the moonlight shone through the glass panes of the window.

He walked over to the window and spread his hands out over the panes. Outside, the tips of the choppy waves twinkled with dazzling effect. For a moment, Titanuus seemed peaceful. He rubbed his head. He'd like to have a pain pill, ibuprofen or something to take the edge off. He hadn't had one of those in years. They brought only more sorrow and trouble. For the most part, Ruger's body handled everything extremely well, inhumanly well, aside from the occasional migraines.

"Come on, Ruger. I need to shake this. We have work to do." He stood. "Block it out. Just block it out, and it will subside."

At the moment, he had too much to think about. His problems were coming at him from all directions. Everything had started with the zillon dragon riders. The alienlike race with ghostly white skin and marble black eyes had tried to assassinate King Hector. It wasn't a customary assassination either, using poison or sharp weapons. The fiends used an assault rifle that looked like an M-16 or AK-47. That tossed Abraham for a loop and put King Hector in a panic. The enemy was using weapons the likes of which he'd never seen. At least Abraham had some idea what they were up against. But a fat lot of good it would do them if they had a lot more of them.

That led to planning the next step. King Hector didn't play games. If you took a shot at him, he took a shot at you, carefully and quietly. Abraham liked the mission. He was ready, but Lewis and Leodor created a problem. They weren't on board. Then, of all people, Princess Clarice showed up, and everything quickly started to unravel. Such was the luck of the Henchmen: turmoil, lots of it.

To make matters worse, that wasn't even Abraham's biggest problem. The fact that he was stuck in Titanuus had taken a backseat to the matters at hand. He, for all intents and purposes, seemed to be becoming someone else, which was madness. He hadn't even taken a sniff at trying to find one of those portals or doorways that would take him back home. The only things attaching him to that reality were his occasional dreams and Jake's backpack.

He rubbed his forehead. "I'd do anything for a Ziploc full of ice right now."

Knock. Knock. Knock.

The soft knocking came from the other side of his door. It was someone's knuckle being gentle on the wooden frame. Abraham opened the door.

Bearclaw stood outside. The warrior was all business behind his broad face and wild jet-black hair. In his direct manner, he said, "Crown Island is in sight."

"Perfect." Abraham grabbed his sword, buckled it on, and headed on deck. The entire crew, aside from Cudgel, who steered the ship, were gathered on the foredeck. Their wide eyes stared out over the foremast, which jutted out of the front of the ship, fixed on the haunting sight in the distance. He joined them.

"Ahoy," Jander said in a gravelly voice as he leaned out over the front, hanging onto sail lines that ran from the bowsprit to the forecastle mast. "Crown Island."

Located south of the West Arm of Titanuus, the stark sea-stranded landmass lived up to its namesake. A rim of jagged cliff faces peaked and dipped all the way around the island as far as the eye could see. The waves crashed angrily against the foreboding cliffs. Clouds, more like a fog, hung over the island, slowly moving in a ghostly fashion. The sea wind cutting through the choppy miles of rock whistled like a banshee gone mad. The rough waters appeared to be surrounded by reefs of coral and shallows of rock. No big ship could traverse it.

Lewis and Leodor approached Abraham. "It's not too late to make the right decision," Lewis said.

Abraham's jaws clenched. He looked them both dead in the eyes and said, "I've already made the right decision. Bearclaw, get the lifeboat in the water. Tonight, we're going in."

13

LEWIS AND LEODOR PUT THEIR BACKS INTO THE OARS AS THEY ROWED feverishly against the sea. Leodor looked as if he was about to die, gasping with every effort he put in. He wasn't even doing much of the work. Swan sat beside him, and Hazel was beside Lewis, doubling up on the oars. The guardian maidens had insisted on coming. Luckily, the lifeboat was plenty big enough for the crew he was taking.

From the bow of the craft, watching Leodor panting for breath, Abraham asked, "When's the last time you did any physical labor? You look like death warmed over."

"I've dedicated to my life to acting from behind the scenes, not in them. It's a foolish thing to bring me. I'm of no use to you," Leodor said as he wheezed.

Luckily for Abraham, his headache had subsided. He said, "I agree with you, but you're a Henchman now. It's time to build some character. Now dig those oars into the water, grandpa."

The other Henchmen in the boat, aside from furrow-browed Lewis, let out some hearty laughter. Among the small ship's crew were Bearclaw, Vern, Dominga, Iris, Apollo, Prospero, and Skitts's brother, the Red Tunic Zann, who like the guardian maidens, had insisted on coming. He'd left the others back on the ship, including Solomon. Something didn't seem right with the troglin.

The boat scraped over a reef, rocking the craft, and got hung up. Bearclaw grabbed an oar and pushed them free. They navigated through the reefs and shallows toward the rocky cliff faces, looking for a spot to dock the craft and enter the island. Crown Island had the foreboding presence of a prison, the kind where you went in and didn't come out.

"Does anyone see a good place to park?" Abraham said.

"Anywhere on these shallows will be fine. We go in any closer, and we're going to crash into those walls," Vern said. "And in this armor, all of us will sink like stones."

"I won't," Dominga reminded him with a smile. She wore only snug garb made of leather. "But if you sink, I'll try to fish you out."

"Brilliant idea, Ruger. Rowing in the middle of the night. A wise man would have waited until morning," Lewis said as he pulled at the oars.

"There's a method to my madness. Number one, the longer we wait, the more likely they are dead. Number two, I'm hoping those bird men, or whatever they are, don't fly at night."

"Is there a number three?" Lewis asked sarcastically.

"Yes—shut up and row."

"Ruger," Bearclaw said as he pointed a long, broad finger toward the island. "If we can get in behind that jetty, there might be a cover back there."

Abraham looked at the strapping women, Swan and Hazel. "Go for it."

With the help of Lewis and Leodor, the two of them guided the watercraft toward the jetty. Horace sat in the rear, while Abraham kept his spot on the bow. Suddenly, the waves picked up the rear end of the boat and sent it careening toward the rocky outcropping they were aiming for.

Abraham cried out, "Hold on! Everybody brace yourselves!"

The lifeboat moved with startling speed toward the jagged rocks. If the nose of the boat hit the rock, it would be shattered to pieces, and the company would be stranded if not sunk to a watery grave. He flung his arms out and braced his feet against the boat's bench. His fingers touched rock. His arms strained against the weight of the boat, which heaved its full weight behind him. With backbreaking effort, he pushed the nose of the ship away from the rocks, grunting with the strain.

The sharp rocks scraped against Abraham's cheeks and shoulder, but he managed to turn the nose of the boat. The side of the ship bumped hard against the rocks, bucking all the passengers.

Using his hands, and with the help of the others, he pushed the boat alongside the outcropping.

Abraham let out a sigh, looked at the wide-eyed crew, and kind of laughed. "That was a close call."

The back surge of waves heaved the boat upward.

A sharp pain lanced through Abraham's skull as he cracked his noggin on a rock sticking out from overhead. Warm blood ran down into his eyes. He touched it and looked at it on his fingertips. The world started to spin. His body swayed, and he faded into blackness.

14

THE PRESENT

BEEP. BEEP. BEEP. BEEP. BEEP.

Abraham woke up in a modern-day hospital bed. The lights were dim. The air was cool. Several blankets covered his body. He was warm, almost comfortable. He turned his head and looked at the blood-pressure monitor. He was at a perfect one-twenty over eighty. His heartbeat was steady at sixty-five beats per minute. His vital statistics were rarely ever that good.

Beep. Beep. Beep. Beep. Beep.

"Dirty donuts, that sound is annoying," he said and clawed a finger at the oxygen tube stuck inside his nose. "What is this thing? For a dream, this is a little too vivid."

Since he'd been on Titanuus, he'd had several dreams about his past. They were so real that he felt he was reliving it. Often, they came on after a headache. A deep sleep would follow. His past came back to haunt him. This dream was different. He was in a hospital room, but there weren't any balloons. It was like the one after his accident. The room was barren, and a flat-screen television hung from the wall.

"That's new."

The last thing he remembered was trying to save the lifeboat from crashing into the rocks. He cracked his head. Blood was on his fingers. He looked at them. His hands were clean. He rubbed his forehead. A bandage was on it. "Ah, no."

"Did you say something to me?" someone asked in a weak voice from the other side of a sea-green curtain drawn along one side of his bed.

With a grunt, Abraham rolled over on one side and pushed the curtain away. An old white man lay in his bed, hooked up to IVs and oxygen. With a bald face filled with age spots, he must have been at least ninety. He was scrawny, a withered man, but light was in his eyes when he tilted his gaze toward Abraham.

"Hi. Uh, no, I wasn't talking to you, just myself. Er... I'm Abraham."

"They call me Charles. Nice to meet you." Even though Charles had hardly a stick of hair on his head, he had frosty eyebrows so thick that he could comb them over. "I was wondering if you'd wake up before I died."

"Well, I guess you got your wish."

Abraham looked about. The room had that hospital smell of bedpans and cleaning agents. Charles didn't appear to have any belongings at all.

"Sorry, Charles, that probably sounded rude."

"Ah, no, not at all. It's good to hear a voice. Aside from brief interludes with the nurses, I haven't had many conversations." Charles closed his eyes. "Everyone is polite, though. They are always polite when they know that you're going to die. It's their job to make you comfortable, I guess."

Abraham grabbed his railing and pulled himself into a sitting position with a grunt. He managed to figure out how to push the support railing down and swung his legs over the edge of the bed.

The first thing he noticed was his bulging belly. The rock-hard six-pack of muscles that Ruger boasted was gone. He placed both hands on his belly. "This is embarrassing."

"At least you have some fat on you. I'm little more than skin on bones," Charles said. "Heh heh."

"I can see that you are old, but you don't look like someone that is about to die," Abraham said absentmindedly. Like a slap in the face, it just hit him that Sticks, Horace, Clarice, and Skitts were in danger and needed rescue. "Ah, man. This can't be happening now."

"What, being old? I've been old a long time. But I get sick, come here—they move me floor to floor and bed to bed. Like I'm a purse or something. I don't know." Charles made a throat-clearing cough. "You know, you might find this hard to believe, but I used to be a big fella like you. Bigger. I was a bulldozer among my fellow infantry men. Now, I've shrunk down like a husk of mini corn. It sucks."

"You're a vet? Well, thanks for your service. My dad was one. A pilot." Abraham shook his head. "What am I doing? I know this isn't real. It's just another dream."

"Listen son, our lives are what we choose them to be." Charles pressed a button on the side of his bed rail, and the back end of his bed rose up. With a shaky hand, he reached over and grabbed a plastic hospital cup. "Say, do you think that you could fetch me some water? I'd buzz a nurse, but they take forever. Unless Lindsay is here. She stays on top of things, but she's always off on Sundays."

Abraham tilted his head toward Charles and asked, "Sunday? What is the date?"

"September something, I think. I'm good with days, but not so much the dates. The new memories fade like melting snow, but I really remember the old ones. My first wife—she was a house girl.

I met her in the Philippines. Stark black hair and eyes that I'll never forget."

Abraham snatched the cup out of Charles's hand and asked, "What year is it?"

"Oh, that I know. It's 2018."

Abraham's knees buckled as his world came crashing down. Dreaming in the past was one thing, but dreaming in the present —that was a nightmare.

"No, no, no, this can't be!" He flung his room door open. "Nurse! Nurse!"

A nurses' station was nearby. The male and female nurses donning a variety of scrubs were drinking and talking, many eyeballing the screens of their smart phones. All of them stopped what they were doing, and their frozen stares hung on Abraham.

One nurse, a short husky lady with a braided ponytail, wore scrubs decorated with pictures of Hello Kitty. She set down a can of Red Bull and said, "Sir, let's get you back into bed. Larry, call the doctor. Tell him Mr. Jenkins is awake."

Abraham cast his eyes on the nurse. "Tell me, what is the date and year?"

"It's September 18, 2018," she calmly said.

Abraham lifted his chin, flung out his fists wide, and screamed, "Noooooooooooo!"

15

GETTING ABRAHAM SETTLED DOWN TOOK SOME DOING, BUT THE nurse in the Hello Kitty scrubs didn't back down. Her name was Nancy, and when she told Abraham he was acting like a child, that got him. He might be torn between one world and another, but he wasn't going to get anywhere by having a fit. He climbed back in bed.

The doctors and nurses ordered a rigmarole of tests. Abraham played along. After all, if he was having a dream, then all he needed to do was wake up. The best way to do that was to get back to sleep. That would be the quickest way back to Titanuus. He requested something to help him sleep and told Charles and the nurse, Ann, "Good night. It was nice knowing you."

The sedatives worked. His lids became heavy, and he heard himself snore before he fell into a deep sleep.

He woke up in the same hospital room, well rested and bleary-eyed. His pulse picked up. "Dirty donuts, I'm still here."

A rustle of paper came from inside the room. Abraham peered that direction. A man sitting in a chair in the corner was folding up a newspaper. He was old and as bald as a cue ball and wore a navy suit, white shirt, and no tie.

"Luther?"

"Good morning, Abraham," Luther Vancross said as he stood up. He owned the brewery that Abraham drove a truck for. He had age spots all over but moved like a thirty-year-old in a seventy-five-year-old's body. "How are you feeling?"

"That's the last question that you want to ask. Believe me—the last question." He looked over to the right. The curtain was pulled back, and an empty bed was beside him. "What happened to Charles?"

Luther leaned forward and asked, "Who?"

"Charles, the man that looked like an even older you? He was here yesterday. He..." Abraham caught a knowing look in Luther's eye. "Did he die?"

"I believe so. It happened right before I arrived. They were straightening up the room. I didn't know that he was the Charles that you spoke of. Sorry, I guess you got to know him."

With emptiness filling him, he said, "I guess you could say that. Though it was brief. He said something about our lives being what we chose them to be. It was kind of cryptic. I hate that he's gone."

"At least you are alive," Luther said with a faint smile. "It sounds like this Charles was full of years. When the Lord takes you, he takes you. I'm glad that he didn't take you. I would have felt a great loss after your accident."

Aside from his original interview with Luther years before, Abraham didn't have much to do with the man. He did his job and went home, catching Luther every so often back at the brewery. Both men spoke little but did much. But Luther always was a straight shooter.

"What accident are you talking about?" Abraham asked.

"The one in the East River Mountain Tunnel. That is where they found you, battered up and knocked out," Luther said, not batting an eye. He'd always maintained a stern quality about himself. He tapped the folded-up newspaper on his hand. "I'll never forget that call. None of my drivers ever had a bad accident. We've always been fortunate. That's why I only hire good men and women. But that accident was freakish."

Abraham clenched his brow. He believed that Luther believed what he was saying, but he didn't believe it himself. He hadn't wrecked his truck. His truck was fine when he entered the tunnel, and he was alone inside it. He hadn't hit anything. "What was freakish?"

"Your accident. They said a hunk of the tunnel fell on top of you. Or the cab. It should have crushed you, they said."

"Who said that, the army? I want to tell you something, Luther, nothing fell on my truck. Believe me, something else that is strange has happened." Abraham looked the man in the eyes. "Have you seen my truck?"

"No. But if it's totaled, it's totaled. Don't worry about it. Insurance will cover it, and we'll get you a new one—that is, if you want to come back to work."

"No, seriously, Luther—have you seen my truck or the pictures? I want to see pictures!"

"I don't see the point, but I'll do what I can." Luther scratched at his sideburns. "Abraham, no one is blaming you. It was an accident. I'll see if I can get ahold of the West Virginia State Troopers. They should have the accident report. I'm assuming that they worked in coordination with the army, of course. I wasn't at the scene. I just got the phone call."

"From who?"

"Er... a Colonel Dexter. I could call him. I have his card back in my office."

The name rang a bell. Abraham remembered talking to a Colonel Dexter at the gas pumps at Woody's Grill. He'd taken a picture with the man. "Did he have a moustache?"

"I only spoke with him on the phone," Luther said. "I guess, to be fair, he sounded like he had a moustache. His voice was deep, very deep, like a Johnny Cash or Sam Elliot."

Abraham crushed the blankets with his hands. Something stank. It reeked. Bells and whistles sounded off like alarms inside him. "Why don't you get on the phone, call your office, and get that number. I want to talk to him."

"Will you please tell me what you are so worked up about? Look at your heart rate. It's rising." Luther put his hand on Abraham's shoulder. "You need to take it easy. Rest and don't worry about the bills. The brewery has all of that covered. If anything, I think that you have a case against the Department of Highways. I have a great lawyer. His name is—"

Knock. Knock. Knock.

"Mr. Jenkins, you have another visitor," Nancy the nurse said. She looked at Luther. "We try to limit to no more than one at a time if you aren't immediate family. But I'll give you a few minutes."

"Understood," Luther said with a gentleman's nod of the chin. "You're the boss."

Abraham couldn't imagine who else would be coming to see him. He didn't have anyone close left, and Luther was his emergency contact. A shapely woman entered the room. His heart skipped. It was Mandi.

16

MANDI COULDN'T HAVE BEEN PRETTIER. THE DARK-EYED, DEEPLY tanned brunette's hair touched the shoulders of a revealing, low-cut blouse. She wore a jean miniskirt that showed off her nice legs. She held a small vase filled with wild flowers. With a shy expression, she came inside. "Hi, handsome."

"Uh, hi, Mandi." Abraham cast a nervous look at Luther, whose stare hung on the very attractive thirtysomething woman. "This is Luther. I don't know if you've met."

Luther extended his hand and held hers and said, "It's a pleasure. We've met, back when you were a little girl. I used to run around with Herb a good bit. I was at his and Martha's wedding. How is your mother doing?"

"She's just fine but worried about Abraham. She's been sick since she heard about the accident." Mandi released her grip. "Nice to meet you, again, Luther. Um... thanks for letting us know about Abraham. We appreciate it."

"My pleasure." Luther stuffed his newspaper up underneath an arm and said, "I better skedaddle. I don't want to upset Nurse

Nancy. I have a hunch she'd throw me out on my rear like a bundle of newspapers. I'll look into Colonel Dexter for you, Abraham. Now get some rest. You're alive. Be happy." He departed.

Mandi showed Abraham the flowers. "For you. I wasn't sure what sort of flowers you liked, so I picked these along the highway."

"Pretty," he said as he took the flowers in hand. "Uh... I've never gotten flowers before. This is a first." He politely sniffed them and set them down on the nearby food tray. "So, how have you been?"

"Worried," she said as she curled her silky locks around an index finger. "When I heard about the accident, I felt my heart jump. If something bad had happened... Well, I'd feel awful the way we left things."

"You shouldn't feel that way. I mean, I'm flattered. You look great, and you're a beautiful woman." He swallowed and averted his eyes. "I just... Well, I never thought it could work out, and I shouldn't have been so cold to you. I should be flattered." He reached out, took her hand, looked into her lovely eyes, and said, "I guess I'm trying to say that I'm sorry."

Mandi's eyes grew, and she leaned back. "Wow. I wasn't expecting that at all." Her cheeks flushed. She ran the fingers of her free hand through her hair. "That was so open and honest. I'm kinda overwhelmed."

"Well, a lot has changed since I've been gone."

She looked confused and said, "You haven't been anywhere but in this hospital. What happened? Did you have an out-of-body experience?" Her voice grew excited. "Did you see heaven?"

"No, I wish."

She squeezed his hand and said, "If it's hell, I don't want to know."

"No, it wasn't that either."

He sighed. The warmth of her hand was so real. Her full lips were perfect. He wanted to kiss her.

"It's a long story," he said. "You wouldn't believe me if I told you."

She sat down on the edge of the bed. "Do you mind?"

"No."

"So, what were you guys talking about Colonel Drew for? You seemed upset. He helped you out, didn't he?"

"You've talked to him? Drew Dexter. That's his name, right?"

"Yep. He's been stopping in the diner and checking on me. I pretty sure he is not as worried about you as he pretends to be. I think he, well..."

"Likes you? Ha, I'm sure he does. What man wouldn't like a woman with gorgeous legs like that?" He squeezed her thigh just above the knee.

Mandi let out a delightful squeal. "Abraham. What's gotten into you?"

"Nothing. I just know that I'm dreaming." He let out a mad laugh. "Oh, this is so crazy. You have to listen to me, Mandi, and if you will, just keep it between us. Something happened to me inside that tunnel. A big chunk of rock didn't fall on my truck. Or hit my head. And I'm only telling you this because, well, you're nice and have been nothing but good to me, so if I'm crazy, then you need to know it first so you don't get hurt."

She leaned over and caressed his bearded face with a gentle hand. "There is nothing you can say that can scare me. I live out in the middle of nowhere. All I do is watch too much Netflix and cable TV." She squinted. "You look a little different. Those soft eyes of yours have gotten harder. I don't know what it is, but it's sexier. Like there is more of you in there."

"Well, maybe that's because I have a split personality."

17

ABRAHAM FULLY EXPECTED MANDI TO GET UP AND LEAVE THE ROOM. She didn't. She sat on the bed with a smile on her face that grew into a short burst of laughter.

"What?" he asked.

"First off, I've already seen two of your personalities. So you've already surprised me with the last one." She locked her fingers with his. "That was a pleasant surprise. I liked it. It was as if you were coming out of your shell."

"No, that's not what I'm talking about. This is serious. When I went into that tunnel, I ended up passing into another world, a medieval fantasy world. I'm talking knights with swords, monsters, and dragons. I've been fighting all of them. I killed a pirate named Flame Beard."

The smile on her face started to vanish. She said, "You've been listening to too many audiobooks. That's what I think." She shrugged. "But go ahead. Entertain me. I don't have anything better to do."

"You really shouldn't like me this much." He played with his beard. "Look at me. I look like Fozzie Bear or something."

She patted his belly. "Don't be so hard on yourself. I can whip you into shape."

"Ha ha, well, if you saw the other me, you wouldn't have to worry about that. He's in perfect shape."

Mandi tilted her head. "Oh, what do you mean? You aren't you in your *dream* world?"

"I'm a master swordsman named Ruger Slade. I look like the Wolverine guy but bigger and better."

"Ha, now I know you're dreaming. Okay, Ruger Blade—"

"Slade."

"Slade, isn't that an Australian band? You know, the 'Run Runaway' song. Maybe that can be your theme."

He remembered the band and rolled his eyes. "Oh man, don't ruin me." He shifted in his bed. "Do you want to hear this or not?"

"I want to hear it," someone with a scratchy old voice said.

Charles was in a wheelchair being pushed by Nurse Nancy.

"Charles!" Abraham hollered as if he'd just found a long-lost dog. "You're alive!"

The old man lifted his feeble arms and shook his little fists. "They gave me one more week to live. Whoopee!" He broke into a fit of coughing and wheezing.

"Stop getting yourself all worked up, Charles," Nancy said as she rubbed his back. "You don't want to shorten that week."

"The sooner you're off your shift, the more certain I'll be that I'll live longer. When's Lindsay coming back?" Charles caught his breath, twisted his neck around, and glared at Nurse Nancy. "Just get me in bed."

"My pleasure, you ancient goat," Nancy said. The brassy blonde loaded Charles into bed and wired him up to the oxygen and monitors. She made quick work of it then patted his forehead. "See you tomorrow."

"I hope not," Charles said as his wizened eyes watched her exit the room. "She's trying to kill me." He got his first good look at Mandi. "Oh my. She did kill me. I'm in heaven already."

Mandi giggled.

"Charles, where have you been?" Abraham asked.

"Who cares? The only thing that matters is that I'm here now. So, who is your radiant friend?"

"I'm Mandi. It's nice to meet you, Charles."

"The pleasure is all mine." Charles cleared his throat and adjusted the oxygen tube in his nose. "I hate this thing. Makes me look pitiful. But don't mind me. After that last battery of tests, I'm exhausted." He closed his eyes. "Nice to meet you, Mandi. I hope you stick around. You look like a woman that would be good for that guy."

"I will if he lets me," she said.

"Uh... well, Charles, I'm glad you're back. Next time, warn me before you leave," Abraham said.

"Who are you, my babysitter?" Charles waved his hand. "Good night."

Mandi shrugged her brows. "So, are you going to keep telling me your story, or do we need more privacy? We don't want Charles to think you are a nutcase. He might report you to Nurse Dr. Jackie."

"No, I won't," Charles quietly said. His voice trailed off. "I could use a good story."

"Whatever. I don't see the harm in it," Abraham said as Mandi brushed his hair away from his eyes. "Where was I?"

"You said that you were Ruger Slade. A sword fighter."

"A renowned sword fighter." He grabbed her hand. All of a sudden, the urgency to return to Titanuus came back. With awakening passion, he said, "And I was on a mission to save my friends. My Henchmen. They need me. Sticks, Horace, Clarice. They are in immediate danger. There are so many people counting on me. King Hector, Bearclaw, Vern, Iris, Dominga. And my sword even has a name. It's Black Bane."

"That's a pretty vivid dream when you know names for things. I studied psychology in college," she said. "I even thought that I might become a psychiatrist. At least I wanted to. But when I got married and had babies, all of that went by the wayside." She made a sweeping gesture with her hands. "Whoosh. The point is that you usually dream what you know but don't actually identify with new names."

"Wow, that's something I never knew about you."

"I'm a quick study of people. Some I like to study, but most I..." She stopped and looked at Charles.

The old man was sitting up on his bed. A new fire glimmered in his eyes as he stared hard at Abraham.

"Something wrong, Charles?" He glanced at Mandi. "Do I need to call a nurse?"

In a voice as strong as iron, Charles said, "You've been to Titanuus. So have I."

18

ABRAHAM CLEARED A CATCH IN HIS THROAT AND WITH WIDE-EYED wonder asked, "Excuse me? Did you just say that you've been to Titanuus?"

"Oh, yes," Charles said with a healthy luster in his eyes. "It is the home of Black Bane, and you wield it. That's fascinating."

"What is he talking about?" Mandi said. "What is Titanuus?"

Abraham peeled away from the woman and swung his legs over the rim of his bed. "Shh-shh-shh," he said softly.

"I'm not one to take kindly to being shushed," she said, rubbing her bare arms. "But since I have goose bumps popping up all over me, I'll allow it this time."

"Charles, what do you know about Titanuus?" Abraham said with desperate urgency. "I need to get back there now."

Charles's monitors began to beep loudly. His heartbeat and blood pressure spiked. His eyes became spacey and distant, and his mouth opened wide. He clutched his heart and moaned loudly.

"Gooseberries! He looks like he's having a heart attack," Mandi said. She repeatedly pressed the nurse call button located on Abraham's hospital bed. "Nurse! Nurse!"

With a wild-eyed look, Charles snatched Abraham's hands in his. His grip was as strong as a mason's. In a strong cryptic voice, he said, "Find the Big Apple, Ruger. You must find the Big Apple. The tide turns. The Elders awaken."

Nurse Nancy rushed into the room. "Let go of him!" She tried to peel Charles's grip away from Abraham's finger. "Geez, it's like there is Gorilla Glue on them." She stole a look at the monitors. "Charles, let go! You're having a heart attack."

Beep. Beep. Beep. Beep. Beep. Beee...

Finally, the old man's grip broke free, and he fell backward on the bed.

"Get the paddles in here, quick!" Nurse Nancy cried.

"Help him!" Abraham said.

"I'm trying!"

A pack of nurses rushed into the room, pushing a defibrillation machine.

Nurse Nancy removed Charles's gown then grabbed the paddles while a male nurse lubed them up. She rubbed them together. "Charge that thing."

The defibrillation machine made a distinct whine. The male nurse studying the machine gave Nurse Dr. Jackie the go-ahead nod. She lowered the paddles onto Charles's scrawny chest.

A tall and slender black man wearing black-rimmed glasses ran into the room. "Stop!" A physician's stethoscope bounced around his neck. He grabbed Nancy by the shoulders and pulled her away. "Do not resuscitate! Do not resuscitate! It's on his medical power of attorney!"

Nurse Nancy sank inside her Hello Kitty scrubs. "Ah, crap, oh no. I'm so sorry. I forgot."

"Why did you stop for?" Abraham asked. "Bring him back! Bring him back! Why isn't anybody doing anything?"

Dejected, Nurse Nancy said, "I can't. I'm sorry, but this is the way Charles wanted it."

When Abraham reached for the paddles, the doctor stepped in his way. In a firm voice, he said, "Mister Jenkins, you need to settle down. This isn't your responsibility. It's ours. Now, you seem awfully upset. Did you have some sort of relationship with Charles?"

Abraham sat down on his bed. "You could say that, but no, we weren't related."

The doctor nodded and turned away. He checked his watch. "Time of death, 2:10 p.m. Go ahead and take Mister Abney downstairs." He took off his glasses and wiped the lenses with a handkerchief. "Nurse Nancy... come and see me in my office."

Abraham dropped his face into his hands as his stomach twisted into knots. Charles knew about Titanuus. He had been there. Nothing but truth was in his eyes.

As soon as the doctors and nurses left the room, he quietly said to Mandi, "You heard what he said, didn't you? He named Titanuus. That's where I have been. For weeks."

"I heard it. That was intense." Mandi rubbed his arm. "It was intense even before, well"—she had a guilty look in her eye—"before Charles died. I've never seen anyone die before. Not in real life, that is."

If anything, Abraham's doubts about where he was and where he'd been had been eased. He wasn't crazy. He was traveling between two worlds somehow. He knew it in his gut. Everything was too real. The question was how. An explanation had to exist.

"Listen, I need you to do me a favor," he told Mandi. "I mean, I'll understand if you don't want to. But in case I go back out, will you look into a few things?"

She arched a brow and said, "Sure."

"I'll do it on my own, but man, my stomach is fluttering like butterfly wings, and a migraine is coming on again."

"Well, let me get you something for the pain."

"Oh no. Remember, I had a severe problem with that kind of medicine, and I don't want to go through that again." He pinched the bridge of his nose. "I need to maintain a clear head."

"So, what is it that you want me to do?"

"When I was in Titanuus, there were two men from this world that I met. The first one was named Eugene Drisk. He was a professor or something. The other one was another professor named Solomon Paige. He would have gone missing twenty years ago or more. He said he was a hippie nutritionist at Duquesne. Just see if you can find them. And try to find out what that Colonel Dexter is up to. Oh, and do me one more favor. Will you take some flowers to the cemetery? For Jenny and Jake. Just in case."

With a worried look in her eyes, Mandi said, "You're kinda scaring me, Abraham. I don't know what's going on, but I don't want you to leave me again. Abraham." She shook his arm. "Abraham!"

He heard her words, but he could not answer. He didn't want to leave her, but they needed him on Titanuus. Shocking pain splintered his mind. Bright, blinding spots flooded his mind, and he screamed.

19

"He's coming around," someone said.

Abraham's eyes peeked open. The dark surroundings blocked out the skies. Nothing but walls of black rock could be seen. The roar of the waves carried to his ears, but he could smell the salt of the sea. Iris's face was looking right at him. Her round eyes and face had their usual warmness. Her soft hand was on his face. Her touch was warm and soothing, and he wanted to melt into it.

"How long have I been out?" he asked with a groan.

"Several hours. You took a nasty shot on your head. I had to mend the wound from all of the bleeding." Iris rubbed his face with a damp rag. "There was a lot of blood. I almost thought you were dead at first, but I knew better. It would take more than a bump on the head to kill Ruger Slade."

Realizing he was lying with his head on her lap with her bosoms in his face, he rolled over onto his side. His head pounded like a jackhammer. His skull felt as if it were split in half. "That rock about got the best of me."

He peered about. They were in some sort of cave with the top cut out. He could see a small part of the daylight sky. Ugly gnarled trees were growing above, and vines and roots were running down into the strange cave that he lay in.

"Where are we? Where is everybody else?"

"We are secluded while the others are scouting," she said as she reached over and rubbed his back. "Bearclaw carried you over. We are—I don't know—about a mile deep into the island. Crown Island is a strange place. Full of surprises." She flicked away a spider as big as her hand. It looked like a tarantula. "And bugs. Many, many bugs."

"Glad to see that you are among us again."

Squinting, Abraham noticed another person huddled in the corner of the cave. "Shades?"

"At your service, dear Captain." The man was hogtied. "I'd shake your hand, but as you can see, or barely see, I'm a bit indisposed."

"Where did you come from?" he asked.

Shades opened his mouth, but Iris slung a handful of dirt at him.

She said, "He stowed away on the lifeboat. The little bugger was crammed underneath the benches with our gear. I swear, I don't know how he does it. He's not that wee of a fellow. But it is a pain in the ballocks." She flung more dirt at him. "Bearclaw left him here until you woke up so you could decide what to do with him. If there was a vote, we'd vote to leave him here after we rescue the others."

Abraham sat all the way up. The last he'd checked, Shades was locked up in the brig. Somehow, he'd escaped and made the trip to Crown Island with them. He thought it strange that such a sudden change had occurred after he'd come back from his dream or other reality. He'd been in the real world for at least a day, and now he was back in Titanuus. One place was as real as the other. *What if I live in two realities? Is that possible?* Regardless, he had a mission to complete and was actually glad to be back in Titanuus —even if his head hurt.

"Ruger or Abraham, are you still with us?" Shades asked with curiosity. "There is a lost look in your eyes."

Iris got up and gave Shades a stiff kick in the gut. "Be quiet. Nobody needs any more of your agitation."

"It's fine." Abraham stood up. The cave walls were thirty feet up. A narrow passage led out. "Let's go after the others."

"They'll be back soon. Bearclaw said so," she said.

"Yes, Bearclaw said that several hours ago, and that's not soon," Shades said. With his hands and feet tied behind his back, he managed to wriggle his way up onto his knees. "Something is wrong. I've been trying to tell Iris that. I've been around this company a long time, and they should be back by now. Or at least one of them would have checked in. They are very military about that."

That made sense to Abraham. The Henchmen were thorough when executing their plans. They did what they said. And there was a big difference between soon, a few hours, and several hours.

"Iris," he said, "be honest. Do you think Shades might be right?"

"My hands are clammy. I know something is off. But I wasn't going to leave you." She had a guilty expression. "I don't trust that Lewis and Leodor. Those two windbags probably got them into trouble. I'm worried about Horace." She frowned. "Someone should have been back by morning. It's daybreak now."

The conversation about the missing Henchmen made Abraham's hairs stand on end. Something was indeed wrong. Ruger's body could sense it. His sword belt was lying on the ground, so he picked it up and buckled it on.

"Captain... Abraham... Ruger... uh, how should I address you?" Shades asked. "It must be very confusing. I only ask because I want to help. Why else would I come to this wretched island? I want to prove my worth to you. If you could only remember how it used to be. I was one of your best."

"Ha!" Iris said, strapping on a backpack. "He's double tongued. You can trust a hungry wolverine better than you could trust him."

Shades rolled his eyes. "It's not my fault that the ones with less intelligence don't understand me. I'm a complicated man."

Abraham drew a dagger and took a knee in front of Shades. "I'll let you go. I'm certainly not going to let you lie in here and be eaten by spiders or whatever."

Shades brightened. "Excellent. So what title shall I address you by? I don't want to sound disrespectful."

"Ruger will do." He reached to cut away Shades's bindings.

Shades slipped his hands and feet free of the cords with the ease of a magician, and he tossed the ropes at Iris's feet. He looked at Abraham's dagger and said, "No need for that. I could have escaped at any moment and even slipped out when Iris would doze off. She makes little chipmunk noises when she sleeps."

"Hey," she said.

"Whatever," Abraham said. There had been enough delays. He needed to save Sticks and the others. "Grab some gear. Let's go."

Outside, the sun was bright, but a haze hung over the island. The three of them marched to the top of the ridge that they'd been hidden in. With his back to the ocean, Abraham gazed toward the center valleys of the island. It was a jungle, thick with huge twisted trees and wild foliage. Skimming the skies, great birds flew from tree to tree. But something else strange stood out in the middle of the great trees like a thumb. A gargantuan mushroom towered over the tree line.

As the sea winds howled through the rocky seawall, Abraham's spine tingled. "Devil's donuts, they're going to be in there, aren't they?"

20

THE SWELTERING ISLAND JUNGLE WAS ALIVE WITH SNAKES AND vermin. Dripping with sweat, Abraham pushed his way through the bush wherever they couldn't pass. With tiny biting bugs stinging his arms, he forced a path through the dense thickness. "Remind me to leave Crown Island off my list of vacation destinations."

"Will do," Shades said. "I think."

They managed to track the Henchmen's path a mile deep into the island. The company had left a trail. They numbered too many to pass subtly, and the guardian maidens and Lewis and Leodor were inexperienced at what they were doing, which didn't help. Normally, the group could pass unnoticed. But not this time. The effort was sloppy.

Trudging along behind Abraham, Iris pulled free of some colorful flowers covered with briars. "Are there any jungles that aren't miserable?"

"I don't know. I haven't been in that many," he said.

Shades picked his way through the brush and came up behind

them. "I think staying on the boat would have been a better idea. It's no wonder that the windreavers fly. Who could live in this misery?"

"Us for now." Abraham noticed fresh blood on a fern's leaves at his feet. A bright-yellow mosquito was feeding on the blood. He flicked it away. "We have blood."

They moved into a clearing among the trees and prickly bushes. Bushes had been plowed through, and deep foot impressions were on the ground. Some were men's, others beasts'.

"A skirmish. A bad one," Shades said. He was on one knee with his hand on the ground, looking at some footprints in blood. "Whatever they fought won. Something carried off the dead. They are still heading the way we are going, toward that mushroom."

"Seems strange that the windreavers would fight on the ground," Abraham commented.

"It's possible that the windreavers serve something else. A higher power. An Elder," Iris said. She wore an onyx-shaped amulet with dull brass trim around black jade. "The primitive places make living sacrifices. It's possible that they prepare a feast to the Elder of the Sea or another."

"You guys sure have a lot of Elders," he said as he eyed the blood on the ground.

"I don't mean to pry, but don't you have Elders where you come from?" she asked.

Shades looked up at Abraham.

"Elders are the names of parents and older people. But you mean something different. You're talking about gods. People in my world worship many idols, much like your elders. Money is the most notorious one. I only believe in the one true God. No time to discuss that now. We've got Henchmen to save from the clutches of whatever is in that mushroom."

"Ah, the Elder of Coin," Shades said with brightening eyes. "I like that one."

The trio continued the agonizing trek through the rough terrain until some faint pathways cleared. Abraham led the way, sword in hand and ears perked. Birds' calling, insects' buzzing, and varmints' chittering carried over the sound of their feet on the path. Tracks were on the ground, pressed-down woodland and footprints. True to their discipline, if the Henchmen were overwhelmed, they would sometimes scatter. Signs of that were all along the path, as well as signs of something else, a beast, heavy like a horse, with hooves for feet.

An animal-like snort erupted from the jungle ahead.

Abraham and his companions froze. Slowly, on tiptoe, they advanced. They stopped behind bushes rich in cranberries the size of a knuckle. A blue-winged robin flew out of a nest within. The trio hunkered down at the sound of a great beast snorting again.

He mouthed the words to his companions, "What is that?"

Iris and Shades only shrugged.

With the smallish man and hearty woman by his shoulders, he split the bush with his hands and peeked through the gap. A weird pack beast stood on eight powerful legs. It looked like an ox, stoutly built, with a broad head and nose, but had the curled horns of a ram. It stood as tall as and twice as wide as a horse. It had a saddle built for two. One man sat in the saddle, carrying a long spear. His head was a bone-white skull without a stitch of hair or skin on it. The rest of his body was that of a man, strapping, with body carvings, tattoos, and a necklace of finger bones dangling around his neck. His skin was pasty white, and he wore only a belt of daggers and a hemp dress around his waist.

Iris pressed her body into Abraham's and spoke softly in his ear. "Ghouls. The henchmen of many Elders."

Super ghouls is more like it, Abraham thought. They weren't ghouls as he thought of them. He pictured ghouls as a bunch of twisted grave diggers that only came out at night. They preyed on rats, bugs, and birds. This group of ghouls was different. They were warriors, wild men of the jungle with skull faces—a perversion of the living and the dead.

Shades tapped on Abraham's shoulders. He was looking around the right side of the bush, and he pointed.

Abraham hunkered down beside him. Apollo and Prospero were sitting on the ground, back to back, corded in jungle vines. Their faces were bloody and swollen. A second ghoul lorded over the top of them. The ghoul cracked each man on the head with the shaft of his spear and shouted in a bizarre language.

"I can free them if you distract them," Shades whispered to Abraham. "I can free them if you don't distract them. Say the word. It's your call."

"Hold on," he said.

The ghoul screamed in Prospero's and Apollo's faces. Prospero spat on the ground. The ghoul grabbed Prospero by the hair and slammed his head into Apollo's then laughed, mocking them. Quickly, the ghoul tethered the strung-up Henchmen to the beast. The ghoul in the saddle kicked his heels hard into the beast's ribs. The beast lumbered forward, and the rope went taut. Prospero and Apollo were dragged down the jungle path with the second ghoul walking right behind them.

As Abraham watched with horror, he said to Shades, "Go cut that rope. I'll take care of the ghoul."

"What do you want me to do?" Iris said.

"Keep an eye out. There's bound to be more." He looked at Shades. "Keep it quiet."

"Quiet is my middle name," the rogue said.

"Let's go."

21

APOLLO AND PROSPERO BOUNCED DOWN THE PATH. DRAGGED AT A brisk pace, both men fought their way to their feet, only to fall down again and again. Then they did manage to make it upright, but with vain effort, for the ghoul tripped them with his spear. Together, the scraggly Henchmen toppled and busted their knees on the jagged path.

Abraham gave Shades enough time to slip out ahead of him. After a mental count of sixty, he made his move. He dashed down the path with Black Bane in hand, as silent as a deer. The ghouls lumbered with an easy gait, oblivious of the death coming upon them. Ten steps away, Abraham's soft feet touched a dry twig, which made a loud snap.

The second ghoul spun around with casual coolness. Tiny fires like burning diamonds lingered evilly within its eye sockets. The ghoul made an uncharacteristic move, tossing its head back and letting out a deep, demonic cry.

Abraham unleashed a lethal swing that took the ghoul's head

from its shoulders. The body collapsed, and the bone-white skull bounced on the ground. It was still screaming.

"Bloody meat pies, will you shut up!" He kicked the skull like a football, and it went shrieking into the jungle.

"So much for the element of surprise," Apollo called out.

He and Prospero had been cut away from their tether. The battered men stood beside Shades, who'd just cut them free.

"I hope you brought some extra steel with you," Apollo continued. "We're going to need it. Those ghouls don't fight in pairs. They fight by the dozens. The jungle's thick as soup with them."

"You're responsible for your own gear, Henchmen. Not me. My guess is that he has it." Abraham pointed at the ghoul riding the great beast, which had turned around.

The beast clawed its hoof across the ground and snorted. The ghoul lowered its long spear like a lance.

"Trouble's coming," Abraham said. "Step aside."

Iris came charging up the path. Her eyes were as big as saucers. "The jungle's alive. They come." She looked at Apollo and Prospero, who were both empty-handed. "Those aren't going to do you much good. Let's do this."

Apollo and Prospero stuck out their right hands.

Iris grabbed them and started muttering. The wind picked up her hair, and a soft pink glow emanated from her eyes when she started chanting. The men's hands that she held turned into sharp ends like machetes.

Apollo said, "That will do."

Prospero let out a pleased grunt.

As fascinating as Abraham found the moment of transformation, he didn't have time to linger. The ghoul on the beast started its charge down the path. Its great hooves thundered underneath its slavering snarl. It lowered its curled horns that same moment the ghoul lowered its spear.

Abraham felt his body come to life as adrenaline charged through him. He felt invincible. He let go and let Ruger take over. He lifted his sword, charged down the path, and screamed.

Ten feet from a colossal collision with the beast, he leapt high in the air. He cleared the beast's horns and the ghoul's stabbing spear. He hit the ghoul like a cannonball, and it tumbled from the saddle. Both men hit the ground and rolled, one over the other. The ghoul got the upper hand. His strong fingers locked around Abraham's neck and dug in deep.

With a swing of his fist, Abraham cracked the skull of the ghoul with the pommel of his sword. The ghoul's teeth clacked together in laughter. Abraham struck again and again. The blows glanced away from the skull, which was as hard as stone.

"Get off of me, Skeletor!" Abraham pulled a dagger and plunged it into the ghoul's side.

The ghoul let out a gasp as dark blood spurted out of its side.

Abraham bucked underneath the weakening ghoul. He flung the body aside and slipped a dagger into its heart. "I have the power!"

The ghoul died.

The clamor of battle rose.

Abraham popped back to his feet. A gang of ghouls were locked in battle with Apollo and Prospero. The pair of fighters fought with wild fury against the spear-wielding fiends. Apollo sank his hand, turned into a machete, into the body of a ghoul. Prospero butchered another with a swift downward chop that went through the meat of the shoulder. "Kazuna!" he roared.

Farther down the path, Iris ran from a brood of ghouls and vanished into the jungle.

Shades was nowhere to be found.

Abraham ran back down the path after Iris. As he passed the skirmish of Apollo and Prospero in his path, he sliced two ghouls down with one swing. Not breaking stride, he churned after Iris. He leapt a fallen tree and came upon the ghouls that had her trapped in front of a tree. Iris's eyes were aglow with pink fire. Her fingertips massaged the air.

Four ghouls rushed her at once with lowered spears. They would impale her in a moment.

Abraham couldn't get there in time. Iris was doomed.

Jungle vines dropped out of the branches like living snakes. The vines coiled around the ghouls and ripped them up off their feet.

Before Abraham could take a swing at them, the vines ripped the ghouls apart. Black guts spilled out of them.

Iris wiped an oily black smudge from her face and flashed a smile at Abraham. "They fell right into my trap."

"Impressive. If I'd known that, I would have stayed and helped Prospero and Apollo." He scanned the bodies. "They are dead, aren't they?"

"For now. Let's hope the jungle feeds on them." She ran after him as they hurried back toward the path.

They busted through the brush back onto the path. Prospero and Apollo were battling for their lives. Worse trouble was coming. The beast came with snorting fury to trample all of them.

Abraham yelled at the top of his lungs, "Get out of the way!"

If they heard it, they didn't give a sign. The wild bearded men kept fighting.

The ox beast didn't slow a step.

22

Ten yards away from colliding with Apollo, Prospero, and a knot of ghouls, the beast veered left. The bearded warriors shoved away from the ghouls. The battling knot of skull faces stumbled right into the stampeding beast, which trampled the ghouls. Bones cracked, and guts splattered underneath the behemoth's hooves.

Suddenly, a head popped up atop the beast. It was Shades. He sat hunched over in the saddle, tugging hard at the reins. "Get out of the way! Get out of the way! I can barely control this thing!" He pulled the reins hard backward.

Ruger stood in the path in front of Iris with his sword ready to strike.

The ox beast skidded to a halt. Its wet nostrils snorted snot all over the ground.

Shades peeked out from over the top. "I think it's another dumb animal. Naturally, a smart man like me can learn to control—"

The beast bucked.

Shades sailed high in the air. He reached up and grabbed the branches overhead. His fingers locked in a cluster of leaves. Then his grip started slipping. Beneath him, the horned beast jumped upward. Its straight rows of teeth nipped at Shades's toes.

He curled up and yelled, "Slay it! Slay it!"

Abraham caught the horned beast coming down and stepped into a sword swing that cut its neck open. The beast hit the ground with a resounding thud. It bucked a few times and died.

Meanwhile, farther up the path, Apollo and Prospero were finishing off the ghouls with spears. Their hands that were once as sharp as machetes had turned back to normal. They were up to their elbows in blood and gore.

Shades dropped out of the tree and landed without a sound beside the beast. He propped his foot up on it and crossed his arms. "Remember this. I'd like a portrait of it."

"You didn't slay it," Iris said.

"True, but the person looking at the painting won't know that," Shades said.

Apollo and Prospero wandered over. They noticed their sword belts hanging from the saddle of the beast. They picked them up, and each strapped on his two long swords and crossed them behind his shoulders. "I thought more would be coming. We were fortunate. This must have been the last patrol," Apollo said.

"What happened to everyone else?" Abraham asked.

"Ambushed. Scores of them." Apollo spat a bloody tooth onto the ground. "Traveling with Lewis and Leodor was like dragging a wagon full of pottery. They wouldn't shut up. We should have left them with you, but they insisted. We scattered. Made the most of it, but the ghouls had the numbers. Bearclaw surrendered. We hung back and followed but got trapped."

"Trapped how?" he asked.

"Fell into a pit," Apollo said while Prospero clawed the grit out of his beard. "I'm not sure if everyone else is caught. I hate to say it, but I assume they were."

A rustle came from the branches. Someone pushed through the vegetated tangles. It was Zann. His face was all scratched up, and he had bug bites all over him. The Red Tunic held his hands up. "It's me," he said, in a murmuring southern drawl. "I heard the commotion and thought I'd take a look. Glad it's you."

"Is anyone else about?" Abraham asked.

"No. I followed all the rest up to where I could see that crazy mushroom. I heard the scuffle and came back. Walked right into a massive spider web and got bit a thousand times." Zann peeled some webbing off himself. "I used to hate bugs. Now, I hate jungles too."

Abraham nodded. "All right, then. This is it. Let's go."

23

A GIANT MUSHROOM SAT IN A JUNGLE GROVE AND TOWERED ABOVE the trees. The tremendous obelisk of oddity appeared to be at least half the size of a football field. Stout at the bottom and with an umbrella of a top, the gargantuan mushroom was petrified. Vines snaked up the mushroom's sides. Small colorful flowers budded between the countless grooves. The place was unlike anything Abraham had seen before.

"That's weird. A mushroom castle." He and the others were hidden in the jungle less than thirty yards away from the mushroom. They'd been observing the comings and goings around the mushroom for quite some time. A broad dirt road made a ring around the mushroom, where ghouls and their oxenlike beasts circled the castle. On top of the mushroom, the windreavers could be seen, darting through the skies and landing on top. They would vanish on the roof. For all intents and purposes, the mushroom castle was well guarded.

"Any ideas?" Abraham asked his crew.

Shades toyed with the fine hairs budding on his chin. Apollo and Prospero were silent. Iris and Zann shrugged.

"Excellent suggestions."

He got the feeling that it would be up to him to figure out what to do. After all, he was the Captain. At first thought, he figured they could enter in a disguise by posing as the ghouls. He thought that their skull faces might have been some sort of mask. He was wrong—their heads were living skulls. The creepiness sent spiders walking up his arms. They needed to find another way in.

Finally, Shades spoke up. "I can get in there and take a look. At least we'll know what we are up against."

"So can I," Zann said in his slow country-boy accent. "I need to get my brother out of there."

Shades rolled his eyes. "I think it's best that I travel alone. I don't need anyone to slow me down."

"I don't need anyone to slow me down either," the lazy-eyed Zann said.

"You're being serious?" Shades said with incredulity.

"Don't I look serious?" Zann said.

Shades eyed Zann up and down and said, "No, you look useless."

"Enough chatter," Abraham said. "It's broad daylight out, and we'll probably have to wait until nightfall. I don't think anyone will be able to waltz over there without being seen."

"Sure I can," Shades said. He slunk away toward the mushroom castle.

"Anything he can do, I can do," Zann said as he took off after Shades.

Abraham opened his mouth as he watched them go. The men were already beyond earshot. He was about to object but thought the better of it. He needed to trust his Henchmen.

"Are you really trusting Shades to go in there with that boy?"

Iris said. The thirtysomething woman had a motherly tone in her voice. "You can't trust him."

"We've been about to trust him this far," Abraham said. He kept his eyes fixed on the road circling the mushroom castle. Teams of ghoul guards made a slow march around the mushroom, sometimes crossing paths with one another. Two teams of ghouls carrying their spears passed each other, and as the ghouls separated and meandered down their paths, Shades and Zann silently darted behind the ghouls' backs and huddled by the mushrooms. Abraham could barely see the men blending in with the vines. "Whoa. That was slick."

Two of the ghouls turned around. Their bright diamond eyes scanned the ground between them and the forest and the mushroom. They looked right at Shades and Zann.

Abraham's heart quickened as he gripped his sword handle. He said under his breath, "Get ready to bail them out."

The ghouls turned back around and continued their patrol. Shades and Zann began climbing the vines up the mushroom castle. The structure stood over one hundred feet tall. It had to have been massive inside. The pair of men scaled the walls like monkeys and vanished into the stem like rats scurrying into holes.

"They are in. We wait," Abraham said. In a kneeling position, he switched knees.

Iris sat down beside him and hooked her arm in his. "I hope Horace is well. I hope they all are, but mostly Horace. I like him much better since he gave up the tobacco. I liked him, but it always made his teeth so ugly. I couldn't stand that. Now, he's truly handsome. Not like you, but you know, for a bullish man like him. A different sort."

"We'll get him back," Abraham assured her. "All of him."

From inside the mushroom came a low moaning like a great

brass horn. The birds in the surrounding trees scattered out of the branches by the thousands. The critters of the jungle scampered.

Iris covered her ears. The sound became louder. The ground trembled beneath them.

The jarring noise became so loud that Abraham couldn't hear himself speak, and he said in a loud voice, "Do you have any idea what that sound is?"

With her fingertips plugging her ears, Iris shouted back, "An Elder awakens! An Elder awakens!"

24

ABRAHAM FOUGHT THE URGE TO COVER HIS EARS. HE KEPT HIS EYES fixed on the mushroom castle. The vine leaves and wild flowers shook and bowed on the petrified construct. The ghoul patrol took to their knees and bowed. The cavernous sound softened, and a chanting came from within the macabre structure.

Abraham looked at Iris and asked, "What makes you think that an Elder awakens?"

"Only an Elder makes a sound like that. Their very breath can shake the earth. The scrolls of the Sect say so." She unplugged her ears. "Was it not like this when we encountered the Elder spawn? Sounds so horrifying that they turn your bones to jelly. If it awakens, then it will be hungry."

"Then we better get in there," he said.

"We are ready," Apollo said. He had both swords in hand.

So did Prospero. "It's time to fish our brethren out of there. That thing within sounds hungry. Let's feed it some steel."

Abraham caught a glimpse of Zann popping out of one of the mushroom's portals. The wiry man shimmied down the vines, checked both ways at the road, and darted back into the forest. He met up with Abraham and the others. His hands trembled as he fought for his breath.

Abraham put his hand on the young man's shoulder and said, "Take it slow. What did you see? Where is Shades?"

Zann caught his breath. "Everything was fine until that sound started. My heart felt like it headbutted my ribcage. So, we navigated through this canal toward the center. It's like the inside of a beehive inside the mushroom—all sorts of coves, different shapes and sizes. There was a ledge that overlooked the center of the mushroom. It reminds me of the arenas and coliseums in Kingsland, except it's all on the inside."

The chanting coming from the inside of the mushroom grew louder.

"What did you see? Where are the Henchmen?" Abraham asked, shaking Zann's shoulder. "Did you see them?"

Zann nodded. "Yeah, I saw them. There were loaded up in a wagon, like the ones we used to transport prisoners in the king's army. One of those beasts was pulling the wagon toward the center. Those bird people were looking upward in the dome of the mushroom, squawking like crazy. In the dome of the mushroom, something moved. It was a black glob, gelatinous, wet, and sticky, a churning bulging mass. Tentacles dripped out of its body and wiggled like snakes." He shivered. "That's when that thing spoke. I felt it from my toenails to my chin. Shades told me to go." He looked Abraham dead in the eye. "I didn't have any trouble running. My feet did it for me."

"We're going in," Abraham said. "Apollo, Prospero, make sure those ghouls don't get the jump on us. You have the back side. Iris, you can stay or go. Whatever powers you have, have them ready."

"I'm coming. I can't let you have all of the fun without me. Besides, Horace needs me," she said.

Abraham nodded. "Lead the way," he told Zann.

Zann nodded and took off in a straight line for the mushroom castle. He led the climb. Abraham followed, with Iris behind them. Down on the ground, Apollo and Prospero sneaked up on the kneeling ghouls and butchered them. Zann entered the portal, and the group wormed their way into the canal. A few dozen feet in, they could stand.

The corridors were a network of hollowed-out stone. Nooks and crannies of all shapes and sizes were everywhere, partially covered in moss and mold. They sped down the tunnels in the direction that the sound was loudest. They emerged on a ledge overlooking a natural arena. Windreavers were perched along the ledges by the score. The ghouls moseyed about by the hundreds on the ground floor. All the lost Henchmen, bound with ropes, were being led into the center, where they were tied up to individual posts fixed in the ground.

"This is bad. Really bad," Abraham said.

The Henchmen were outnumbered over twenty to one. He looked up into the mushroom's dome. The numbers were just as Zann said... but worse. The heavy glob half filled the cap. Cords of slimy tentacles dropped from its guts. A great circular mouth full of razor-sharp teeth opened and closed. It started a slow descent down the walls.

"That's disgusting. How are we going to kill that thing?"

"It's an Elder. It can't be killed," Iris said.

"It's an Elder of what, slime?" he asked.

She shrugged. "We need Leodor. He might have some idea on how to stop it."

"I don't think we're going to stop it. We need to get everyone out of here," he said with widening eyes as he watched the glob descend. "That big thing moves fast."

Apollo and Prospero filed in behind them and peeked over the rim. "I see it's going to be another one of those days," Apollo said. "What's the plan?"

"We need to cut loose our company and get them the heck out of here." Abraham scanned the ground. "That wagon pulled by the beast might do. We're going to have to load them up and drive them straight back through that tunnel. Those beasts pulling the wagon should make a path. What do you say?"

"Death before failure," Apollo said.

Abraham nodded. "Yeah, it's going to be a real tequila wine mixer."

A shrieking scream erupted from down below. The glob slunk to the ground. Its tentacles, dozens of feet long, lashed out and caught Sticks by the waist. The slimy tentacles pulled her off of her feet. The rope binding her wrists and tethering her to the pole snapped taut. With a pain-stricken face, she hung parallel over the ground, quavering like a strummed banjo string. She cried out, "Help!"

Abraham took off down the stairs, yelling, "Sticks! Sticks!"

25

THE INSIDE OF THE MUSHROOM FLARED OUT LIKE THE INSIDE OF A football stadium. The levels tiered up ten feet at a time. Abraham jumped from one level to the other, catching the attention of the surrounding windreavers. The windreavers started to chirp and beat their wings. Abraham paid them no mind. Sticks was seconds away from having her arms pulled out of her sockets. Panic filled the devotedly expressionless woman's eyes.

A spear ripped right passed Abraham's ear from behind. The mushroom became a hive of anger. He didn't break stride.

"Hold on! Hold on!" he yelled.

Sticks screamed something back at him

Out of nowhere, a smallish man sped across the arena floor with a dagger in hand. He made it to Sticks ahead of Abraham by thirty feet. It was Shades. He cut through the rope with one quick swing. Sticks snapped forward, careening toward the black glob's opening and closing slavering mouth. She flopped on the ground no more than twenty feet away from those foul clenching jaws.

The tentacle holding her by the waist dragged her limp form toward the mouth.

Abraham churned on. He stretched his stride and closed the distance between her and him. Tentacles whipped at his feet and body. He bounded over one, rolled under another, and sliced the third clean through. He arrived at Sticks only ten feet away from the monster's mouth. Small tentaclelike tongues shot out of the monster's mouth.

"No!" With a single downward chop, he sliced the tentacles away from Sticks's waist. A smelly, sticky, gooey puslike substance squirted out. "Run," he said. "Run!"

Sticks tried to crawl away to safety, but another tentacle snared her leg. Her fingers clawed at the ground as she started to be dragged back in and yelled, "You call this a rescue?"

———

Horace sawed the ropes binding his wrists against the sharp square edge of the post he was tied to. The twine rope coiled around his wrists started to fray. Even with great effort, getting free would take an hour. He would be dead by then. "Remain stalwart, Henchmen!"

The mushroom's arena broke out into absolute chaos. A handful of Henchmen erupted from the terraces, bringing a roaring shout of encouragement from the prisoners. At the same time, the black glob, some sort of ancient Elder, had come to life. Tentacles sprang from its mouth like snakes, and that fiend's slithering things came for them. That was only part of it—the other part were the windreavers and the ghouls. They were in a full-frenzied attack and had set their sights on the Captain.

"Be patient, big one. I'll be back for you," Shades said as he slipped by Horace and sawed at Dominga's cords where she was hung up on the next post over. "Ladies first."

"Take your time. I don't need you." Horace put his shoulder into his post. The six-inch-wide pole wobbled. Using his strong hands, he rocked the post back and forth. It broke free in the hard ground. With a loud grunt, Horace ripped the post out of the ground.

Bearclaw and Vern let out wild cries. "Wreak havoc, Horace!" Vern shouted.

With eight feet of hard wooden post in his hands, Horace took a swipe at three charging ghouls and knocked them over. "Kiss wood, abominations!"

Two tentacles coiled around his ankles and ripped him from his feet. A windreaver glided over him and dropped a hunk of stone.

The boulder landed square on Horace's belly. He let out a gusty "oof!" and the tentacles reeled him in toward the black glob's mouth.

———

Shades cut Dominga free, which had a domino effect. He gave her a blade, and she cut loose the guardian maidens while he freed Bearclaw and Vern. The bigger men burst into action, and along with the rigid guardian maidens, Hazel and Swan, the foursome unleashed an assault on the ghouls. Locking up in hand-to-hand combat, they took away the ghouls' swords and abused the fiends with them. Streams of black blood dripped onto the ground.

The last people Shades cut free were Lewis and Leodor.

While the old man rubbed his raw red wrists, Lewis glared at Shades and said, "Next time, free me first."

Shades made a quick bow and sarcastically said, "As you wish, son of the king."

Lewis turned away. Weaponless, he marched straight toward two ghouls coming at him with swords. Lewis darted between their simultaneous thrusts, twisted a sword from one ghoul's hand, and heel-kicked the second one in the gut. With a sword in hand, he disemboweled the one he'd disarmed with a lightning-quick stroke. Then he split open the white skull of the other. A rush of more were coming his way. "Leodor, do something! I'm not doing all of the work myself."

Leodor gave Shades a firm push. "Step aside, child of the star." He flicked his fingers. The bony appendages emanated a green fire. He spread out his fingers, pointed at the rushing knot of ghouls. Green darts shot from his fingertips, and the darts shot through their foreheads. They tumbled to the ground. "That's power."

Windreavers soared overhead, dropping rocks. Shades danced away from the shower. Leodor took a direct blow to his skull.

The hordes kept coming. The battle got worse.

26

THE GUARDIAN MAIDENS CUT PRINCESS CLARICE LOOSE FROM THE post by sawing the rope with a spear.

"Get me a weapon!" Clarice said.

A windreaver soared overhead and chucked a spear down at her. With catlike agility, Clarice jumped aside. The spear bit into the ground, inches from her toes.

The dark-headed guardian maiden, Swan, and the light-haired Hazel cocked their spears back over their shoulders. Taking aim with the skill of well-trained soldiers, they launched their spears.

The windreaver that attacked Clarice twisted away from Swan's spear, but Hazel's caught it right in the abdomen. The windreaver let out a squawk and spiraled downward. It crashed skull first into one of the hitching posts.

Two ghouls carrying swords rushed Clarice. The first ghoul moved with a notable limp, and the other's skull face had a busted socket. The swords they carried were corroded, but steel still shone from underneath the rust. The notched edges were keen in some spots.

Clarice ducked underneath a sideward swing from the limping ghoul. She hopped out of the way of the second ghoul's cut. The strapping fiends lifted their swords high and struck out at her at the same time. She hopped backward. The swords missed her chest by an inch. She tripped over the legs of the dead windreaver and fell to the ground. The ghouls pounced.

"Save the princess!" Hazel cried out. Without a weapon, the guardian maiden hurled herself in front of the ghouls. She absorbed the full brunt of their attack.

The ghouls' swords hacked deep into Hazel's body armor with vicious blows, and blood flew.

Clarice screamed, "No!"

Abraham chopped at the tentacles as quickly as he could. He freed Sticks more than once, but keeping up was hard as the tentacles kept coming out of the black glob. He severed one slimy cord after the other and shouted, "Sticks, get out of here! I can handle this!"

"I don't think so," she said as she made acrobatic leaps and rolls away from the tentacles. "There are too many of them." She kicked one tentacle away and jumped another.

"Get in that wagon, and get everyone out of here!" Abraham sliced through two tentacles at once. "This is a rescue mission. Be rescued!"

"Incoming!" Horace said in his bearish voice. He was being dragged by many tentacles coiled around his feet toward the great opening and closing mouth. He had the hitching post and was clobbering the tentacles, but they did not release. Eyeing Abraham as he was dragged helplessly toward the black glob, he said, "Death before failure, Captain!"

"Everybody is going the wrong way!" Abraham said. "Hench-men, all of you get out of here!"

Escaping was easier said than done. In addition to the black glob were the scores of ghouls and windreavers launching attack after attack. Everyone was engaged in a life-and-death struggle. Where there were blades, there was blood—lots of it.

A new wave of tentacles spat out of the black glob's mouth. Abraham sliced through half of them. The other half wrapped up his wrist and ankles. With a fierce yank from the tentacles, he hit the deck. The black glob drew him in toward its clenching jaws. He wasn't alone. Sticks and Horace were heading that way as well. Wrestling against the tentacles, he said, "Meatballs and spaghetti! This isn't good!"

The black glob reeled them in toward its hungry mouth.

"I can smell the foulness within! Like the sewers of Dorcha!" Horace bellowed. "There is nothing but rotting death in there!" He looked to Abraham. "I have an idea. I'll go first and buy you time. It's been a pleasure to serve, Captain *Abraham*."

"No, stop, Horace, what are you doing?" he asked. He was on the right, with Horace in the middle and Sticks to the left of Horace.

Horace managed to hop on his butt and inch ahead of Abra-ham. He came within a few feet of the black glob's mouth. Horace lifted up the post, and as soon as his boots touched the rim of the glob's chomping mouth, he shouted, "How about a toothpick?" With a well-timed effort, he shoved the post into the monster's mouth. The great jaws froze. The gelatinous black glob let out an angry moan.

Horace gave a big, bearded smile. "It's working!"

The black glob's mouth twisted left and right like a dial. Its massive gooey body trembled all over. Abraham found a sliver of hope in the futile moment. Horace had bought them time. It could go a long way.

The post inside the monster's mouth snapped in half with a loud pop. Its teeth clacked together. The tentacles that held them were severed. They were free.

Horace let out a throaty cheer and pumped his fist in the air. "Death before failure!"

A nest of slimy tentacles burst out of the slimy Elder's mouth, enveloping Horace. In one easy yank, Horace's big body was jerked off the ground, and he vanished inside the blackness of the monster's mouth.

27

Abraham's fighting heart sank. The gutsy Horace was gone.

"No," he muttered.

As the dead tentacles fell away from his limbs, another surge of them came. He and Sticks jumped and twisted. The tentacles were too many, overwhelming them with slimy coils that bit into their limbs and bodies.

With vain effort, he tried to cut against the tentacles locking him up, with fierce motions of his wrist. He cut, but that wasn't enough. "Sorry, Sticks," he said.

As the tentacles slowly reeled her in toward the monster's mouth, she said, "It's not your mistake. We never should have been caught."

"I say, what is all of the commotion about?" Black Bane asked, speaking into Abraham's mind.

"Black Bane! Do something! We're about to be devoured by a glob. Stop it!" he said.

"Are you calling me Black Bane or someone else?" the sword asked.

"You! You never told me your name. You forgot it!"

Wriggling against her bonds, Sticks asked, "Who are you talking to?"

"The sword! It's a long story!"

"Hmm... I suppose Black Bane will do. It's a fine name for a sword, but I'm not so sure about for a person," the sword replied. *"Let me see what I can do. Drawing magic from different worlds can be tricky. What sort of spell are you needing? A shield. Perhaps flying. I liked flying, I think."*

With the black glob's mouth only a few feet away, Abraham yelled, "Fire! Lightning! Just do something!"

"No need to yell."

The engravings on Black Bane charged up with the hot glow of lava. The handle heated up quickly in his hand. "What am I supposed to do?"

"Point and shoot."

Abraham was more than familiar with the concept. He'd been to the firing range with his father dozens of times. Also, he was a pitcher. The problem was that the sword was pointed toward the ground. Tentacles pulled down his arms, making it impossible to aim.

He huffed and puffed. The hard muscles in his arms went to work, and Ruger's body responded. He grabbed the handle in a firm grip with both hands. With the muscles in his forearms bulging like roots, he lifted the sword and pointed it toward the glob. "Cut loose the chaos!"

A crooked stream of burning energy blasted out of the sword's blade as if fired from a cannon. The fiery bolt slammed into the glob's body. Shockwaves rolled through its gelatinous makeup. It let out a heavy moan that filled the arena. The black glob crept away from the wroth power. Its tentacles loosened their iron hold on Abraham and Sticks.

Abraham climbed to his feet and let the sword unleash its power on the monster. "Die, you pile of manure. Die!"

The black glob spat a huge black glob out onto the ground. It landed right before Abraham's feet. He didn't change his efforts, keeping the stream of energy pointed at the monster. With alarming speed, it crawled back up the wall and into the cap of the mushroom, more than half filling the ceiling. The bolt of power sent out one final surge as the last blast of energy released from the sword. The black glob made an ear-jarring shriek. Its body heavy and bulged, and it exploded.

KA-POOOOOM!

The ceiling rained down big globs of goo, showering everyone in oily sludge.

The ghouls and windreavers scattered.

Covered in glistening ebony slime, Abraham said, "That was gooey. Ghostbuster gooey—like a burnt marshmallow." He smacked his sludge-covered lips. "But that ain't marshmallow. More like burnt dung."

"Tastes like life to me!" the small black blob at Abraham's feet said.

"Horace!" Abraham said.

Horace popped up. "Aye!" He pumped his fist in the air. "Henchmen! Henchmen! Henchmen!" All the others rallied around the men and joined in. "Henchmen! Henchmen! Henchmen!"—except for Lewis and Leodor.

Abraham walked over to Lewis, stood by his side, and put his hand on his shoulder. "What is wrong? Aren't you used to victory?" he asked the refined prince, who was now covered in muck. He wiped his finger over the man's cheek, revealing the white underneath. "Don't worry. You'll eventually get a taste for it."

28

THE HENCHMEN MADE IT BACK TO *SEA TALON* AND CONTINUED THE journey north through the Sea of Troubles. All of them were sticky with black glob goo and blood. The blood from their battle wounds washed off easily. The glob was a different matter. It was more like a tar. It clung and stank on all of them.

Only one of them had died on the trek into the detestable Crown Island. Hazel the guardian maiden was given a flaming burial at sea. The crew watched the pyre of floating smoke and flame from the rear decks of the ship. It sank with the dreariness of Crown Island in the background.

Horace said a few words. "She lived with loyalty and died like the guardian she was."

All the eyes of the hardened company were dry, save for Princess Clarice's. The sixteen-year-old fought hard to control her sobbing, but her chin quivered. She clung tightly to her other guardian maiden, Swan. Like a loving aunt or older sister, Swan stroked Clarice's tangled locks.

"Everyone," Abraham respectfully said as the funeral pyre was swallowed by the waters, "let's get back to work. Mend your wounds and fill your bellies. This journey has only started." As everyone got back into action and moseyed down the decks, he looked at Swan. "Let me have a word with Clarice."

The raven-haired woman with eyes as hard as stone deepened her frown.

"It's a polite request," he said.

Swan's nostrils flared. She kissed Clarice on the head and walked away.

Clarice wiped her eyes, which were fixed on the burial spot at sea. "What do you want?"

"I just wanted to say that I'm sorry about the loss of your friend."

"Hazel has been with me since I was born." She sat down on the railing and held on with shaky hands. "That should have been me that died. Not her. She gave her life for me. And just like that, it's gone. I didn't have the right to take that."

Abraham lifted a boot up onto the railing, leaned forward with his eyes on the shiny wavetops of the sea, and said, "It's a good thing that you care."

"What is that supposed to mean? Of course I care."

"Where I come from, there are a lot of entitled people, like you, that don't care. Life has little meaning to them."

"I'm not like Lewis. He's that way, not me."

He nodded. "I can see that. But her death is your fault."

She glared at him and said, "I know that."

"No, I don't think that you do. At the moment, yes, she gave a sacrifice for you, but it was you that put her in the dangerous situation," he said. "You see, you disobeyed your father. You stowed away on this ship. You didn't give any consideration to the consequences of your actions. And now, your friend is dead."

Clarice turned rigid. Her eyes had the poison of snakes. "How dare you? I'm the—"

"Princess! Yeah, I know that. But you're on my ship, and you're part of my Henchmen. From now on, you act like it. Keep your impulses to yourself. They get not only you into trouble, but others as well."

With her mouth hanging open, she stood up, shut her mouth, gave him a burning look, and stormed away from the deck.

Abraham didn't even watch her go. He'd said what needed to be said. Clarice, Lewis, and Leodor were proving to be nothing but trouble. They were dragging the Henchmen down. He couldn't have that.

Sticks slid into view. "Pretty tough on the girl," she said. Her clothing was sticky with black tar, and she had cuts and scrapes all over. Her hair was tied back in two twisted braids.

"You disagree?"

"No, you're the Captain. She needed it. I think what you said was spot-on." Sticks planted her rear end on the railing. "Let her go plant her face in a pillow."

"You don't cry, do you?"

"No. It's a waste of water."

He chuckled. He needed the laugh. The day had been a long one.

Sticks cocked an eye at him and said, "Your sword talks to you?"

"Huh, well, when it wants to." He locked his fingers on Black Bane's handle. "I was going to ask you or Horace about that. Did the other me ever talk to the sword?"

"Not out loud, that I recall."

"What about the power that I used? I mean, I cast lightning out of the tip."

"The old you used some strange powers. But he never

attributed it to the sword." She licked her fingers and rubbed at a greasy spot of tar on her elbow. "This stuff is nasty. Yech. Anyway, the older you acted like he could do anything. Horace and I always suspected there was something with Black Bane. After all, the Elders made it. So *they* say."

"Who is *they*?"

"Isn't that always the question?" The straight-faced woman shrugged and spat over the deck. "I say, who cares? We live. We die. Don't dwell on it."

"You really know how to liven up a party, don't you. If for some reason you ever make it to my world, I'm taking you to a Catalina wine mixer."

"A what?"

"Nothing." He took his hand away from his sword and said, "Just keep this between us, but I think a wizard from another world lives in it. Like I live in Ruger's body, someone else lives in this sword. It's very weird. Like Excalibur with a personality."

"What's Excalibur?"

"A legendary sword from my world."

"So, your world is like this world?" she asked.

"It used to be, I suppose. I'm not so sure about the magic. But the supernatural was more prevalent in biblical times with wizards like Jannes and Jombres." He slapped a knee and smiled. "But what do I know? I didn't live back then, but I can't rule it out either." He pushed out his chest and said, "Frankly, I'm just rolling with it."

Sticks gave a concerned smile. "Are you well?"

"I can't say. For all I know, I've gone crazy, but let's keep that between ourselves. I'm going to go track Solomon down. I'll see you later."

"Your cabin?"

He lifted two fingers and started to think of Mandi. "Uh, possibly."

"I'll kill him!" someone shouted from the main deck. "I'll kill him!"

29

IT TOOK SOME DOING, BUT ABRAHAM QUICKLY BROUGHT THE commotion of angry voices under control. Apparently, Shades had somehow fondled Swan inappropriately. He claimed it was a misunderstanding, and he claimed it from the safety of the crow's nest. Meanwhile, Swan had her sword out, eager to butcher the slightly built man. She tried to climb the ropes, but her clumsy effort only brought on chortling laughter from the crew. Swan apparently couldn't climb ropes to save her life.

The red-faced Swan put it all on Abraham and said, "Put that man in the brig! Cast him in the sea! No man touches me like that and lives!"

"Touch you how?" Abraham asked.

"I don't want to discuss it. Bring him down here, and let me cut him open. I'll have satisfaction!"

"I saw it, Captain," Tark said from the next-highest deck. "He squeezed her rump like a melon from the marketplace. He got both hands on the hind end. Both small hands, that is. I'm surprised she noticed it. She's got an ample rear end." He made a curved gesture with his hand. "Like an apple."

Swan waved her sword at Tark and said, "Keep your eyes off my hind end! I'll kill you too!"

Tark's light eyes grew big.

The Henchmen ruptured with chuckles.

Even Abraham couldn't help but laugh. As he regained his composure, he shouted up to Shades in the crow's nest. "Come down here, apologize, and let's be done with it."

"Do you think an apology will do?" Swan said to him with an angry white stare. "I will have satisfaction. I will have vengeance. That rodent is not worthy to touch the sanctity of a guardian maiden. He has soiled me."

"He squeezed your butt," Iris said. "You don't need to start a war over it even though you could probably fight one on it."

Swan paled. She was a tall, strapping woman, almost mannish in build, with a tailgate that seemed to bring with it a natural air of authority that she wasn't entitled to. "You gap-toothed trollop. How dare you speak to me like that. I'll kill you too!"

"At this rate, she is going to kill everyone," the puffy-lipped Vern remarked with a chuckle. "Everyone, keep your hands to yourself, or the princess's bodyguard is going to cut them off and shove them up your nose."

"Okay, that's enough!" Abraham threw his arms up. "We are all Henchmen, and we don't cut each other's throats. Sorry, Swan, but an apology from Shades will have to do."

Burly, bald, and bearded, Horace said, "Er... Captain, they are not Henchmen. They don't have to live by the same standards that we do."

Abraham remembered that neither Shades nor Swan was branded. Without the brand, he didn't have full control over them.

Lewis strolled into view. "Ah ha, yes, the guardian maidens live by their own rigid standards. And when I say rigid, I mean rigid. Certainly, you remember, don't you, Ruger? Or am I talking to the other man in the shell, Abraham?"

Abraham didn't know what the man was talking about. Swan had a seething look.

"Can't you let this go?" he asked.

"No," Swan said in her husky voice.

"Ruger, you know me, I can't always control my impulses when faced with a such a charming woman," Shades shouted down from above. "The moment I encountered her, I was... smitten."

"I won't be groped like a tavern trollop. I am a guardian maiden. This sullied man must pay. You should know that," Swan said to Ruger.

"Fine, Lewis, fill me in." Abraham hated to ask, but it was something that he should obviously know but didn't. "What am I missing?"

"The guardian maidens are virgins. Pure of heart. No man can touch them without permission," Lewis said happily. "Not me and certainly not that man in the roost."

With her arms crossed over his chest, Dominga said, "No wonder she is so uptight." She bumped forearms with Vern and Iris, who stood beside her smiling.

"So, let me get this straight. You want to fight Shades. To the death," Abraham said.

"It is our way," Swan said. She took off her sword belt but removed her poniard. "A dance of daggers will do. I aim to teach him a lesson, but I'll kill him if I want to. I have the right."

Abraham gave Sticks and Horace a lost look. They shrugged their brows at him. Apparently, this was a legitimate conflict, and he could do nothing about it.

"This is insane. Swan, you should set your pride aside and let me punish him. Cheese and crackers, all of this from a bump on the rump." He threw his hands up. "Shades, get down here. This lady wants to dance. Give her a dance."

Shades climbed out of the crow's nest and down the mast like a spider. "I love to dance. And with this fabulous vixen, it will be a pleasure."

Swan glared down on Shades and said, "Grab a dagger. You're going to need it."

30

A CIRCLE OF PEOPLE FORMED AROUND THE TWO COMBATANTS. THE fight was on.

The belligerent Swan glared at Shades and said, "Arm yourself, little man!"

Shades showed his slender fingers and said, "There won't be any need for that. I'd never stab a woman. Especially a ravishing beauty like you."

"You are a fool," Swan said in a cold tone. "I will not show mercy on you."

"Ooh... you know how to say the things that I like," Shades said with a smile.

All Abraham could do was watch and hope that Swan didn't kill the mouthy man. As he stood with his hands crossed over his chest, Vern took wagers from the others. The Henchmen were whispering among themselves. Some of them, like Cudgel, were grinning. Apollo and Prospero were huddled together, gathering their own money.

Swan spun her poniard in her hand and cut it quickly back

and forth. She'd proven to be a skilled fighter, slaying ghouls and windreavers alike. Shades, however, appeared to be a different sort of foe. He moved quietly and quickly in his cloak.

"Take off that cloak," she said. "I need to see that you don't have any tricks up your sleeve."

"Oh, I'd be happy to." Shades spun the cloak off his body in a showy display. He hung it over his arm as a butler would and made a quick bow. He was bare chested and little compared to the other men on the crew. His body had a thin layer of fat and some muscle showing. He was fit, but not as fit as most. White and red scars from battles and beatings covered his back and chest. He'd been through something—a lot of something. "Oh, sorry, I accidentally removed my jerkin. I hope you like what you see, dear guardian maiden." He flexed his meager arms.

Bearclaw chortled.

Swan, whose skin appeared unblemished, blanched as she eyed him top to bottom. She set her jaw again and said, "You talk too much. One last chance to take a weapon."

Dominga flicked a dagger at Shades's feet, where it stuck deeply into the planks. She said, "Don't be a fool. Take it."

Shades tossed his cloak aside, bent over, and grabbed the dagger with one hand. Straining with effort, he tried to pull the dagger free with a grunt. He dropped to both knees and pulled at it with both hands. The dagger didn't budge.

The Henchmen busted out with bellowing guffaws.

Abraham couldn't hold his laughter back. Even Sticks couldn't contain her smile.

Swan's face turned as red as a beet, and she cast a hot stare at all of them. "Foolish hyenas! I'll give you something to laugh at!" Cat quick, she lunged and stabbed at Shades.

Without the dagger, Shades rolled out of the way in one silent, smooth motion. He popped up to his feet and hopped away from a slice across his belly.

"Cut him open like a fish!" Iris shouted.

Shades shot her a look. He backpedaled, dodged, dived, and rolled away from Swan's lethal strikes with the grace of an acrobat. The more he moved, the angrier Swan appeared to become. She thrust hard and fast.

The Henchmen shouted cheers of encouragement.

The combatants worked the inner circle. Swan's nostrils flared. Shades shot a devilish smile at her. With a grunt, she rushed him and let loose an overhead cut. Shades spun underneath the strike and slipped behind her body. She overextended and lost sight of him. She spun around, but Shades moved more quickly than she. He stuck to her, back to back, without touching her. She turned around slowly, a lost look in her eyes. Even when she would spin more quickly, Shades remained smoothly behind her. He put his finger to his lips when she stopped.

The Henchmen couldn't contain their laughter.

Swan looked over her shoulder and kicked backward. As Shades leaned left, she drove her left elbow into his ribs. With a painful *oof*, he sagged to the ground. She pounced on top of the smaller man. Straddling him, she pinned him down by clamping one hand over his throat.

She poised the dagger above his eye. "What do you have to say for yourself now, worm?"

Shirking underneath her gaze, he said, "The flesh is weak."

"I'll show you how weak it is." She cocked back the poniard and started to thrust.

"Swan! No!" Princess Clarice shouted in a voice that all could hear. She had been down below earlier, but the commotion of battle must have caught her attention.

"This man violated me. He violated the guardian maidens," Swan said, out of breath and panting.

"I tried to apologize," Shade said, "but everyone knows that these hands can't be trusted. Not when beholding such rare and divine—"

"Shut your mouth hole!" Swan said.

The princess walked over to Swan and calmly said, "Set your weapon aside. That's an order."

"But..." Swan said, dejected. She stuck the dagger in the deck right beside Shades's face. When she stood up, she found Clarice looking up into her eyes, and she swallowed.

"Swan," Clarice said. "I hereby release you from your vow to me. You are no longer a guardian maiden. I am no longer princess. I am a Henchman. You choose to be what you choose to be."

A silence fell over the ship. Lewis stood nearby, leaning against the mainmast with an eyebrow lifted.

Swan's jaw dropped. "Princess Clarice... I know no other task."

"Neither do I. You'll just have to learn like me."

31

As the ship sailed on, Abraham finally tracked Solomon down. Compared to a luxury cruise liner, *Sea Talon* was very small. However, finding Solomon wasn't so easy. The troglin had a knack for hiding. In this case, Solomon had hidden himself in plain sight. He'd locked himself in the brig. That was the last place Abraham looked.

"You really don't need to be inside there." Abraham stood outside the cell's bars, which were locked. "You aren't an animal. Care to tell me what is going on?"

Solomon sat on the floor with his head down. "I don't feel like troglin are meant to be sailors. The motion of this ship is torment to me. It puts me on edge, and that makes me hunger."

"You mean, you want to eat people?"

Solomon nodded. "It's a sick thing. I'm becoming a ravenous cannibal. I swear I did nothing to deserve this."

"We'll cast our nets and start fishing. Will fish fulfill you?"

"I don't know that that will sustain me. I could handle some sushi. About a ton of it." Solomon lifted his hairy face and managed a sharp-toothed grin. "But this isn't a fishing vessel."

"No matter. The Henchmen always surprise me. I'm sure they'll catch something. A shark, maybe."

"Jaws would be delicious about now."

Abraham slid down the wall and sat down. "I had another experience."

"Really, you mean, a dream? What happened on that island?"

"That's a long story, but you'll pick up on it." He rubbed the nasty bump and gash on his head. "We were rowing the lifeboat to Crown Island when the surf rode my head into the rocks."

"I can see that. Do tell more."

"I woke up in a hospital. There was an old man in the other bed. Uh…" His eyes searched the ceiling. "Charles. Charles Abney was his name. He was old but very lively. There was a whole lot of goings-on. But do you know what he said to me?"

Solomon's belly rumbled. "No."

He turned his head toward Solomon and said, "He said he'd been to Titanuus."

"But that was a dream?"

"It didn't feel like a dream. It felt as real as this, or as real as it ever was." He bumped his head gently against the wall. "My boss was there, Luther Vancross. And Mandi was there too. We had a very deep conversation."

Abraham spent the next hour going over the details, and Solomon hung on his every word.

"I'm telling you, Solomon—this place is real, and that place is real. I feel like we are part of a bizarre experiment. In my dream, I was back in my body too. Just like I had an accident, but in a way, I don't believe it."

"Maybe you are Ruger Slade, dreaming that you are in another world and in another body," the troglin offered.

"What? No, that can't be it. Anyway, if I go back again, maybe I'll get more answers. I told Mandi to look into a few things. I wanted her to find out what happened to you and look into that Eugene Drisk."

"That's very kind of you. I'd be very curious to know what happened to me too. I wonder if my gangly body has been running around grocery stores terrorizing butcher shops for the last twenty-plus years."

"What do you mean?" he asked. "You think that the troglin inhabits your body?"

"I don't know how it works. It just made sense to think of it that way. Anyhow, go on."

Abraham rubbed the back of his head and said, "I think I lost my train of thought." He snapped his fingers. "Oh, when I get a bad migraine, that seems to trigger it. I've always had them since the plane accident. It's what got me addicted to painkillers. So, you don't have dreams like I do?"

"No. I'm envious. I'd do anything to go back to our world, even for a day—drink beer, smoke pot, and eat pizza. That's what I'd do."

"You can't think of something more practical to do? Like see your family?"

"I just want to relax, man. My family is pretty intense, hence my early inclinations towards recreational drug use." Solomon chuckled.

"I think we could make pizza if we wanted to. We could introduce this world to a lot of things."

"Indoor plumbing would be delightful." Solomon scooted away from the back way to the front of the cell. "Abraham, I think you are enjoying this world more than the last. Would that be an accurate statement?"

"I hate to say it, but I think so. Back home, I didn't have

anything but my beer truck. I felt guilty all the time. It was hard to overcome. Everything reminded me of them," he said. "I know that's not right. Is it?"

"Who is to say but you? But if you let this world take over, then you might not ever make it back to the other," Solomon said.

"The only thing back home is Mandi. But we haven't even been on a date. I feel guilty when I'm with her, but here, I don't feel as much guilt."

Solomon tilted his head back. "Ah, what happens in Titanuus stays in Titanuus."

Abraham chuckled. "That's messed up, but I guess so. We could probably make a killing if we opened up our own casino here."

"Assuming that no one else has thought of it. Perhaps."

"What do you mean by someone else?" Abraham asked.

"Well, dude, we can't assume that we are the only ones here, now can we? If we are seeing modern items, and I've met you, and you've met me, then it's safe to say that *we are not alone*."

"Holy baloney. I just remembered something. The old man, Charles—he told me to find the 'Big Apple.' Does that mean anything to you?"

"Aside from what I know of it back home, no. I've never heard the expression before. Not here, anyway."

"I guess we are going to have to start asking around, then." Abraham got up. "It might not hurt to ask around now. Hang tight. I'll see what I can do about getting you something to eat."

Solomon came to his feet. The hairy troglin had to bend sideways as his head hit the ceiling. He reached through the bars and grabbed Abraham by the arm. "Don't get caught up in this world. Remember, we don't belong here. I want to go back, and I'm counting on you."

"I know. I gave you my word. I'll keep it."

"You can't please everyone all the time," Solomon said. "At some point, it will have to be one or the other. We can never have it all."

Abraham pulled away and said, "We'll see."

32

S*EA* T*ALON* AND ITS CREW SAILED FOR DAYS WITHOUT ANY MORE incidents on the turbulent waters. The pirate galleon made its way safely over the Head of Titanuus and was now making its way south, past the Pirates' Peninsula, located on the East Arm. Early in the day, the great sun shone over the sea. Tark and Cudgel were in the crow's nest, using spyglasses. They were far out at sea, where the land could not be seen. That left Abraham uneasy.

Sticks stood beside him, overlooking the port side of the ship and staring farther out to sea. She leaned against his body. He put an arm around her shoulder. The last few days had been quiet. In the evenings, they slept together in his quarters. She had been very affectionate, more so than before. They didn't speak about it, but he had a feeling it had something to do with him saving her life. He was getting used to it and feeling less guilty.

"Feels like there is nothing out here but us, doesn't it?" he asked.

"I know I'm glad I'm not alone. I'd hate to be lost at sea. It's massive," she said.

"Have you ever wondered if there are other lands like Titanuus out there? In my world, there are many."

"I couldn't care less. So long as I'm on land, I'm happy, even though being on this boat with you has had, well, some advantages."

"Women find sailing romantic." He toyed with her braid that hung over her breast. "Do you?"

"I don't know about that, but it seems to make the sex better."

"Oh, so you're just using me."

"It's either you or any one of them," she said as she glanced at the working crew. "But you do have the larger bedroom."

One thing he liked about Sticks was her matter-of-factness. And she was certainly a lot more woman than she appeared to be. With her came mystery and excitement, which made the voyage more delightful.

"Let's hope we don't sail too far and run into one of the Elders. I'd hate for one of them to capsize our boat." Abraham looked toward Horace.

Manning the wheel of the ship, the warrior had his face to the wind, and Iris stood behind him with her arms wrapped around his belly. Her hands beat on it gently like a drum.

Abraham scanned the deck with a shade of a smile.

Vern and Dominga sat on the bow with their legs dangled over the rim. They held hands. He talked. She giggled.

Somehow, impossibly, Shades and Swan were speaking openly. They were both swabbing the deck. He constantly spoke with flattering words while she tried to fight back her smiles.

"It's becoming a regular Love Boat around here," he said. "At this rate, we'll be starting new families. Is there an Elder of Love or Romance?"

"The Elder of Passion, they call her. They say her essence is the same wind that kisses the seas. Perhaps she is kissing us now," she said with a playful smile. "Do you want to go back to your cabin?"

Without any guilt, Abraham tossed her up on his broad shoulder and said, "Sure. What happens on Titanuus stays on Titanuus." He slapped her on the rump. As he turned away from the ocean, he found himself face-to-face with Lewis and Leodor. "I don't want to hear it. We are going after the Underlord, just as King Hector wants. I'm not diverting on some other quest. It's Hancha or bust. Get over it."

"We've agreed to let you lead us down that treacherous path," Lewis said with a bored gaze. "And it wasn't I that wanted to interrupt your little tryst. It was Leodor. Now that he's come around, he has something to say."

"Something useful, I hope." Abraham set Sticks down and faced the viceroy.

Leodor had taken a rock to the skull back at Crown Island, and it showed. Half of his face was bruised. He looked like death warmed over, but the glimmering intelligence in his saggy eyes was still there. He'd been under the deck, getting treatment from Iris the last few days.

"Well, spit it out, Mister Magoo," Abraham said. "I can't wait to hear the next twist from your chicken lips."

With his hands tucked inside the sleeves of his tar-stained robes, Leodor said, "It was always my wish to expressly serve the king. Putting our differences aside, Lewis informed me that you had made an inquiry about the Big Apple. Is this true?"

Abraham arched a brow and said, "Yeah, that's true. What do you know about it?"

"Interesting that you should ask. I know this name, not intimately, but I know it well enough." He winced, took his hand out of his sleeve, and touched the lump on his head. "I know exactly what it feels like to be hit with a boulder. It hurts. I've gained perspective for the games of brawn that men like you play. As I was saying, the Big Apple is an odd name, but it does pass the lips of the Sect from time to time. He is a player in the grand scheme of things."

"He's a man?" Abraham asked.

"I can't say if it is a he or she. All I can say is that there is. Sorry, I didn't mean to mislead you." Leodor licked his pale lips. "Do you still have port on board?"

"Plenty," Abraham said. "Tell me more about the Big Apple. Who is he, and let's assume he is a he in the *grand scheme of things*."

"The Big Apple is a smuggler of goods and information. It's people like him that the Sect use for their benefit. That is how they have eyes and ears in all places. They take the donations to the Elders to finance it." Leodor took a gratifying snort of air into his nose. A wince followed.

Sticks touched Abraham's hand and spoke up. "Spit it out. Where is the Big Apple?"

"Don't speak like that to the viceroy, wench," Lewis said.

"You aren't on any different footing than me, oh mighty prince," she fired back.

"Why, because I'm not sleeping with the Captain?"

"No, because you don't have the big walls of a castle to protect you."

Lewis sneered. "I don't need a castle to protect me from the likes of any of you. I can handle myself quite well." His eyes shifted to Abraham. "Even without a magic sword."

"Is that so?" Abraham asked. "Care to find out?"

"Any time and any place," Lewis replied coolly.

33

LEODOR STEPPED BETWEEN THE TWO BRISTLING MEN. "THERE HAS been enough fighting over the past few days. I don't think my head can stand the racket. Abraham, I'll make your task simple. After all, it is only information. This smuggler, the Big Apple, he resides on the Pirates' Peninsula on the East Arm. But that would dissuade you from your current mission. But"—he lifted a bony index finger—"perhaps the Big Apple can provide information that can serve us just as well. The trick is finding an audience with him."

"Why is that?" Sticks asked.

Leodor looked at her as though she were stupid and said, "Because nobody in Kingsland has ever seen him."

Abraham met privately in his quarters with Horace, Sticks, and Solomon. Horace kept his distance from and his eyes on Solomon.

The guardian didn't care for the troglin at all. Abraham ran everything Leodor had said to him by them.

"What do you think?" Abraham asked.

"I think whatever you think, Captain. You lead. I follow," Horace said.

"You know that I'm all for it," Solomon said. The troglin looked crammed inside the cabin even though he was sitting down.

"And you?" he asked Sticks.

She was straddling a wooden chair that she'd turned backward. "I can't help but wonder if Leodor is pulling the wool over your eyes. He's a Henchman and shouldn't be deceiving you. It would be to his peril."

"That's what I was thinking. I was also hoping that I wouldn't be the lone voice in this line of reasoning." Abraham stretched his hands up to the ceiling as the boat rocked to the side. He looked at Horace. "And I expect the rest of you to have input, whether you think that I'll like it or not."

Horace clawed his fingers through his beard and said, "I trust that the brand will do its work if there is a betrayal. It has. It will. We've had deserters. They've never been seen again. Once, the blue demon plucked a man from the earth and took him away in the sky. I forgot his name, with so many, but it was before your time."

"I say, nothing ventured, nothing gained," Solomon added. "Perhaps this Big Apple is one of us. He might have the answers that we seek."

"Yeah, well, that's what I'm hoping for. In more ways than one. Horace, take the ship to Pirates' Peninsula. It's time to get docked."

"Who's going on land?" Sticks asked as she got out of her seat.

"We'll start with a small group. We better keep the others back with the ship in case they need to bail us out," he said. "Why, who did you have in mind?"

"We've let Shades linger because we needed him to guide us through Hancha," she said. "And he wants to be branded again. Have you come to a decision on that? Does he stay or go?"

"Go," Horace volunteered.

"He's been cleared of any wrongdoing that we accused him of," she said, "aside from the incident in the prison. I know it sounds strange coming from me, but I have to admit we need him. With the brand comes loyalty."

Horace frowned. "I'll support whatever the Captain decides. But I don't like the way he operates."

So far, Shades had proven to be nothing but loyal. He'd been a huge help on the ship and in the skirmish on Crown Island. "I'll bring him along. We'll see how it goes. If he fouls up, he fouls up, and we'll leave him."

34

THE PIRATES' PENINSULA RESIDED IN EASTERN BOLG TERRITORY. Both Western Bolg and Eastern Bolg were enemies of King Hector. However, the Pirates' Peninsula and the East Arm were neutral territories run by an anarchist pirate government. The seafaring pirates, fishermen, merchants, and smugglers didn't answer to anybody. They served themselves and whoever paid the most. At least, that was what Leodor told Abraham.

Sea Talon docked at one of the large ports. Hundreds of vessels of all sizes were in the bay, including a smattering of warships from other territories. Hardy men and women in short clothing worked like ants on the piers, loading and unloading in the hottest part of the day. The sweat-drenched people were busy, eyes forward, and talking bitterly in the heat.

Abraham and a small company of Henchmen casually strolled down the docks toward the bustling activity of the seaside city often referred to as Pirate's Harbor. Pirate's Harbor started on the beaches and ran right up into the rolling hills. His company included Sticks, Shades, Iris, and also Leodor, Lewis, Clarice, as well as Swan, who insisted on coming. He wanted to keep the party small and not appear intimidating. Too much muscle might draw attention. But Solomon came too. He dressed in a stitched cotton vest and wore a skirt altered to fit him. Apparently, troglin were often hired as bodyguards in northern territories. Hence, typical of the Henchmen, they posed as merchants with a small squad of moderately heavy guards. From Abraham's point of view, they fit right in with the multitudes. Aside from that, he didn't have any idea where he was going. He let Sticks lead the way.

Pirate's Harbor was a large, expanding cluster of stone buildings with clay-tiled roofs and mud and stone roadways. The buildings had no porches. They were more or less tall, narrow buildings of stone side by side, which ran deep and away from the roads. The sound of seabirds and harsh voices haggling were commonplace. Men and women in fisherman coats walked the streets, smoking pipes. Vendors with carts loaded with fish shouted at them from the streets. The ocean breeze did nothing to carry away the pungent smell of fish and sweet tobacco.

Sticks led them up the network of streets past numerous windows of dolled-up women shamelessly flaunting their bodies and catcalling.

"One shard, one trick. Two shards, three tricks," called a rosy-cheeked strumpet who sat in a windowsill—all the windows of that building had red shutters on them.

Solomon waved at the women and grinned. "A red-shutter district. I guess it is fair to assume that every city in every world has one."

"It's the oldest profession in the world, they say," Abraham said.

Lewis sneered at the women and said, "This place is disgusting. Nothing but animals in houses. I hate commoners. They have the standards of a sow."

"Yes, we know how you feel," Iris said. "But you're worse than a commoner now. You're a Henchman, two steps lower than a shepherd."

"Never," Lewis muttered.

Sticks stopped in front of a tavern that had a wooden sign mounted above the door. The sign read The Greasy Pelican inside a drawing of an oversized beak of a bird. She opened the door. Smoke and loud voices and the twangy sound of stringed music rolled out of the doorway like a slap in the face.

"After you," she told Abraham.

He crossed the threshold of the stone-built building. The room was deeper than it was wide, and round tables, half empty, covered the floor. Surly men and hearty women in short clothing chattered all over the room. The laps of men of all sorts were filled with women in skimpy outfits. The smoky room was filled with a vibrant, exotic Arabian beat. At the far end of the room was the bar and a stone staircase that led up to three balconies over-looking the room. The Henchmen filed in. No one paid them any mind until Solomon, bringing up the rear, entered.

All the way in the back, the bartender pointed at the group. Looking dead at Solomon, in a loud and edgy voice, he said, "We don't serve his kind in here!"

35

THE CONVERSATIONS INSIDE THE TAVERN CAME TO AN ABRUPT HALT. The eyes of the patrons took long, hard looks at the Henchmen. Hands that were once wrapped around the handle of a tankard of ale found new homes on the pommels of weapons.

Abraham moved front and center.

The barkeep marched out from behind the bar and came right down the aisle. He was a burly, cigar-smoking older man with short, wavy jet-black hair and a pockmarked face. He wore a greasy white apron, and his sleeves were rolled up over his hairy, meaty forearms. He stopped a few feet short of Abraham and blew a ring of smoke in his face. "Get out. Don't make me tell you twice."

"Where I go, the troglin goes," Abraham said, "and I'd be happy to throw in a few extra shards to accommodate you."

Puffing smoke like a steam engine and with his arms crossed over his chest, the barkeep said, "It ain't the troglin I'm talking about. It's you. We serve plenty of troglin. They're our best customers. And troglin serve them." He shouted back over his shoulder. "Hey, Gertie! Get out here!"

The swinging kitchen door behind the bar flung open. A troglin in a pink apron bent down and stepped through. Wiping her huge hands on a towel, she said with irritation, "What is it, Sam? I'm busy, you know."

Abraham looked at Solomon, and Solomon was looking at him. Solomon shrugged. Gertie the troglin was a much younger version of Solomon, with a coat of rich brown fur. She wasn't built much differently from Solomon, though she was taller and had noticeable bosoms tucked behind her apron. Abraham scratched his head. "I don't understand the problem."

"You don't?" Sam the barkeep said. "The problem is you, cupcake. Trouble is written all over your face. I know that type. I've seen all sorts. You waltz into my bar, have a few drinks, and the next thing I know, I have broken furniture and blood on the floor. No challenges here. This is a well-run establishment."

Abraham scanned all the hard-eyed and disheveled people in the room. Surely, a handful of cutthroats were among them. Half of them could have fit in with his crew if they weren't so shabby.

"You're joking, right?" Abraham asked.

"Do I look like someone that jests?" Sam said.

Gertie strolled in behind Sam, towering over everyone. She tossed her dish towel over her shoulder and asked in a sweet and womanly voice, "Do you want me to escort these bums out?"

"Bums?" Lewis fired back. "Who does that walking flea catcher think it is?"

Gertie's massive hand shot out and grabbed Lewis by the collar of his coat. She lifted him up with one hand and said, "You have bad manners, little man."

Lewis's hand went to the handle of his dagger, but Abraham's hand stopped him from pulling it out.

"Stop. We'll go peacefully. Sorry for the trouble, Sam." He looked up at the female troglin, whose stormy blue eyes were locked on Lewis. "Will you please put my comrade down, Gertie?"

"Since you asked nicely." Gertie set down Lewis, who rubbed his throat and straightened his coat. She eyed Solomon and asked, "What are you looking at?"

"One hairy beauty," Solomon replied.

Gertie crossed her arms and said, "Dream on, old-timer."

The modern vernacular Sam and Gertie used left Abraham mentally scratching his head. He nodded at Sam and said, "We're going."

Shades piped up and said in an uncharacteristically whiny voice, "But we are supposed to meet with the Big Apple here."

"Shhh," Leodor said. "That's personal business."

Blowing smoke out of his nostrils, Sam said, "Bloody barnacles. Why didn't you say so in the first place? Have enough sense to keep your voice down when you talk about the Big Apple. Gertie, find them some tables. Give them some privacy too." He faced his patrons, lifted his arms, and said, "It's cool. Go back about your business."

The pirates and patrons carried on. The rattle of tankards and pouring of ale renewed. The stringed instruments were strummed again with the same Arabian beat. Gertie led them to the center of the tavern, where a curtain hid a short platform. She pulled back the curtain far enough for them to pass through. Three sets of tables sat on what looked to be a small stage. "Make yourself comfortable," she said. "I'll have a waitress bring you some pitchers of ale and wine. It's happy hour. Enjoy it, and try not to cause any more trouble." She walked away as everyone was seated. The platform boards creaked beneath their feet.

Clarice sat down in the chair that Swan pulled out for her and said, "We didn't cause any trouble. They did." Her nose crinkled. "What is that smell? It cuts through the body odor. I like it. Saucy."

Solomon and Abraham were sitting at the same table with Sticks. The troglin elbowed Abraham and tipped his chin toward the center of the tavern floor. A waitress in a floppy shirt and white blouse crossed the floor with a serving tray on her shoulder. She set the tray down in front of a pair of tattooed men with golden hoop earrings, licking their lips.

"That's pizza," Solomon said, elated.

"It sure looks like it," Abraham said with widening eyes. More pizzas were on tables throughout the room, loaded with all sorts of mouthwatering cheeses and toppings. "I wasn't expecting this. Were you?"

"I've spent most of my time on the Spine. If I knew about this, I would have been here long ago," Solomon said. His mouth watered as he watched a pirate pull away a slice that stretched with cheese. "Oh man, that looks good."

Abraham turned to Sticks and asked, "Did you know about this?"

"About what?"

"The pizza?"

She straightened her back and said, "I've seen it before— briefly, when we were on one of our missions that Twila sabotaged. Never tried it. It looked weird to me. Many weird things in the north."

"You can say that again. I get the feeling that this might have something to do with the Big Apple. Do you?" he asked Solomon.

"If it smells like a big apple, it must be a big apple. It explains the modern influence of their character." Solomon's belly rumbled. "I hope they have every meat topping imaginable on it."

Abraham caught Sam waving him over to the bar. "I'll be back."

"Order me at least ten of those pizzas. I'm really getting hungry," Solomon said.

"I will." He crossed the room to the bar that Sam stood behind.

Sam the barkeep was wiping out the inside of a mug. "I wanted to let you know that the Big Apple will prefer discretion." He eyed the curtains. "Didn't want you to get spooked when the girls closed them. The word is out on your arrival. The Big Apple will come soon."

"Really? That seems quick," Abraham said as he watched two leggy waitresses close the curtains.

Lewis and Leodor sat alone and were frowning. Clarice, Swan, and Shades were at another table, pouring the wine just served to them. Sticks sat with Iris and Solomon. They vanished behind the curtain. Abraham tilted his head. Shades had made up the meeting with the Big Apple. If that was the case, Abraham wondered how the barkeep knew the Big Apple was coming. He played along but felt a spider crawl up his spine. "Say, Sam, I'd prefer it if you kept the curtains open. I like to keep an eye on my company. You understand. Some of them can be trouble."

"Sure, I understand," Sam said. He put a tankard of beer down in front of Abraham and whistled to the girls who had closed the curtains. "Have a beer. It's on the house."

Abraham took a tankard and a sip. "Thanks." He watched the waitresses slowly open the curtains. Every seat at the tables was empty. The Henchmen were gone.

36

At first, Abraham thought the Henchmen were playing a joke on him. The tingling nerves running through his extremities told him different. His hand went to his sword. He turned to Sam, grabbed him by the collar, and pulled him over the bar. "What sort of mischief is this? Where are they?" he demanded.

Red-faced, Sam said, "I don't have any idea. Magic isn't my area of expertise. Serving ale is."

Abraham had Sam laid out on the bar. He lifted him up by the collar and slammed him back down. "Don't play games with me!"

The surly patrons came to their feet. Some left. Others drew small, pointy weapons. Gertie lumbered through the swinging kitchen door, carrying a huge iron frying pan. "Do I need to get busy with this?" she asked.

"Don't even try me, lady." Abraham put more pressure on Sam's chest. The stout man puffed for breath. "Spit it out, Sam. I'm not the kind of man that plays games."

"I hate to insult you, partner, but you're the fool that waltzed into the Peninsula with a bounty on your head," Sam said. "People know you. You're Ruger Slade. I haven't seen anyone as brazen as you since, well, you."

Abraham's grip loosened.

Sam continued. "The Big Apple knew you were here the moment you stepped off your ship. You just happened to wander into my tavern. I didn't ask for it, but all of them would have been waiting on you. You probably would have been safe if you hadn't mentioned the Big Apple. But you did. Or at least, that runt did. I tried to warn you, but you gave me no choice."

Gertie came around the bar and crept up on Abraham.

"Back off, bigfoot," he said.

"Don't you know it's not polite to comment on a lady's feet?" she asked.

"Those aren't feet. Those are oars, and that's not what I meant. What is with this place and the vernacular?" In a way, Abraham liked it, but it was confusing at the same time. This tavern had a different vibe to it. He'd experienced some modernism in Stronghold that Eugene Drisk left behind, with pancakes and syrup and a touch of slang, but this was different. It seemed extreme, almost jarring. "Where do you go from here, Sam? Does the Big Apple want me dead?"

"Boy, you really don't remember much, do you? The Big Apple doesn't want you dead, but plenty of other people do. I can't read his mind, but I'd say he might be protecting you from them. His associates will be here soon. You should go with them or never see your friends again."

"I'm not going anywhere without my friends." He looked back at Gertie, who stood only a few feet behind him. "Where are they?"

"Only the Big Apple can answer that." Gertie flicked her long fingers at him. A stream of pink dust flew from her hand into his face.

Abraham couldn't dodge the dust, and it covered his face like flour. He tried not to breathe, but it was too late. He lost all feeling in his limbs. The sword he'd drawn slipped out of his grip. All he could think as he drifted off to deep sleep was, "Not again. Home, here I come."

37

ABRAHAM WOKE WITH A JERK. SOMEONE HAD SPLASHED HIM DOWN with a bucket of stagnant water. He spat the foulness from his mouth as sat up. He was inside a dungeon cell and stripped down to his waist. The only thing he had left were boots and trousers. On the other side of the cell bars was a beefy goon wearing a leather helmet that covered his eyes and nose. His chin jutted out.

He banged his bucket on the bars and asked in a gruff voice, "Are you awake?"

"No, I'm still asleep and having a nightmare, apparently." He rubbed his temples. He'd fully expected to wake back up at home. Not that he wanted that to happen. His mind was cloudy, however. Whatever Gertie had flicked at him was nasty stuff. Even Ruger Slade couldn't handle it.

"I'll be back," the goon said. He turned and walked away down a dim dungeon corridor and vanished around the corner.

Abraham climbed to his feet. The dingy cell had a wooden cot with the framework broken and the fabric torn. Rotting straw was spread out on the floor where he'd been lying. His arms and legs were shackled with tight chains. He checked the tautness of the chains. The links were thick, unbreakable.

"Dirty donuts."

He was in a lone cell at the end of a row. In the aisle ahead of him were more stone cells, guarded by steel bars.

He called out, "Hello?"

No reply came. A black rat the size of a squirrel squirted from one cell and vanished into a cell across the aisle.

He called out again. "Hello?"

Abraham wondered where his friends were. All of them had disappeared like an act from a David Copperfield show. Either that had been an illusion, or some powerful magic was behind it, magic the likes of which he'd never faced before. He wondered where it had come from.

At first, he thought Leodor might have had something to do with it. After all, the viceroy had had the idea to venture after the Big Apple. Perhaps everything was a setup from the beginning. The only thing Abraham could hope for was that the brand kept Leodor in check. The mystic should be in the same danger as the others. He hoped they weren't dead.

The sound of soft footsteps caught his ear, more than one set. They became louder. The guard from earlier rounded the corner at the end of the aisle, followed by a much smaller man, about five feet tall, shirtless, and layered in balled-up muscle. He had two small horns like a goat's on his head, and his face was impish. He wore a collar with three bright-yellow gems in the middle. Another figure glided in behind both men, a tall, slender person with robes that covered the gaunt body like vapors. His or her hooded face could not be seen—only blackness.

The little muscle-bound man with horns marched out in front

of the others. His eyes had a devious intent. He stood a couple of feet from the bars of Abraham's cell, put his fists on his hips, and said in an impish voice, "Ruger freaking Slade."

"Do I know you?" he said.

"Hmm-hmm, oh, you don't know me, but I know you. Doesn't everyone? Hmm-hmm." The horned man tilted his head to the left in a quick, birdlike fashion. "I see in your eyes that you are lost. Tell me—what are you looking for? Hmm-hmm."

Figuring that he didn't have anything to lose, he said, "The Big Apple."

"And you've found him," the little man said.

"You're the Big Apple?"

"In the flesh," the Big Apple said.

Big Apple, my butt. More like little apple. He's messing with me. He has to be. With his hands still glued to the bars, he said, "That's an interesting name. Can I ask how you came upon it?"

"I gave it to myself." Big Apple tapped his fingertips together. "Hmm-hmm. I can see something deeper in your eyes. Tell me. What are you thinking, Slade the Blade? I want to know what you are thinking."

"Reggie Jackson."

Big Apple's eyes brightened. A pleased smile formed on his lips. "Tell me more."

"Times Square. Manhattan Island. The Statue of Liberty."

Big Apple rocked up and down on tiptoe. "Interesting. Very interesting." He rubbed his fingers across his mouth. "You have made a connection." He turned and looked at the guard and the shadowy figure. "Give us some privacy."

The guard and the robed person moved back down the aisle and out of sight.

"Was that a thing or a person?" Abraham asked.

"That's my wraith. Fleece. I control it. My personal protection. Once a very powerful wizard and now my slave. Hmm-hmm." Big Apple lifted a finger. "Now that we are alone, it's time to swap stories. Who are you really? How did you learn about me?"

Opting to believe he was in a dream anyway, he let loose. "I'm Abraham Jenkins. I used to play for the Pittsburgh Pirates. I was told to seek you out by a man named Charles Abney, back in the real world. Sometimes, when I black out, I go back and forth."

"You learned about me through a dream? Humph." Big Apple nodded. "I don't know any Charles, but I have met many people like us. However, most of them, as you know, are hunted down and killed." He circled a finger around his ear. "They think that we are madmen. Hmm-hmm."

"So, what's your story?" Abraham asked.

"I'm Edgar Gravely. From Queens. I was born with cerebral palsy. It was manageable for a long time, and I even had the exciting job of being a janitor at Yankee Stadium. But I had no life outside of that. A real loner. My parents were decent, but they died young. I think taking care of me killed them... or at least took a lot of years from them." Big Apple was as bright-eyed as ever. "But now I'm here, and even though I'm a horned halfling, I like it."

"A horned halfling? Aren't you big for a halfling?"

"I have to say I like it. And I'm not looking back. Do you under-stand me, Abraham Jenkins? I'm not looking back." Edgar thumped his chest. "This isn't *Lord of the Rings*. This is Titanuus, a real fantasy world, a world of second chances, and I'm thankful for mine. In this world, I have knowledge that others have." He poked a finger to his temple. "Like me, you should take advantage of that."

"I sort of feel like I already have."

Big Apple gave a big grin. "Of course you should. You're freaking Ruger Slade, the baddest swordsman that ever lived. I'd kill if I could have been you." Big Apple came closer to the bars. "You have no idea what you are, do you?"

He shrugged.

Big Apple let out a belly full of laughter and walked away, saying, "You are about to find out."

38

HOURS LATER, A GROUP OF GUARDS IN LEATHER HELMETS AND WORN tunics escorted Abraham out of the dungeon. They marched him, shackles and all, up a windowless stone staircase, level after level. He had no feel for the place and couldn't tell whether it was inside a building, like a castle, or in the belly of a mountain.

Finally, the stairwell came to an end, with a broad landing at the top and a wooden door with black iron fixtures. One of the guards with more belly than brawn pushed his shoulder into the heavy door and shoved it open. The door dragged over the ground, and a gust of salty air filled the stairwell. Moonlight spilled through the opening.

Rough hands shoved Abraham outside and closed the door behind him. He stood in the darkness of night alone.

Abraham wandered forward with the irons rubbing his ankles. The floor was solid stone. Sheer rock walls twenty feet high surrounded him. The area was square, about thirty yards wide, like a courtyard or arena. Great torches burning with flame lined the top walls from the inside of the arena. Shadowy figures sat behind the rim of the wall, their faces obscured from the light.

More doorways were there, similar to the one he'd walked through, one on each wall. They were closed.

A familiar voice spoke above the wind. It was Edgar, Big Apple. His voice was amplified and carried all over. "Welcome to the Rim, Ruger Slade. There is a bounty on your head. A sizeable one. But I have plans for you."

Abraham spun in a slow circle. His eyes adjusted to the darkness behind the rim of the wall. He could see the faces of many people, sitting in stands overlooking the arena. Men and women of all sorts were dressed in clothing, armor, and colorful garb. Finally, his eyes landed on Edgar. The horned halfling sat on a big wooden chair like a throne. Two comely women with painted bodies and skimpy exotic clothing clung to the small man's sides. More guards and the wraith, Fleece, stood nearby.

Abraham walked toward Edgar as though he were in a scene taking place in a much smaller Roman coliseum. "What's this all about, Edgar? I thought we were making some ground."

"No, no, no," Edgar said with a waggling finger. "I am the Big Apple. Always the Big Apple. Don't draw my temper. Hmm-hmm." He leaned forward, his hands gripping the ends of the arms of his chair. "You have enough problems to deal with."

"Well, aren't you the mighty little man." He looked about. "Let me guess, at any moment, those doors are going to open, and I'm going to have a fight on my hands." He wiggled his fingers. "Is this a fistfight?"

"No, it's a fight for your life, sword master. Do you see all of these people in the stands? They came to see you fight. They came to see you die."

"Fight or die, huh? It has a nice ring to it. The only problem is that I don't have a sword. I'm not much of a swordsman without a sword."

The Big Apple reached behind his chair. He lifted a sword and scabbard out into view and laid it across his armrest. Then he rested his muscular forearms on it and said, "The legendary Black Bane. It's worth as much as you. Today is a great day to be the king of the smugglers. This weapon, well, it stays here, with me. I want the fights to be fair, after all." He tipped his head toward one of the guards wearing a leather face helmet.

The guard tossed a sword into the arena. It was a short sword designed like a gladius.

Abraham picked it up. The edge was notched, the blade tarnished, and the pommel worn. He turned it side over side. "Nice toothpick. So, who am I supposed to fight with this?"

Big Apple stood up on his chair and pointed to the doorway on the far side of the arena. He looked at Abraham and snapped his fingers. The shackles that bound him fell to the ground.

In his enhanced voice, Big Apple said, "Let the chaos begin!"

The door opened. Six men wearing ragged clothing and carrying swords spilled out of the opening. Their eyes locked onto Abraham, and they lifted their weapons and charged. The crowd lurking behind the wall came to their feet with wild howls.

39

ABRAHAM SIZED UP THE WOULD-BE KILLERS IN A SPLIT SECOND. THE killers were the kind of men you'd hire to do dirty work, tough men who fought in gangs who grouped up and bludgeoned people. They ran hard, holding their long swords like loaves of bread. The fastest one drove in on Abraham with his sword lifted high.

Abraham thrust his gladius into the man's chest. *Glitch!*

The attacker's mouth dropped open. His sword fell from his fingers.

Smooth as silk, Abraham grabbed the long sword before it hit the ground. He spun around the dying man and hewed down another attacker with a fierce chop across the man's exposed temple. With his fist filled with sharp steel, he turned into a tornado of death. The attackers didn't have time to know what hit them.

Stab!

Chop!

Slice!

Glitch!

In a handful of seconds, Abraham left six men dying in pools of their own blood. He tossed the gladius aside and picked up another dead man's sword. He spun them both together in a twist of shining steel.

The blood-hungry crowd erupted in throaty cheers. They pumped their fists and flailed their arms in a wild frenzy. They began to chant.

"Slade the Blade! Slade the Blade! Slade the Blade!"

Edgar applauded in his chair. He jumped out of the chair and sat on the wall. He motioned Abraham over. "That was fantastic! I'm eager to see more. Hmm-hmm. Look around. You made many people happy and many sad. See, see the long faces. Many want you dead."

Abraham wished he knew exactly why they wanted him dead. He didn't know a single face in the crowd. He did, however, like them roaring for him. It reminded him of the days when tens of thousands of people had chanted for Jenkins the Jet. He loved that. Now, his hot blood churned again. Or at least Ruger's did. "What's this all about? Is there something in it for me? If I win, will my Henchmen be freed?"

The Big Apple tossed his head back and laughed. "You are making demands, and you haven't even started yet. You have much to prove before you have a say in anything."

"You're a real pal."

Big Apple smiled. "I know."

He stood back up on the rim and clapped his hands, and the door underneath him opened. A swordsman dressed in layers of fine golden clothing stepped through. Big Apple's voice amplified again, and he spread his arms out wide as the crowd of hundreds quieted. "Now a real challenge. A sword for hire, a legend of the shadows, the killer of all that cross his steel, Fonay Zar of the Barbican."

Whispers spread throughout the square arena. Abraham backed away. Fonay Zar wasn't some chump like the men whom Abraham had just slaughtered.

The swordsman had light-brown hair and striking features. The lean fighter moved into the area with the grace of a panther. His sword was finely crafted, a straight length of steel with a white bone handle. The edge appeared as keen as a razor. Fonay Zar held out one sword and said, "A blade for a blade unless you are a coward, Ruger Slade."

The swords in Abraham's hands were nothing close to a superior weapon like Fonay Zar carried. They might as well have been strips of steel with edges on them, by comparison.

Ruger tossed one blade aside. He saluted with the crude sword in his hand and said, "Let's see what you got."

Fonay Zar bowed. He then went into a showy display of swordplay. The shining blade flickered like lightning around his body. The blade's edge whistled and cut through the air like a living thing. His technique and form had no flaws. He was perfect.

Abraham ground his feet into a fighting stance, high guard position, and said, "Wow, that was amazing. But the wind still lives, and so do I. Bring it on, golden boy."

Fonay Zar crept forward with his sword cocked over his shoulder in the wrath guard position. The crowd applauded. A few steps from Abraham, he switched to the high guard position and attacked.

Sword tips kissed. *Clang!*

Abraham hopped backward. Fonay Zar moved with the speed of a striking snake. The man's light eyes were as cold as steel.

Fonay Zar pressed the attack. He lunged with one quick step and stab followed by another. Abraham backpedaled like a bull.

The man he fought was as smooth as silk. Abraham parried one blinding stroke after the other. He countered with a sideward slash.

Fonay Zar slid away and smiled. He flexed his arms and said, "You are strong like a bull. Yes! So much I have heard about you. Fast as a cat too. You are all I ever hoped that you would be, Ruger Slade. And now, I get to kill you." He stepped back over one of the dead bodies. "Then I will be the greatest swordsman in the world."

"No, you're going to be another one of those dead guys." Abraham cracked his neck side to side. "I promise you that. Soon enough, you're going to have blood all over your pretty clothing."

Fonay Zar's smile vanished. "Your blood, yes, but my blood, never." Fonay Zar charged Abraham and brought his sword down in a flurry of precise strokes.

Abraham parried them aside. He felt every bit of the blows in his hands and arms. The cheap steel he wielded didn't absorb punishment like Black Bane did. The cheap length of steel shared it. He parried and countered, only to be countered again. The tip of Fonay Zar's sword flashed before his eyes.

The audience shouted with raucous elation. New chants began as the master swordsmen went back and forth.

"Slay the Blade!"

"Slay the Blade!"

"Slay the Blade!"

Fonay Zar shuffled backward and thrust forward as if shot out of a cannon. Abraham twisted left. He was too late. Fonay Zar's sword clipped him through the shoulder. Blood spat down his arm. He jumped away.

The audience broke out in a frenzied howl.

"Feeling tired, Ruger?" Fonay gloated. He cut his sword inches above the ground. "You look tired. I can't promise I'll make your death painless, but I'll try to make it quick. Even though I think that the audience would like to see you bleed to death."

"It ain't over until it's over," Abraham replied.

"A futile expression. Where did you hear that?"

"*Rocky* one and *Rocky* six."

"I've never heard of those places." Fonay Zar flipped his sword around and made a quick bow. "It's been a pleasure."

I need to finish this guy and finish him quick. Come on, Ruger. I feel like you're holding back. What gives? Abraham rifled through his memories filled with pages of sword technique. The memory that stuck was that when equally matched, often the fighter with the superior weapon won. It made sense. He didn't have Black Bane, which made him every bit of a hair quicker. That fraction of time made the difference between life and death. Any risk he might take would be fatal.

He squared off on his opponent once more and said, "The pleasure is all mine."

He pounced at Fonay Zar. Blades collided. His blade broke.

40

ABRAHAM TWISTED AWAY FROM FONAY ZAR'S DEATH STROKE. HIS blade had snapped off at the hilt, leaving him all but empty-handed. He threw the handle at the swordsman. The handle flickered over Fonay's head.

The audience jumped onto their feet and screamed their lungs out.

"It will almost be a shame to see it end like this," Fonay Zar said. He crept toward Abraham. "You were every bit a worthy opponent."

Without taking his eyes off Fonay, Abraham backed toward the dead men. Plenty of swords were on the deck. All he needed to do was snatch one of them.

Fonay darted toward Abraham and sliced, herding Abraham away from the field of the dead. "No, no, no, you had your chance."

"I don't know about that," Abraham said. His shoulder burned like fire, the wound freely bleeding. "I should have had a choice of a better blade."

"From what I can see, you had six choices. You chose poorly."

With sweat dripping down his face, Abraham said, "I know this. I've never cut a man down in cold blood. That's the brand of a coward."

Breathing easy, Fonay circled the arena with him and said, "This is not an arena of honor, my friend. It is an arena of death."

"Oh well, I had to try." He continued to square off with Fonay, keeping his eyes fixed on the man. He had one chance—just one —depending on what Fonay Zar did. "Remember this. You might be good, but you'll never know for sure if you are better than me."

"I don't care. All they'll remember is that I slew you with my sword. In the end, that is all that matters." Fonay Zar poised himself in the high guard position and attacked.

The moment Fonay lifted his sword the slightest to initiate the downward chop, Abraham dove at the man's legs. The sword stroke came down in flash of silver and bit into the ground. Both men wrestled over the ground in a tangle of limbs. Fonay's wiry frame proved to be as fit as a wolverine's. Natural strength powered his lanky limbs. His grip on the sword handle was iron.

Abraham headbutted the man in the nose, and the bridge crunched. He pinned the younger fighter's sword arm down and chopped his hand into the wrist. The fingers opened, and the blade slipped free. Abraham grabbed the sword, rolled away, and sprang to his feet.

Fonay jumped back to his feet with a look of bewilderment. His light eyes darted to the swords on the ground. They lay behind Abraham.

"Looks like you have blood all over your pretty outfit. It gives it character." Abraham knelt down. He set down the good sword and picked up two of the bad ones then tossed one bad one at Fonay's feet. "Pick it up!"

Fonay glanced down at the inferior weapon.

The crowd chanted.

"Pick it up! Pick it up! Pick it up!"

Fonay Zan picked up the sword. He squared off with Abraham, who now carried a sword of the same poor craftsmanship as his.

Abraham looked the man dead in the eyes and said, "For once, you're going to fight like a man! And die like one!"

Abraham attacked. His sword slipped through Fonay's defense and cut the man clean through the neck. Fonay dropped to his knees, clutching his bleeding throat. He toppled backward and died.

The crowd went silent.

Big Apple had a grin all over his face. He applauded again. "Such honor. Such honor. Honor can be deadly."

Abraham took a knee beside Fonay Zar. He removed a light golden sash from the man's waist and wrapped up his shoulder, then he picked up Fonay Zar's sword. The weapon had great balance and was half the weight of the ones he'd been wielding.

He looked up at Edgar, the Big Apple. "Is that it?"

"No," the Big Apple said. "Not even close."

"Fine, but I'm keeping this."

"Good, because you're going to need it."

41

ABRAHAM STOOD NEAR THE MIDDLE OF THE ARENA, PANTING. HE swayed. Blood and gore coated him from the tip of his sword to his shoulder. All the rest of him was covered in blood. The dead of all sorts were piled up all around the square arena. Two dead lions and a giant white-haired ape were among them. Men were there, the Black Knights in blackened armor from the Old Kingdom, who fought with spiked chains, daggers, and axes. They were great, gruesome, and gaunt alive. Now, they lay in heaps of flesh and bone sliced asunder, dead.

A minotaur lay on the ground. Its head was chopped off. One horn was missing. Fifteen men in forest-green robes with eyes the color of silver had come at him with spears and throwing stars. They were from the peaks of the Dorcha territory and had been called the Monks of Mayhem. They soiled the hard ground now. More were there, many more—sword fighters by the dozens. He'd fought as if he had fire in his veins. Abraham killed them all. Or Ruger did. Abraham got his first real glimpse of who Ruger really was. He was a killing machine who fought as if fire were flowing through his veins. He was invincible.

The flies and mosquitos came to feed on the dead at dawn. Their buzzing numbers overwhelmed the crowd. The Big Apple's guests began to file out of the arena, their throats raw from the screaming. They had nothing left in them. Ruger Slade had escaped time after time after time. His enemies had no choice but to move on, with heads hanging in defeat.

Edgar the Big Apple sat on his wooden throne, bright-eyed and bushy-tailed. The girls who accompanied him were sleeping. Fleece, the wraith, hadn't moved since the battles started, but his robes rolled like smoky vapors around his tall body.

Abraham dragged his sword toward the main wall, where the smuggler sat. He lifted his chin and asked, "What's next? Dragons? Giant vorpal bunny rabbits? A pink unicorn that breathes fire? Let's make a deal and see what's behind door number three."

Edgar tugged at the collar on his neck, which had three yellow gems in the middle. His nostrils flared. He fanned the air in front of his face and said, "Whew! I should have dragged the carcasses off after you killed them. But I never thought that you would even make it this far. Not without Black Bane." He tapped on the sword scabbard lying across the arms of his chair. "What to do? What to do? Wow, I wish I could have been you, even though this body isn't so bad compared to my old one."

Only pockets of people were scattered about the rim of the arena. The morning sun shone on their sweaty foreheads. The crowd had cheered for and against Abraham. His titanic efforts against the odds swayed the crowd. The haters left. The hopeful stayed. He didn't recognize any of them. "Come on, Big Apple. Let me and my people go. After all of this, I think I've earned it."

"I decide what you have or have not earned. Hmm-hmm." Big

Apple scratched his nose. He waved his hand in the air. "Let me consult with an old friend."

On the far side of the arena stands, two figures stood. Casually, they walked around the arena toward the Big Apple's chair. The sun shone in Abraham's eyes. The moment they rounded the first corner, they came into focus, a man and woman, both of whom he recognized. The man, tall and fit, light hair receding, wore a black vest over a maroon shirt. A gun was holstered on his hip. It was Lord Hawk, leader of the Shell. Ruger had tangled with him at the hideout where he found Solomon. He was handsome, with a strong chin and natural charm. Beside him was the gorgeous myrmidon woman, Kawnee. The woman was from the race of fish-like people who lived on land and in the sea. Her alluring eyes were solid black. The scales on her sensuous body shone in the sunlight, her leather garb accenting the natural curves of her body. Her arm was hooked in Lord Hawk's.

Lord Hawk clasped hands with Big Apple. "It's been quite a show. My kind of show, old friend. Thanks for the invite. Even though the results have been disappointing so far." He looked down at Abraham. "We meet again."

"The pleasure is all yours," Abraham said. "Big Apple, what does he have to do with this?"

The horned halfling smiled. "I am the Smuggler King. I have many associates. The Shell is part of that. Lord Hawk is another one with a bounty on your head... and the troglin's."

"The troglin. You want the troglin back?" Abraham said.

Lord Hawk put his foot up on the wall, leaned over, and said, "He was a special pet."

"You treated him like an animal."

"Well, he is a troglin. Smells like an animal, it's an animal." Lord Hawk spat over the side. His hand was on his gun, which hung at his side. He surveyed the dead. "Quite a mess. It makes me think of all of my men that you butchered."

"There is a price for stealing and kidnapping," Abraham replied. He looked past Lord Hawk, and his eyes caught Kawnee's for a moment as she winked at him. Moving on to Big Apple, he asked, "Is this a parlay?"

"No, it's a reunion." Big Apple stood up on his chair. "Lord Hawk, what do you think?"

"Well, it's early. We have the entire day ahead of us." Lord Hawk patted the grip of his gun. "I say, let him fight some more. A lot more."

"Hmm-hmm. What are you in the mood for?" Big Apple said to Lord Hawk.

Lord Hawk looked dead at Ruger and smirked. "How about the Wild Men from the Wound?" He turned his head back toward Big Apple. "You still have some of them, don't you?"

"I have plenty. How many shall I set free?" Big Apple asked.

Lord Hawk opened up his hands casually and said, "All of them."

42

NONE OF THE FOUR DOORS LEADING INTO THE RIM'S SQUARE ARENA opened. Abraham could hear scuffling behind them. The rattle of chains and harsh voices could be heard behind the iron hinges. In the stands, Big Apple and Lord Hawk and Kawnee had turned their backs. They were drinking from large goblets and talking in quiet voices.

Abraham licked his parched lips. He was as dry as a bone. All his sweat was gone. Blood had caked on his flesh. Ruger might have been tough, but even he was subject to dehydration. With a dry throat, he shouted up to the group and said, "Grant me a request and let me drink."

Everyone stopped and looked at him. Big Apple asked, "What is the matter? Is the master swordsman thirsty? Hmm... hmm. Flesh and bone cannot conquer him, but a lack of water will."

"You didn't bring me out here to die of thirst. You brought me out here to fight. I don't think a skin of water will hurt anything."

Big Apple and Lord Hawk shrugged at each other. Lord Hawk threw an arm over Kawnee's shoulder and said, "Look at this beauty. She's a myrmidon. Sea people. She doesn't complain of the sun or beg for a drink."

"She's hasn't been fighting her butt off for the last several hours, either," Abraham fired back.

Lord Hawk kissed the pretty myrmidon woman on the cheek and said, "I'll let her decide. Just remember, dear, he killed your love, Flexor."

Kawnee might not have been thirsty, but she blinked a lot. The gills on the neck of her pale-green skin opened and closed rapidly. She slipped away from Lord Hawk, bent over, and grabbed what looked like a skin of water from underneath the stadium benches. With the grace of a queen, she moved down the bench planks to the edge of the wall. She leaned over the wall and held the skin out. "Come, and I will give you a drink."

Abraham walked up underneath Kawnee's outstretched arms and swallowed. The damp water skin hung suspended twenty feet above his face. A drop of water dripped down onto his cheek.

Kawnee tipped the water skin over, and water poured from the spout. She flipped the tip back up.

The water splashed onto Abraham's face. He barely got a drop in his mouth. He could see the playfulness in her eyes, only between her and him. The others could not be seen.

He mouthed the words, "Thank you."

Kawnee lifted her eyebrows. She took the water skin, put it to her lips, and gulped it down. She drained the remaining water by squeezing the contents of the water skin. The cool liquid splashed all over her face and down her chest. She twisted the water skin in her hands. That last of the drops dripped onto her tongue. She flung the water skin down at Abraham's feet and walked away.

"Bravo!" Big Apple cried, elated.

Lord Hawk clucked with laughter along with the guards and the handful of people still left.

Abraham frowned at the discarded skin. He picked it up and squeezed out a few drops that landed in the dust. "You know, for a fish lady, you make one lousy water boy. I didn't want your lousy H$_2$O anyway." He flung the skin up into the stands.

Lord Hawk swatted it down and said, "What is the matter? Don't you want a refill?" The audience started laughing again.

Abraham walked back into the buzzing flies and stink of the arena. He had bigger things to worry about than water. Survival came to mind. Lord Hawk had mentioned the Wild Men of the Wound. The name of the men didn't ring a bell with him, but the Wound did. He'd seen it on the maps of Titanuus. It was located in north Eastern Bolg. It was a great chasm, something like the Grand Canyon. According to Sticks, the Wound was said to be the fatal wound that the eternal being, Antonugus, had killed Titanuus with.

He began picking through the weapons of his enemies. He'd killed most of them with lethal precision—gouged hearts and slit-open bellies and necks. He couldn't afford to let them get a second swing. He had a sinking feeling inside his guts. The next wave that Big Apple sent was going to be bad—really bad, if that was possible.

The Black Knights of the Old Kingdom had been well equipped. Aside from their blackened armor, they had thick belts called girdes. Abraham suited himself up with a worn belt and loaded a few daggers he found into it. He still carried Fonay Zar's sword. The weapon wasn't Black Bane, but it was a difference maker. No other weapon could match it, but he needed one, a good one. He caught a shine of an axe head underneath one of the monks whose arm he'd cut off. The small wiry fighter had come at him with a pair of nunchakus.

He pushed the body aside with the heel of his foot and said, "You ain't no Bruce Lee." He picked up the axe, which had a wicked-looking singular head of steel, with a long beard and sharp chin. It was a true cleaver that one of the black knights had carried. He tossed it up and watched it flip end over end and caught it. "You'll do. You'll have to."

Big Apple and his small brood were all staring at Abraham. They had stopped talking and appeared to be waiting, the same as him.

A hard knocking came from the door below Big Apple's thronelike chair. One of the guards appeared on the upper deck. The brute hustled down the steps and whispered in Big Apple's ear.

"Good lord, your breath smells!" Big Apple shooed the man away. "Go, go bathe and brush with something besides manure. Man, these people have no hygiene. I got it." He tapped his fingertips together. He looked Abraham dead in the eye. "Hmm-hmm." He drew out the next two words, which had a familiar ring to them. "They're here."

Abraham spun around slowly.

The people who had left the Rim returned in a quick and orderly fashion. They had their hands full of bottles of wine, tankards of ale, and trays of food, much as one would see in a sports stadium. The hungry glazed look in their eyes returned.

They began to chant. "Wild Men! Wild Men! Wild Men! Wild Men!"

Big Apple raised his mighty little arms and clapped his hands.

All four of the arena doors opened at once. The Wild Men lumbered out of the great doors.

The crowd's chants turned to stone-cold silence.

Abraham's skin crawled into his toes.

43

THE WILD MEN OF THE WOUND WEREN'T MEN IN THE CUSTOMARY sense of the word. Instead, they moved on all fours, knuckles on the ground, like white apes. Twenty appeared in all, five coming out of each door, grunting loudly when they entered.

The grimy men had shaggy manes of hair, bodies bulging and flexing with natural muscle with every movement they made. Like dogs, they moved deeper into the arena, snorting and sniffing the air. The half-naked men's large eyes grazed over Abraham before falling on the dead. Abraham stood still. The sight of the wild men jostled Ruger's senses. The hairs on his arms stood on end, which was a rare event. Nothing bowed the iron in Ruger Slade's limbs, but the Wild Men did.

They moved about the arena in small packs, their heads scanning side to side. They shoved, pushed, and rubbed up against one another. One of the Wild Men picked up the head of a Monk of Mayhem. He tossed it to another wild man, who caught it, stared at the decapitated face, and grunted. That Wild Man cocked the head back over his shoulder and slung it into the back of the head of another. That Wild Man rolled underneath the blow, popped up, and attacked the one that threw the head at him. They wrestled over the blood and the dead like fighting dogs.

While two of the Wild Men fought, the rest of the primordial pack milled through the slain. One Wild Man picked up a spiked flail. He swung it up and brought it down with great strength into a dead corpse. He kept swinging, turning the body into hamburger. Others were doing the same thing. They picked up weapons, toyed with them, and tested them out on the fallen.

One of the Wild Men sat back on his haunches. He held a sword in his hand and thumbed the edge. His eyes hung on Abraham. The others continued to pick through the weapons. Half of them armed themselves while the others seemed content to fight with their mallet-sized fists or thick fingernails that could tear open flesh.

"I should have put some armor on," Abraham muttered underneath his breath. "Times like this, a swordsman needs it." He eyed the pack of men. So far, they had shown very little interest in him as they sorted through the battlefield. Abraham tried to figure out who was the leader of the pack. If he took out the leader, that might scatter the others long enough to give him an advantage.

"What are you waiting for, Ruger?" Lord Hawk said from above. "Make some conversation with them. Say hello. The Wild Men love to chat."

"Oh, these are Wild Men," Abraham said. "I thought this was your family reunion."

"Ha ha!" Big Apple laughed, pointing at Lord Hawk. "He got you."

"You know, I'm really going to love watching them rip you apart, Ruger. And I know that the crowd is going to love it too!" Lord Hawk lifted up his fist and pumped it in the air. "Wild Men! Wild Men! Wild Men!"

Abraham took a deep breath.

The Wild Men clustered together, spread out, and encircled Ruger. The ones without weapons—ten in all—lurked on all fours, grunting and barking like hounds. The others stood tall and formidable with their backs bowed and metal weapons in hand. They cast deadly looks on Abraham from their dark eyes. The wide circle of the savage pack tightened.

The people in the stands chanted more loudly, "Kill the Blade! Kill the Blade! Kill the Blade!"

Abraham had slain over two dozen men in the past few hours. These men were different. They were a pack of wild-eyed animals hungry for blood and fearless of death. He could take down a few, but if they came all at once, their superior numbers would overwhelm him. *Come on, Ruger, what are we going to do?*

A Wild Man on all fours bolted out of his stance and charged.

Abraham brained the man with his axe.

The Wild Men growled and began to salivate. Two more barehanded Wild Men charged Abraham from opposite sides. They pounced like gorillas from several feet away.

With a flash of his sword, Abraham lopped the head off of one and cleaved the other Wild Man in the face. Both men dropped dead at his feet. Abraham jumped over the dead men and charged the biggest Wild Man of all, the one who carried a sword and had eyed him earlier. That Wild Man whistled under his breath just before the others attacked. He must have been the leader. Abraham drove a knee into the jaw of a Wild Man standing in front of the leader. He stabbed his sword at the leader's neck.

The Wild Men's leader slipped out of the way like a wild jungle cat. He made sharp whistles through his teeth. The throng of Wild Men came to life. All of them descended on Abraham in a frenzied wave.

Abraham sprinted after the leader.

The long-haired brute ran like a deer while screaming and holding his sword high. He spun around and backpedaled on bare feet away from Abraham.

Abraham closed the gap.

The Wild Man stopped on a dime and stuck his chin out.

Abraham lowered his sword and aimed for the heart. The Wild Man coiled his legs and leapt high into the air. Abraham passed beneath the Wild Man and cut the man's foot off. The leader let out a wild cry and fell into the knot of charging men. Abraham kept running.

With his attacker howling for his blood, he sprinted into the nearest corner and turned. "Come on, dogs!"

The Wild Men of the Wound converged on him as one.

Abraham hammered away at the rank knot of sweating bodies with his sword and axe. His sharp edges mangled bone and flesh. Blood sprinkled and splattered in the air. He chopped at the churning mass with everything he had in him. He moved like a human Cuisinart. His attackers became meat for a butcher shop. He ruined their sinewy flesh. *Slice! Hack! Chop!*

Strong limbs penetrated his defenses. Hands locked around his legs and arms. The Wild Men locked him up. They hit, punched, and bit. They brought Abraham down to his knees. They ripped his weapons from his grasp. Hard fists punched him senseless. He fought back. They beat him down, grabbed his legs, and dragged him across the ground, screaming like a pack of howling wolves.

44

WITH THE CROWD CHEERING, THE WILD MEN DRAGGED ABRAHAM around the arena in triumph. They came to a stop near the middle and pinned him down by the arms and legs. Abraham wrestled against his captors. His own great strength could not match their numbers. One of the Wild Men kicked him in the ribs.

"Guh!"

A second Wild Man punched him in the face.

The leader of the Wild Men hopped into view. Blood dripped freely from the wound where Abraham had chopped the savage's foot. The leader used his sword as a cane for balance. He pointed at Abraham's foot with his free hand. He hopped closer to Abraham and hovered over his legs. Two savages pinned his jerking leg down.

"I guess it's nothing personal," Abraham said. "A foot for a foot. Just make it quick."

The Wild Men's leader lifted his sword.

A ball of blue fire soared across the arena, smote the leader in the chest, and knocked him from his feet. The Wild Men let out cries and scattered.

Abraham rolled up on one side. Iris and Leodor stood in one of the doorways. Balls of energy exploded out of their hands, smiting the Wild Men. The people in the stands stampeded out of the stadium.

Big Apple jumped up and down in his chair yelling, "No! No! No!"

In the stands and on the arena floor, the Henchmen came. Horace, Bearclaw, and Vern hustled through one of the doors and engaged the Wild Men. Horace gored two of the men at once on the end of his spear. Bearclaw savagely ended one Wild Man's life with a single stroke. Vern's long sword flickered in and out of body after body.

Clarice and Swan carved up one savage together.

Prince Lewis's lethal strokes were as smooth as silk.

By the time Abraham got to his feet and snatched up a weapon, all the Wild Men from the Wound were dead. Up in the stands, Solomon, Sticks, Shades, Dominga, Tark, and Cudgel had Big Apple and the wraith, Fleece, surrounded. The guards were dead, and Lord Hawk and Kawnee were nowhere to be seen.

Big Apple sank down in his throne and clapped his hands slowly. "Well done, Ruger Slade. That was extraordinary. Hmm-hmm." He scratched one of the little horns on his head. "Now, before you try anything stupid, such as kill me, I think we should talk first."

"If you want to talk, come down here, and we will talk," Abraham said. The Henchmen gathered around him. He wasn't sure how they'd escaped or come together, but the timing couldn't have been better. "Don't be shy."

"I like it up here," Big Apple said. "It's my comfort zone."

"Solomon, why don't you give him a hand?" he said. "And keep an eye out for Lord Hawk. He was here earlier."

Solomon's eyes grew big. "He was?" With a quick glance over his shoulder, he approached Big Apple. Fleece moved in front of him. "I don't think Mister Curtains is going to let me."

"Leodor, what is the deal with that thing?" Abraham asked.

"It's a wraith," Leodor said with a frown as he stuck his hands inside his sleeves. "Not to be taken lightly. Do not touch it. They are known to have very bizarre powers. In some cases, their breath can be lethal."

"I've experienced plenty of that already." Abraham wanted information from Edgar. Despite how much he wanted to kill the horned wretch, the time to play nice had come. He had to remember that this might be a game and none of it was real. "Edgar, how about the two of us have a nice little chat? Mano a mano. Capisce?"

Edgar stood up and said, "Very well. I always was a good listener. Give me your word that you won't kill me."

"I won't."

"Or your Henchmen?"

Abraham glanced at Horace. "They won't."

Cheerfully, Edgar said, "Then come on up."

"No, you come down."

Edgar rolled his eyes. He jumped down from his throne, walked the benches, and jumped off the wall. He made an acrobatic somersault in the air and landed on his feet. He strode up to Abraham and said, "Let's walk."

Abraham wasn't surprised by the horned halfling's bravado. He walked the walk and talked the talk of a five-foot-tall muscle man. They separated themselves from the others. "You might not want to go home, but I do. But first, I have to help King Hector."

"Ah, man, why do you want to help King Hector? The entire

world hates him, even his people in Kingsland." Edgar shook his head. "You are on the wrong side of this. You should be on my side. We could rule this world together, you and me."

"I want to go home."

"Ha! No you don't. Hmm-hmm. I can see it in your eyes. You like this place, the same as I do. It's addictive. Listen to me. We have knowledge." Edgar put his finger to his forehead. "That is priceless. Hey, I heard that you had some pizza in the Greasy Pelican. Hmm-hmm. Where do you think that recipe came from? We can have so much fun in this place."

"I gave my word to the king."

"No, you gave your word to a dream."

45

A DREAM. CERTAINLY, A STRONG CASE COULD HAVE BEEN MADE FOR that, especially with Abraham's last experience back in the real world. Charles Abney, the old patient, had mentioned the Big Apple. Now Abraham was standing face-to-face with a horned halfling from New York City. It was convenient, all too convenient. Covered in flesh wounds, he limped along and asked, "Should guys like us be helping each other?"

Edgar's face tightened, and he shook his head. "Hmm-hmm, I told you the last thing I want is to go back to the body I was in. I'm very content with this one." He flexed his biceps. "And the girls like it. And even though I am small, I'm strong as a bull. Horned halflings are special people."

"Will you tell me how you got here?"

"Nope."

"Fine, listen, I'll find out on my own one way or the other. But what I want now is to help the king. Zillon dragon riders tried to kill him using an assault rifle. I saw it myself." He looked down at Edgar. "Do you know anything about that?"

Edgar clasped his hands and smiled. "I know everything—you see, everything. It is the beautiful thing of being me." He lifted his fingers as he spoke. "One, I know that King Hector is seeking out Arcayis the Underlord. He believes that man is behind the attempt. Two, I also know that you are seeking to reassemble the Crown of Stones."

Abraham slowed.

"Ah, you are surprised that I know that, aren't you?" Big Apple said with a grin. "I told you that I know everything. You see, the Sect and I work close together. We use each other for information. Of course, they think they are using me more than I am them, but it's the other way around."

They finished one lap around the inside of the arena. Everyone else was standing around and watching.

"King Hector wants the Crown of Stones," Big Apple continued. "With it, he thinks that he can save the world and unite the kingdoms. I'm telling you, uh, Abraham, that will never happen."

"Why not?"

"For one"—Edgar stuck out a pudgy index finger—"more trouble from our world is coming every day. And number two—"

"Whoa, whoa, whoa, what do you mean more trouble every day?"

"You know, more stuff like guns and people. People with ideas like me. We aren't the only ones. There are many otherworlders in Titanuus. Be wary. I will tell you this. The Sect is snatching up them and their knowledge. They have been for quite some time. They are ten steps ahead of King Hector in this game where this world is quickly changing."

Abraham nodded, wanting to keep Edgar talking as long as he could. More information was more weaponry for his arsenal. *Keep yapping, you little goat.* "What is number two?"

"Those magical gemstones that you want to complete the

crown—well, the Underlord has all of them save for one. Hmm-hmm."

"I don't believe it."

In a scratchy old voice, Edgar said, "That is why you failed."

Abraham tilted his head and said, "Funny. It's been a long time since I heard that line. Anyway, if he has most of the stones, wouldn't he have enough power to overrun Kingsland?"

"I don't know. I think he wants King Hector to punch himself out. But there is the matter of the King's Steel. It's the strongest metal in the world and only mined near the House of Steel. The Underlord respects its power. He wants it for himself too. But, metal or no metal, the way I see it, you and your Henchmen are the only hope that he has. I believe he is comfortable in destroying all of you one by one, the same as he did before with the assassin, Raschel. She was a good one, wasn't she?"

"You really do know too much. But since you are so smart, where is the Underlord?"

"Why would I tell you that?"

"Ah, so you do know?" Abraham asked.

They finished their third lap.

"Of course. I'll tell you this much. Why? Because I like a long shot. Being a smuggler, I'm a betting man, and I need friends on both sides when one wins and the other dies."

"All right, spit it out."

"The Underlord resides in Little Leg, near the zillon dragon-riders' peaks. It's a fortress or cathedral, something like that. I've never been. It's near Cauldron City. All I know is that he stays there all day, all night, running his operations. Oh, and those assault rifles that you were talking about, I'd expect more of them. Possibly worse. Arcayis the Underlord has been storing up arti-facts from our world for quite some time. I'd be careful."

"I don't think I'd be any other way." Abraham stopped and

faced Edgar. "Still think it's strange that you would offer anything useful."

"You fought with honor. I liked it. Besides, you don't stand a chance, but I'm willing to at least give you a fighting one. Perhaps I have a soft spot for a homeboy. May the Elders bless you. May they curse you too."

"Have you ever seen an Elder?" Abraham asked.

"Heck no. Hmm-hmm. These people worship everything. It's Elders this and Elders that." Edgar shrugged his arms and shoulders. "They are a bunch of pagans. They worship dog skulls, flowers, even funny-looking pastry dishes. Like pizza. Ah, when I made pizza, they started an all-new cult."

"What about the saying 'The tide shifts. The Elders awaken'?" Abraham asked.

"Pfft... these idiots say that all of the time. They don't know what that means."

"You sound like someone that has more faith in our world than this one."

Edgar lost his smile and said, "There is a world created by God and a world created by man. I made my choice."

"What does that mean?"

"I've told you enough. Hmm-hmm. Figure it out yourself."

46

The Henchmen equipped themselves at Pirate City with horses, rations, and gear. They left *Sea Talon* in the hands of Jander, one of Flamebeard's former crew. Apollo and Prospero stayed back on the ship as well with a few other crewmen. No other volunteers stayed. Abraham led the company south, riding close to the shoreline toward Hancha.

Abraham rode out front with Sticks and Horace riding beside him. As usual, Dominga and Tark were scouting ahead on foot. Behind Abraham were Bearclaw and Vern, followed by Cudgel and Iris. Lewis, Leodor, Clarice, and Swan were in the rear, with Shades and Solomon—who was on foot—bringing up the very rear.

No one said so much as a word. Abraham gave the orders. They followed. The mission hadn't changed: kill the men that had tried to assassinate the king, the zillon dragon riders—not to mention the man who had most likely given the order, Arcayis the Underlord.

The beaten paths cutting through the forest hills weren't hard to follow. The roads were well traveled in the south.

Iris stitched Abraham up. His wounds still burned and were sore. He could still feel the hard claws of the wild men raking across his skin. Certain doom had fallen upon him, but he escaped, thanks to the loyalty and bravery of the Henchmen.

With the sun sinking behind the trees, Abraham, who had been mulling over the latest torrid series of events, broke his silence. "What happened on that stage at the Greasy Pelican? All of you vanished."

Sticks touched her stomach and said, "I don't know, but I puked my guts out after it happened. We poofed from that stage into a dungeon. Ugh, my stomach twists like a vine from thinking of it. That thing, though—the wraith in the stands of the Rim. It was there when we arrived."

"We could have killed it," Horace said.

"How did you escape?" Abraham asked.

"Shades. He squeezed through the bars, killed the guards, and freed us." Sticks's horse trotted ahead of Abraham's. She tugged on the reins and waited for him to catch up. "The problem was we didn't know where you were or where we were. That took some time. We beat it out of the guards. Once we figured it out, Shades headed back to the ship. I led the rest of us in to find you at the Rim."

"You have my gratitude. I was seconds away from having my foot chopped off. And that was only the start of it," he said. "Your timing is impeccable."

"All in a day's work." Sticks's brown hair was tied behind her head in twin braids. Her single bandolier of daggers crossed her shoulders. She was missing a few of her blades. Blood stained her clothing. She had a mark on her upper left arm, which was swollen and bruising where one of the Wild Men had bitten her.

She'd bitten the savage back with a dagger into the temple. "Care to tell us more about your conversation with the horned halfling?"

"Let me guess—inquiring minds want to know?"

"What?" she said.

"Never mind." Abraham sat slightly hunched over in the saddle and patted the side of his horse's neck. The horse was a chestnut brown with a black mane. He didn't have much experience with horses in his past, but he'd come to like them.

"Big Apple the Smuggler King says that he came from the same world as me," Abraham continued. "His real name is Edgar Gravely, and he likes it here. He doesn't want me to do anything that will screw it up for him."

"You can't trust horned halflings. They are nothing but trouble," Horace said. His sausage fingers combed through his beard. "I've crossed them before. They are as bad as the troglins."

"They eat people?" Abraham asked.

"No, they lie. They steal. They are trouble." Horace coughed, reached down, and grabbed a water skin. "Trouble."

"Well, he is a smuggler," Sticks said as she made a rail-thin smile at Abraham. "Horace doesn't care for the peoples beyond Kingsland, if you haven't figured that out. He thinks they are all trouble."

"They are all trouble," Horace fired back. "And that one has horns. Who would trust a wee man with horns? We should have killed him."

"We need information. We can't kill off the source of information. Besides, Edgar isn't really a horned halfling. He's an otherworlder like me." Abraham chuckled. "I just called myself an otherworlder. Interesting. Anyway, we'll track down these assassins in Cauldron City. That's our mission. Kill whatever zillons are associated with Arcayis and take the stones of power or whatever they are."

Horace bit off a crusty fingernail and spat it away. "The zillon dragon riders live in the high places."

"Your point is?" he said.

"They live in the high places, Captain. That's what I know, not because I have seen, but I have heard."

"That's a big help. Thanks, Horace."

Horace gave an affirmative nod.

Lewis and Leodor rode up alongside Abraham.

"Great, my favorite Henchmen," he said with a shake of his head. "Let me guess, you came to offer more advice."

"No... well, yes." Lewis said. His right arm was bandaged just below the shoulder. "Who wouldn't want the prince's advice?"

"Perhaps you mean Lewis the Lewd's advice," Sticks said.

With a sneer, Lewis said, "You better mind your tongue, you scrawny wench. Or I'll have it twisted out of your face."

"Lighten up, Lewis," Abraham said. "Try being nice to the ladies. It gets you a lot farther than being mean to them."

Lewis rolled his eyes.

Leodor cleared his throat and said, "I overheard you talking about Cauldron City. What is our business there?"

Abraham looked at Leodor as though he were stupid and said, "To find Arcayis. Big Apple says that he resides there."

Leodor shook his head and replied, "The only thing we will find in the Cauldron is certain death."

47

Abraham rolled his eyes. "Listen, spooky old man, I don't know if you figured it out yet, but facing certain death is what we do." He looked dead at the older man. "Now, are you going to be part of the problem or part of the solution, Chinless One?"

Leodor blanched.

Horace laughed. "Har! Chinless One. I like it." He poked a finger Leodor's way. "It's because you don't have a chin. Aye!"

Leodor covered his small chin with his hand. "I have a chin."

"You have a baby chin," Abraham fired back.

Sticks trembled in her saddle, bent over with her own silent laughter.

He turned on Lewis. "And you have a chin like Waluigi."

Touching his chin, Lewis said with insecurity, "What is a Waluigi?"

Lewis had very handsome, chiseled features with a slightly prominent chin. Aside from the scar on his lip, he had no flaws at all. That was all the reason for Abraham to pick on him. "A

Waluigi is a person with a giant chin that can poke an eye out in my world."

"I'm not a Waluigi," Lewis said. "I'm a prince. Don't call me that again."

Abraham looked away. The joke turned into something else as he remembered his son, Jake. The two of them had played a lot of *Mario Kart* together. Waluigi, dressed in purple overalls, was Jake's favorite character. Abraham and Jake used to joke about people with big chins. Jake would point and innocently say, "Waluigi." He reached down and touched Jake's Pirates backpack. He hadn't opened it in a while, but he always slept with it near his side.

"Joking aside, Leodor, do you care to fill us in on why Cauldron City can bring about our doom?"

"Cauldron City is not the problem. The Cauldron is. We don't want to venture into the Cauldron."

Abraham arched a brow. He didn't want to sound ignorant by asking, but he did anyway. "Are they different?"

"Cauldron City is not so different than any other city, but it resides in the shadow of the Cauldron," Leodor said. "The Cauldron is a fortress where many members of the Sect preside. They study. They train. They manipulate. The Underlord is now chief among them. No doubt, he will be expecting our arrival. And the zillon dragon riders, well, I think we can only assume that they are on his side as well. Their spiny pinnacles overlook the Cauldron. The Sect has eyes everywhere. I thought it pertinent that I pass this warning along."

"Have you been to the Cauldron?" he asked.

"Yes. My training as a mystic began there when I was young. It's the same with many chosen members of the Sect."

"Was Iris trained there?"

"No, she didn't come from a background of privilege," Leodor said with a glance behind his shoulder. "She uses a perverted form of Titanuus's powers. Her kind is not chosen to wield the stream, but some find it without proper training. Very reckless."

"You better watch how you speak about my lady, Chinless Man, or you might end up being a headless man as well," Horace said.

"Don't threaten me, big belly. I can turn your skin inside out," Leodor replied.

Horace grunted. "I'd like to see you try."

"The point is, as formidable as you might feel, even with Black Bane, you are storming a fortress with only a handful of men and women." Leodor moved his brows up and down. "You'll need a better plan than that. I'd focus on the zillons. They tried to kill the king. Perhaps the Underlord was not behind it. Of course, the zillons are another matter entirely. They have dragons. We don't."

"This is our mission," Abraham said. "There won't be any turning around. Aside from your chronic warnings, do you have anything positive to offer, Leodor?"

"No."

"I didn't think so. What about you, Lewis? What dreadful insights would you like to share?"

Leodor and Lewis turned their horses away and headed toward the rear of the company. With hard eyes, Bearclaw and Vern bumped horses with them as they passed.

Abraham hollered back at them, "Thanks for all of the help, guys! Real team players! You know, there is a saying back in my world: 'If you don't have anything good to say, don't say anything at all.'"

Horace nodded. "I like it, Captain."

"Yeah, well, I like it too." Abraham scowled. "But those two windbags are getting on my nerves."

48

THAT NIGHT, ABRAHAM WARMED HIS HANDS OVER A SMALL campfire. Solomon was with him.

The shaggy gray-haired troglin still wore his maroon vest. He was squatting near the fire and toying with the buttons. "If I'm not mistaken, I think these buttons are made of plastic. They feel like plastic."

"They aren't plastic. They are brass. I can see the shine still on them." Abraham pitched a stick onto the fire.

No one else was around. Several fires had been set up at the campsite in a clearing surrounded by great trees.

Abraham stared deeply into the fire. "But I guess anything is possible. They have guns. I have a backpack. Why not?"

Solomon scratched his neck and said, "I wish I would have got a crack at Lord Hawk."

"Yeah, I bet you did."

"He treated me like an animal. Tortured me. I'm not prone to violence, but I think I'd rip his arms off."

Abraham smirked. "No doubt you could, Chewie."

Solomon tilted his head. "Huh?"

"Nothing."

"Tell me more about Big Apple. Do you believe him?"

"I believe he's an otherworlder like us. I can't say whether or not his story checks out. He gave me the distinct impression that he had no interest in going back to our world. He said he had cerebral palsy." He flicked a twig into the fire. "I can't say I blame him."

"Sounds like this Edgar is sowing his oats for the first time. I don't think that I can blame him either." Solomon sat down cross-legged, stretched his arms upward, and yawned. "You know, I'm getting a lot less rest now that I'm a Henchman. But at least I'm off that boat. I tell you, Abraham, I don't think I'm going to sail back. I'd rather ride a horse back to Kingsland."

"No, you're coming with us. We stick together, one way or the other."

"I know." Solomon looked heavenward. "Just saying."

The night crickets chirped all around.

"I've gazed at the stars a thousand times since I've been back. I don't recognize a one of them. When I was a boy, my dad got me a telescope when I was ten—a birthday present."

"You like astronomy?"

"No, I couldn't have cared less. I liked girls. Those were the stars that I wanted to see." Solomon showed a smile of sharp teeth. "My first girlfriend was older. Not when I was ten, but in high school. I was a sophomore, and she was a senior. She taught me a lot about things. We'd even get together when she came back from college. She was a huge stoner and went on to become a law-school teacher. What a waste. I wonder what she's into now."

"She's probably a senator. What was her name? On second thought, I don't want to know."

"Heh, now that you mention it, her father was in politics. Congressman, I think. I didn't pay much attention. Anyway, her name was Alice. Kinda square, but she'd surprise you." Solomon lay down in the dirt. "I never paid the stars a lick of attention until I got here. What in the hell happened to us, Abe?"

"I don't know, but I have a feeling that the horned halfling does." He sat back and looked skyward. "He doesn't want us to find out either."

"We had the upper hand. We should've taken advantage of it. Maybe he does know the way home."

"I gave my word to take care of the king first. If I see that through, then he'll take care of me. At least, that's the plan."

Solomon sighed. "I think you like it here. Perhaps too much. If it were up to me, I think I'd take a crack at going back home. That's what I'd do."

"You aren't me, and I'm not you. Did you ever stop to think that you might be here for another reason?"

"Aside from some sort of punishment, no." Solomon rolled up onto one side. "Let me guess. You think that you are here to save the world, don't you?"

Abraham shrugged.

Solomon let out a hearty laugh.

"What?" Abraham said. "It's better than thinking that I'm here by accident."

"You jocks are all the same, aren't you?" Solomon's usual mild tone became bitter. "Every jock I ever knew had a hero complex."

"Hey, if the shoe fits…"

"Pah!" Solomon got up, dusted the dirt off his vest, and said, "I think I'll sleep elsewhere."

"Solomon? Come on, man."

The troglin vanished into the woodland as if he'd never even been there.

"Bigfoot, eat your heart out."

"Ahem."

Abraham turned his head. "Oh, hi, Shades. Have a seat. Solomon's spot is still warm."

Shades had his hood off. The smallish man brightened. "Don't mind if I do... Abraham? Is it all right that I call you that?"

"I'm good with both. What's on your mind?"

Shades sat in Solomon's spot and warmed his hands by the fire. "I was wondering if you had given any more thought to Manding me a Henchman."

"From what I can see, you earned it. But I have to ask why. You don't seem like the type that would want to be a Henchman."

"I take offense," the silky-voiced man said. "Why would you discriminate between me and the others?"

"You come across as the self-serving type."

"Like Lewis and Leodor?"

"Ha, well, not like that. More like a thief or a rogue. You want to have something so that you can get something out of it." He pointed at Shades's face. "Besides, it appears that you have a brand."

Shades gently touched two fingers to the starlike scar on his cheek. "This little beauty mark. Ha, it's nothing."

"How'd you get that beauty mark?"

"Er, well, if I told you that I was born with it, would you be satisfied?"

"No."

"I don't want to lie about it either. It's my cross to bear. And, well"—Shades shrugged—"it's embarrassing."

"I don't think anyone in this group should have anything to hide. We have to trust one another."

With an easy smile, Sticks leaned back and said, "Oh, come now, do you really think this group doesn't hold secrets from one another? You are leading a bunch of criminals, for the Elders' sake. Look." He pointed toward Lewis and Leodor, huddled over their own fire. "Those two conspirators tried to kill the king." He made his rounds group by group. "Tark and Cudgel are common thieves. Dominga, a thief. Sticks, a former harlot and thief."

"Harlot?"

"Er, I mean Dominga. Not Sticks. No, Sticks has always been a thorn among the roses—er, I mean a rose among the thorns. And don't get me started on Iris." Shades leaned forward and said under his breath, "She's a mystic. Never trust a mystic. One like her practices the arts of the dark druids. Not a good thing, even by the Sect's standards."

"Well, aren't you a fountain of information?" Abraham would be lying to himself if he didn't admit that Sticks being a former harlot stung a little. Shades's words twisted in his heart. *Don't take it personal. Remember, this might not be real. And so what if she was?* He set his jaw and said, "You know, you have a fine way of deflecting attention away from the mark on your face." He touched the stitches Iris had sewn into his arm after the last battle. "Listen, bub, we are all a bunch of dirty rotten scoundrels. But with me, the slate is clean. It's all about what you do moving forward."

"If that is the case, why won't you brand me?" Shades said with an unusual tightness in his voice. "I haven't given you any trouble. I've been the best ally a friend can be."

"Sorry, Shades, but I have to trust my gut on this." Abraham lay down on his side and looked into the fire. "Say, you're from Hancha. What can you tell me about Cauldron City or the Cauldron?"

Shades stood up. "Sorry, Abraham. It will have to wait." He walked away.

Abraham made a big yawn. The battle, the ride, and the aching wounds had finally caught up with him. "Fine by me." With the crickets chirping and the small fire's embers popping, he fell asleep like a baby.

49

BACK HOME

ABRAHAM WOKE UP INSIDE A PADDED WHITE ROOM. HE SAT UP. HIS arms were bound to his chest. He wiggled around and screamed, "Nooo!" He was in a straitjacket. He popped up to his bare feet. "No. No. No. No. No."

His heart fluttered—not the good kind of flutter but the bad kind. Helplessness assailed him. Wide-eyed, he walked the padded floor and bounced against the soft walls. The walls were dingy white. Everything had a stale smell. He looked about. A white camera shaped like a globe was anchored into the corner of the ten-foot-high ceiling. He looked dead at it.

"Hello? Can you hear me? What is going on?"

He paced, continuing to call out for help. The padded walls absorbed his pleas. Seeing the faint outline of a door, he threw his shoulders against it. He kept that up until he fell down in the center of the room, lathered in sweat and panting.

This can't be real. I'm not crazy. I belong in Titanuus. He squeezed his eyes shut. *Take me back to Titanuus!*

For the longest time, Abraham lay on his back with his eyes

wide open. He had no idea where he was or what had happened. He had gotten used to bad headaches and blacking out and finding his way home again, but this was different. He'd fallen asleep by a campfire while talking to Shades. Now, he was in what he assumed to be the real world. He rolled over and looked at the camera. A tiny red dot glowed like a red eye underneath it.

"Why am I here?"

That was the bigger question. It made sense that he had wound up in a hospital before in a coma. He could believe that it was the result of an accident. But now he was in a loony bin of some sort. *Why?*

"Oh no," he said softly. The only thing he could think of was that he'd possibly spoken to the wrong people, and they had locked him up. He rolled over and scratched his itching nose against the floor. "This is crazy. Why would they have locked me up? I'm a nice guy, and I couldn't have said something that stupid. I wonder if that Nurse Nancy had something to do with it. She seemed to be kinda mean." He looked at the camera. *Oh great, I'm talking to myself. The first sign of crazy.* He sat cross-legged and faced the camera. "Could I please talk to someone? I'm Abraham Jenkins. The last thing I remember was being in a hospital after a truck accident." He tossed out more information about himself— where he was from, who he was, and even his driver's license number. "Please, someone talk to me."

Time passed. The only company he had was the chronic hum of the caged fluorescent lights above him. The bulbs were bright, but a few of them had gone dim and flickered. He lay on his back and stared at them for many long minutes. He closed his eyes and tried to sleep, but the straitjacket's constricting nature made getting comfortable impossible. His shoulders and arms itched, and he couldn't scratch them.

Abraham walked on his knees to the door and pressed his ear

against it. The only thing he could hear was his heart thumping in his temple. He tapped his forehead against the door. He wanted to slam his skull into it but refrained. *Remember, they're watching.*

The question is, who is watching? How did I get here? Where is Mandi? Does she know about this? Did she put me in here? Perhaps Luther Vancross did. Maybe all of them think that I'm crazy.

Maybe he was.

He took in a deep breath of air from the stuffy room and shook with a shuddering sigh. He leaned back against the door and closed his eyes. He tapped his toes together. *I want to go to Titanuus. I want to go to Titanuus. I want to go to Titanuus.*

One of the flickering fluorescent bulbs went black.

Abraham huffed a depressed laugh. "I'm going to have to fall asleep eventually. Don't dwell on it, Abraham. Don't dwell on it."

He moved to one of the corners in the wall, the one below the camera. He closed his eyes and breathed deeply. His sore muscles began to ease. His breathing slowed. His eyes became heavy. *Yes, sweet sleep, take me away.* His chin dipped into his chest.

The door to his padded cell opened.

50

TWO MEN IN THE SEA-GREEN UNIFORM SCRUBS OF AN ORDERLY walked into the padded room. One of them carried a long metal stick with two prongs on the end. He was black, older, short haired, and built like a football lineman with his playing days long behind him. His nose was busted. The other was a white farm-boy type, young, about the same size as his counterpart. He had a black eye and a front tooth missing. Their wounds looked fresh. Both men wore frowns.

Their names were sewn into their shirts. The black man's read Otis, and the younger fellow's read Haymaker.

Abraham tried to make it light. "Good morning, fellas, or after-noon or evening... Uh, I hope it's time for my bathroom break because I really have to go."

The orderlies exchanged a glance.

The black man, Otis, stepped forward and stuck his prod into Abraham's ribs.

Abraham jumped from his seat. "Gah!" His nerves caught fire

from head to toe. Cringing in the corner, he asked, "What did you do that for?"

"Because if you get squirrely, you are going to get more of that," Otis said in a deep voice. "Get up! And don't play games with me today, fool."

"Okay," Abraham said. Judging by the heavy stares in both men's eyes, he knew they meant business. And he certainly didn't want to get shocked again—it sent fire right through him. "Okay."

The orderlies got him up on his feet and led him out of the room. With their strong hands locked on his arms, they led him down the hall. The floor tiles were cold. Abraham's cold feet burned with every step. The floors felt as if they had tacks in them for some reason. The hallway was dim, the cinderblock walls were painted off-white, and the lights above showed off the dinginess. The place was definitely a hospital of some sort. They passed many closed doors. Some had portal windows, and others didn't. It was a dreary place.

At the end of the hallway was an elevator with metal doors so shiny Abraham could see his blurred reflection in them. *I look shaggy. Scary. No wonder I'm locked up. I look like I haven't combed my hair or trimmed my beard in weeks.* The big men were about the same size as him. Haymaker pressed the elevator button.

"So, is this the way to the bathroom? I really hate to sound like a baby, but I have to go."

Otis waved his metal stick in his face.

"I mean, I did have to go."

The elevator dinged, and the doors split open. The rough-handed orderlies guided Abraham inside. The doors closed. Haymaker hit the button. The elevator went up.

Abraham nodded. "Going up. A good sign."

He counted the floor buttons on the elevator panel—eleven floors. Haymaker hit the eleventh-floor button.

"The top. Even better."

Otis stuck his stick right underneath Abraham's chin and said, "Quiet."

The elevator stopped. The doors opened. The orderlies let him into the room. It was an office with a bunch of empty cubicles. The same fluorescent lights hung in the ceiling. Most of the bulbs were out.

The carpet didn't hurt as much on his feet as the cold tile floors in the hallway. The men led Abraham to the back of the offices into the corner. Otis knocked on an oak door.

"Come in," someone said in a sharp voice.

Otis pushed the door open by its nickel-plated handle. The office was very big, nicely decorated with warm wood-paneled walls and the heads of game. Deer, elk, and black bear heads were mounted on the wall. The overhead lights were off, but the cloudy sunlight of a hazy morning shone through the windows. Bookshelves, display cases, and sports memorabilia were there. A man sat behind an expensive cherry-wood desk in a high-backed burgundy leather chair with his legs propped up on the desktop. His face was hidden by an open newspaper, but Abraham could see curly locks of brown hair over the rim of the paper.

"Sit him down and gear him up," the man behind the desk said.

"Yes, sir," Otis and Haymaker replied. They took the straitjacket off Abraham. As they did so, they put two chrome-plated shackles on his wrists, with three small stripes of green light glowing on the cuffs. They shoved Abraham down into a green leather chair in front of the desk. "He's ready, Doctor."

"Good. Now leave us," the clean-shaven doctor said.

Both men exited without a word, closing the door quietly behind them. The man behind the desk dropped the paper from his face, folded it up, and placed it on the desk. He had a receding hairline, curly brown hair, and a round face and was in his late fifties, clean-shaven and dark eyed. He wore wire-rim glasses shaped like octagons. His expression was stern with a slight smile. He wore a camo hunting suit and clasped his rough hands on the desk. "Good morning. I am Dr. Jack Lassiter. Tell me who you are."

"Abraham Jenkins." He looked at the cuffs on his wrists.

"Don't worry about those," Dr. Lassiter said. "So long as you behave yourself and don't do anything stupid, like before, you'll be just fine."

Abraham lifted his chin and asked, "Before? What do these things do?"

Doctor Lassiter smiled. "Heh heh heh. It's a little therapeutic invention of my own. It will make that cattle prod that Otis carries feel like a tickle of a feather."

51

ABRAHAM RUBBED HIS WRISTS. "OH. I'LL STAY PUT. THAT CATTLE prod was enough. It almost shot the pee out of me, though." He looked over his shoulder at a door in the corner behind him. "And, well, I still really need to go."

"Keep the door open."

"Thanks, Dr. Lassiter." He got up, crossed the room, opened the door to a small, quaint bathroom, and turned the light on. Feeling as though he hadn't gone in days, he relieved himself, washed his hands, turned off the light, and exited. "Again, many thanks, Dr. Lassiter."

"No need to be so formal. Call me Dr. Jack. It's best we keep it simple, Abraham." Dr. Jack pointed at a little black button mounted on his desk. "That's the switch that will make you twitch. Remember that. I'm not the kind of man that jokes about a thing like that."

Abraham lifted his hands and sat down. "I believe you." He wouldn't learn anything about what was going on if he didn't cooperate. He stuck with the nice-guy act. Eyeing the trophy heads mounted on the wall, he said, "So, you're a hunter?"

"I've been sweeping the woods and skinning bucks since I was a boy. A fine sport, hunting." Dr. Jack rocked back in his seat and drummed his fingers on the end of his chair's arms. "What about you?"

"Never hunted much. I was more of a ball-sports guy."

"I know." Dr. Jack reached down into a drawer and pulled out a thick manila file with a red rubber band on it. He took off the rubber band and opened the papers. He licked his thumb and rummaged through the file. "You have had an eventful life. Some very unfortunate turns of events. Very sorry to hear about that."

Abraham leaned forward. "I have to say, you've lost me. Can you tell me why I'm here? I don't mean to be pushy, but I'm very confused."

"That's why I brought you here. Because you aren't the only one that is confused. I'm a bit confused myself." Dr. Jack picked up a remote from his desk. He pointed it toward a large flat-screen television that hung on the wall to his right, and the television came on. "Tell me, what is the last thing that you remember before coming here?"

I was lying by a campfire in Titanuus. That was the first thing that came to Abraham's mind, but he knew better than to say it. His turned in his chair toward the television. "I was in a hospital. I'd come out of a coma. I talked with my roommate, a very old guy, Charles Abner. A couple of friends stopped by—my boss, Luther Vancross, and a woman friend, Mandi." He buckled his brows and quickly lifted a finger. "Oh, and the nurse was Nancy."

Dr. Jack nodded several times. He took notes with a blue pen while Abraham spoke. He shook the pen. "Ah, crap. My pen's out of ink." He flicked it into a wastebasket beside his desk and grabbed another one out of a drawer. "If you are ever in the market for a good reliable ink pen, get the Bic Atlantis. It's my favorite. All of the other ones suck." He scribbled on a separate notepad. "Good. Good. So, you remember talking with your associates. Then what? Who did you talk to last?"

"Mandi. I think I fell asleep after that." He told a partial truth, not wanting to get into how Charles had jumped into the conversation too. "It was the last thing I remember before waking up here."

"Fascinating," Dr. Jack said with a shine in his brown eyes. "If I'm correct, what you are talking about lines up with what happened with the occurrence three days ago."

"Occurrence?" Abraham leaned back in his seat. "Did you say three days ago?"

"Abraham, you're a jock. You've seen your own kind of action, and you've been through a lot. I mean, have you ever been a striker, a brawler? You are a big fella. Rough looking, like a biker. One of those Hells Angels."

"Hey, I've never been into those types of things. I mean, there might have been some scuffles on the baseball fields, but I always tried to break them up." He broke out in a cold sweat. "I was cocky but mellow."

Dr. Jack picked up a piece of paper and said, "Says here that you punched a guy and knocked him out in college. Two teeth out."

Abraham sank in his chair. That had been an ugly day, one that he'd buried deep. He didn't even start the fight—he only went in swinging. The guy didn't see it coming. The young man's face caved in, and his body fell. "Look, that was more of an accident."

"Maybe. Look, all men have a violent nature. But that day, something uncorked in you. Right?" Dr. Jack said in a pushy voice.

"No." Abraham's neck reddened. "I was a talker."

"Did that provoke the fight?"

He bobbed his head side to side. "Probably. I don't know. It was long ago, and everyone was in on it. Wait, I remember, I hit a guy with a ball. In the hip. I didn't tip my hat. The bench cleared."

"Why didn't you tip your hat?"

"I guess I was being a jerk that day, but I learned my lesson. I swear I did."

Dr. Jack puffed up in his chair, flexing and gesticulating mildly with his arms. "You're a big rangy fella. That draws attention. I bet you liked that. Being a jock, you are probably used to getting your way. But when you don't, you get angry, don't you?"

"I, uh... no. No, I don't have a temper."

Dr. Jack made a devilish smile and picked up another piece of paper. "Sure you don't. And what about this man? The pharmacist you attacked. Bill Lowman. Did he provoke you?"

"No, no, I was hooked on pain pills. It was an accident."

"You've been in a lot of accidents. You know that? Accidents that hurt many and killed them." Dr. Jack leaned forward. "I know this is harsh, but trust me, it's therapeutic. Facing the truth. It's the best therapy." He looked Abraham dead in the eye. "Look at you. You're turning red all over. You want to hit me, don't you?"

Yes.

52

"It's fine. Say what you are thinking," Dr. Jack said.

"What is up with the third degree? I've been through all of this. I want to put it behind me. How is it therapeutic to dredge it all up?" He flipped out his hands. "What man wouldn't want to hit someone treating him like this? Especially after all I have been through."

Dr. Jack pecked an index finger on the table. "It's a matter of trust. We need to establish that. You see, I think you believe that you have moved on, but you haven't. I'm going to show you why I believe that. It should shed a little light on my concerns." He turned toward the television. "After you fell into another coma, you had some violent convulsions. Your language was foreign. The local hospital didn't know what to do with you, so you were brought here—a special treatment center."

"Okay. Pardon, but I don't think there is anything wrong with me."

"Pain-pill addiction. Migraines." Dr. Jack shook his head.

"There is something wrong with all of us. But most, we hope, can control it."

"There's nothing wrong with me. I'm normal," Abraham lied. *Abnormal is more like it.* His life had a new truth. He was the best swordsman in Titanuus. Many were dead to show for it. But that wasn't this world. It was another. He scratched an eyebrow and looked at the television. An image came up of a hospital nurses' station.

Dr. Jack glanced at him and said, "Here we go. I kinda wish we had some popcorn. Do you like popcorn, Abraham?"

He placed a hand on his belly. "I'd like about anything right now." He focused on the TV screen. A tall shaggy-haired man wearing a hospital gown approached the nurses' station. He dragged intravenous tubes behind him, along with the monitoring station. Two of the women looked up from their phones and jumped in their seats. One of them grabbed a phone. Nurse Nancy raced into the scene from out of nowhere. She wore a set of Hello Kitty scrubs, much like before. She put her hands into Abraham's belly. She was yelling at him.

Abraham broke out into a cold sweat. *Oh Lord, tell me I don't hurt her. Don't let me hurt her.* He watched himself pick up Nurse Nancy by the waist like a child and set her aside. He moved down the hallway. The camera view switched from the nurses' station to the hallway. In long strides, he made his way down the hallway, head twisting left and right like a trapped tiger's. He glanced upward for a moment in the direction of the camera. His eyes were wildfires. Abraham didn't recognize himself. The man was him but different.

A group of doctors and nurses, male and female, came rushing down the hallway. The men barred Abraham's path. He pushed through them. Two nurses, stout men but not as big, hooked his arms. Abraham slung them face-first into each other.

"Heh heh heh. I know I shouldn't laugh, but I love a good action movie. But this is better because it's real," Dr. Jack said. "Man, that hurt me to watch."

One of the doctors was screaming and waving his hands. He mouthed the words, "Call security! Call security!" The doctor backpedaled from Abraham, stumbled, and fell down. As he walked by, the doctor locked both arms around his leg. Abraham glared down upon the doctor. The doctor let go. Abraham moved down the hall. He poked his head into doors and walked into rooms and came back out. He ripped the intravenous needles out of his arms. He moved down the hall and disappeared from view.

The camera angle changed.

Abraham saw himself move into the lobby, where the elevators waited. He walked by one set of doors when they opened. Four security guards in blue uniforms came rushing out, carrying black billy clubs. A nurse pointed at Abraham and screamed. The guards converged on Abraham.

The first guard to approach Abraham clubbed him in the back of the head. Abraham spun around and backfisted the man in the jaw then snatched the man's club as he crumpled to the floor.

"This is where it really gets good," Dr. Jack said. He gesticulated with stiff open hands. "Wah tah!"

Abraham touched the back of his head and felt a knot on it.

The camera view caught the second elevator's doors opening. Six more guards, armed the same, came pouring out. Abraham, club in hand, squared off on the guards of all shapes, ages, and sizes. Two bum-rushed him with their clubs raised high. Abraham cracked them both in the tops of their skulls in the blink of an eye. The guards fell face-first to the floor.

One of the guards was barking orders to the others, a big black fellow. He waved his arms and was mouthing the words, "Pile on him! Pile on him! There's more of them than us."

The gang of guards bum-rushed Abraham. That was a mistake. He snatched another club from the ground, and fisting the two clubs, he beat the tar out of the inferior men. The black clubs busted out a man's teeth, smote temples, and dislodged an eyeball. Watching, Abraham winced.

Dr. Jack chuckled. "I've never seen a big man so out of shape move so fast. It's uncanny. Inhuman."

Abraham followed the fighter's perfected movements. Lightning-fast strokes. He knew them like the back of his hand. It wasn't inhuman. It was Ruger. A chill ran down his spine.

All the guards were sprawled out on the floor, groaning, bleeding, crawling, or all of the above. The men were wiped out, crying over busted elbows, broken noses, and arms. Three female guards remained. They had their taser guns out and pointed at Ruger.

Smart. They should have tried that first and saved the men from the macho act.

Two of the women guards trembled, but the third came forward, as steady as a rock. She was butch, with spiky black hair. She crept in on Ruger. Her lips were saying, "Give yourself up, big fella. I'll shoot."

Ruger took one step toward her.

She fired the taser. So did the other two.

Ruger's eyes lit up like a Christmas tree.

53

Ruger's body shook inside his skin. His belly jiggled like Santa Claus's. Over a dozen strands of electricity latched onto his chest. The prods sunken into his flesh sent pulsating jolts of electricity through the strings. His hair stood on end, and his teeth clacked together. He swayed but did not fall.

The butch guard shouted to the other two. It looked as though she said, "Give him all the juice you got! Lay down, big fella." She continued to squeeze the trigger on her taser gun, as did the others. "Fall!"

The wild-eyed man swept two handfuls of taser strings into his big hands. With a fierce yank, he pulled them all out. The chest of his hospital-issued clothing showed small bloody marks on it. He dropped the wiry coils down on the floor.

The female guards' eyes widened. The butch one swallowed. She nervously looked at the others then faced him again. She took out her club and took a step forward.

Ruger gave her the no-no finger sign.

She rushed him, screaming. He snatched the club out of her

hand and shoved her backward. The other two caught the meaty woman, and all three fell down.

Ruger turned his back and ran down the nearest hall.

"At least you play nice with the ladies," Dr. Jack said. "If not for that, I'd have figured you were completely out of your skull."

The camera angle changed. The view caught up with Ruger looking out a window. His head quickly turned side to side. He pounded his fist on the glass. He turned and saw an empty linen cart. The shiny metal frame sat on black heavy-duty casters. He hustled over to the cart and picked it up in his long, hairy arms. With a heave, he sent the cart crashing through the glass window. Moving with apish agility, he swung himself out behind the window's broken hunks of glass and vanished.

Abraham looked right at Dr. Jack. "Where did he go? I mean, where did I go?"

"Interesting that you put it that way." Dr. Jack held up the remote and waved it gently. He pressed the buttons. "Fortunately, we have plenty of cameras on the outside. Man, I must have watched this over a dozen times. Every time, I get the chills. But not so much as this next part."

A new picture showed up on the TV screen. It was outside and snowing. The camera showed the outside of a tall, impersonal, hospital-like building. Abraham guessed it was the building with the elevator he'd taken. It was surrounded by the tall trees of a forest. *What is this place?*

Dr. Jack leaned forward in his chair. He patted the remote in his hand and pointed at the screen. "Take a close look. This is a camera shot from the ground level. But up near the top, the eighth floor, well, tell me what you see."

Abraham squinted. A man was climbing the building like a spider. The winds tore at his hospital garb and beard.

Ruger's fingers and toes were lodged inside the cement grooves that ran vertically down the building. He descended slowly, foot by foot, level by level, without stopping.

Abraham's heart raced. It was him, but it wasn't. It could have only been Ruger. He didn't know Ruger for certain—they'd never met—but for some reason, he knew that was him. That was the only explanation he could comprehend. *How?*

"I've seen a lot of crazy things in my life. Crazy is what I do... but this?" Dr. Jack looked right at Abraham when he said it. "This is something straight up out of *The Terminator*. I kept waiting for your skin to come off. I'm thankful that didn't happen. I think."

Ruger made it down the building one level at a time. He didn't move like Spider-Man, but he moved.

"How is my body doing this?" he muttered.

Tapping the remote on his chin, Dr. Jack said, "I've been wondering the same thing myself. To the point that it is making me crazy. Every time I watch, I learn a little something else. Look at you, a big fella but out of shape. For your fingers to cling to those snowy walls, well, your grip would have to be stronger than steel. I understand smaller climbers doing feats like this, but you, a washed-up baseball pitcher turned junk-food-eating truck driver? Uh-uh, I can't buy it. There weren't any pentagrams tattooed on your body. So, I ruled out any demons, even though it's been recorded that demons that possess people give them super strength."

"I'm not a demon."

"No, but it would make a lot more sense if you were. I'd be sleeping better. I know that much." Jack smiled at him and looked back at the television. Marveling, he said, "You know, I must have watched this five times before I caught on to something."

"What's that?"

"Why didn't you take the stairs? Or try the elevator? Any

HALLORAN, P CRAIG

normal person would have done that. But like some sort of alien, you went right through the window. Why? Why? Why?"

That was a good question. If it was Ruger, he wouldn't have been familiar with the layout of modern buildings. He might not have recognized the exit signs over the stairwells. And the red glow of the exits might have deterred him. *Man, if that's you, Ruger, then how are you suddenly in me?* "I don't know," Abraham said. "Look at me. I'm the kind of guy that prefers elevators."

"Uh-huh." Jack's stare was fixed on the television.

Ruger made his way down the wall and dropped from it the last fifteen feet.

"Look at that. You land like a cat. A fat cat, but a cat, none-theless. You should have shattered your leg, but nothing in your body is broken."

Ruger prowled across the hospital grounds. The camera views changed several times as he raced across the campus grounds. A twenty-foot-high fence surrounded the building. Red warning lights were flashing on the tops of the metal fence posts. Ruger grabbed the fence then jerked his hands away.

"That fence is electric." Dr. Jack chuckled.

54

RUGER SCALED THE ELECTRIC FENCE LIKE A MONKEY. HE PUSHED HIS body through the barbed wire at the top, shredding his hospital garb. After dropping to the other side of the fence, he didn't look back. He dashed through the snow and disappeared into the woodland.

The TV screen went black. Dr. Jack tossed the remote onto the table. "Tasers didn't stop you. The electric fence didn't either." He looked at the bracelets on Abraham's wrists. "Don't get any funny ideas. I promise you that those will stop you. Forever, possibly."

"I'm not going anywhere. I want the same answers that you want." He wiped the sweat from the side of his head. "So, where did you catch me? Or how?"

"Good question." Dr. Jack spun in his chair and faced the wall of mounted trophies. "I've been hunting since I was a kid. I love it, my dad did, my grandpa did, and so on. You see that buck up there." He pointed at the wall. "Twenty point. It took me years to get him. I knew he was there, and he knew that I was there. But one day, I got him. We left early, right after dawn. I camped in the same spot for three days. He appeared. One shot took him down."

Abraham played nice, even though massive confusion still raced through his head. "Impressive. He's very big. I take it that I was easier."

"You were a wild-eyed man in the woodland. Lost. Confused. Technically, you didn't hurt anyone... that bad. Aside from the fellow whose eyeball you dislodged." He spun back toward Abraham. "You left a trail of blood that the blind could see. The hounds gave chase. Cornered you in the cliffs. You know what we did?"

"I'm on pins and needles."

"Threw a net over you. My idea. There isn't much a man can do once he's all tangled up and you drag him away."

"Like in the *Planet of the Apes*. Nice."

Dr. Jack made a wicked chuckle. "Good one. A net and tranquilizers. The tranquilizers took a long time to wear you down. I didn't want you to hurt yourself or others, so it was the straitjacket and padded room for you." He leaned forward, clasped his hands, and put his elbows on the table. "So, Abraham Jenkins, can you tell me what in the hell is going on?" He looked him right in the eyes, searching for a sign or an answer. "Tell me what you are thinking. I can help."

Abraham had dealt with his fair share of intelligent people in this lifetime. Dr. Jack was one of them. He came across as the kind of man who was two steps ahead of everyone around him, the kind of man who knew more than he showed. Judging by the heads mounted on the wall, he was a dangerous man too.

"I think I might have been abducted by aliens. You know, we are close to Wytheville. Maybe they implanted something inside of me. It gave me superpowers." He smiled.

"You might want to cooperate."

He lifted his wrists. "I am. Look, I can't explain that. It's as impossible to me as it is to you. Not to mention that I'm sore and burning like fire all over. Can I ask you a question? What kind of special treatment facility is this?"

"It's a WHS center. You've probably never heard of it, but we take care of privileged clients. Consider yourself lucky."

"Why am I special?" He frowned. "I don't get it."

"You are safe. That's all that matters. But we need to diagnose your problem. Your schizophrenia."

"I'm not schizo!" Abraham's knee started to bounce. He could live with the migraines and his past troubles, but he couldn't live with being called crazy. He wasn't crazy. Everything he did was real. There had to be an explanation for it. He was going to find out. He noticed Dr. Jack's finger hovering over the button. "I'm sorry, but no one has ever called me crazy before." He sighed.

"Just like most people that are incarcerated swear that they are innocent, well, people with mental disorders are pretty much the same. Don't take it hard. There is therapy for you. I can, and I will help." Dr. Jack leafed through the papers in the file, wetting his thumb as he did so. "You were roommates with Charles Abney in the hospital. Do you remember him?"

"I do. He died."

"Yes, he did. I shouldn't share this with you—it's privileged information—but seeing how he's gone and he doesn't have any family"—he made that smug chuckle—"well, who is going to know? Besides, if I get caught, it's my word against yours. A crazy person."

"Isn't *crazy* a bit of an insensitive way of labeling people nowadays?"

"Do you take me as a man that gives a crap about political

correctness? Sticks and stones, Abraham, sticks and stones." He fished out a piece of paper from one of his desk drawers and held it up—it was a map. "Charles drew this for me. Does it look familiar?"

Abraham swallowed. *Titanuus!*

55

ABRAHAM TRIED TO PLAY IT COOL. HE TILTED HIS HEAD TO ONE SIDE and said, "It looks like a picture of West Virginia. I mean, if you flip it over." He shrugged. "I've looked at a lot of maps. I'm a local and a truck driver, you know."

Dr. Jack turned the picture around and flipped it over. He scratched his neck. "Huh. I never picked up on that. It actually does closely resemble the mountain state." He set the map down on the desk. "A funny thing. You know, one of my nurses—you met her, Nurse Nancy—overheard Charles talking to you about a something called Titanuus just before he died. She made it sound like the two of you might have had something in common."

With his fingers locked together, Abraham shrugged his thumbs and lied, "I didn't really make much sense of it."

Dr. Jack was playing a cat-and-mouse mind game with him. That wasn't Abraham's strongest suit, but he wasn't one to be played either.

He decided to flip the conversation. "It sounds like you might know more about this Titanuus than I do. Do you?"

Dr. Jack raised his brows. Stiffly, he said, "I hear a lot of things from my patients. Nothing they say surprises me. But one thing that I've become particularly good at is knowing when they are lying. Again, I want to emphasize that you and I need to establish a chain of trust. If we can do that, well, both of us will be better off. I'll be enlightened, and you'll be relieved of the burdens that you carry. You can hopefully return back to society, sooner than later."

"Return back to society?" Abraham rocked forward in his chair. "How long do you plan on keeping me?"

"I don't think you fully understand the severity of your situation. You assaulted several people. It's on video. I can keep you as long as I want. And be thankful—it's either this or prison."

Abraham paled and sat back in his seat. Dr. Jack Lassiter meant business. Abraham wasn't sure what sort of business the man was into or what he really wanted, but he'd made it clear that he was in control. Abraham's eyes swept the room as he searched for something to use against the man, something to remember. He needed to know more about who this man was. At the same time, he thought, *Prison might be the better option.* He cleared his throat. "Dr. Jack, I might think a lot better if I had something good to eat. After all, a lot has happened, and I'm starving."

"You'll eat. You'll eat sooner if you open up with me." Dr. Jack closed the file and tossed it in the drawer. "Do you have anything else that you'd like to add?"

"No."

"Then this session is over. Otis! Haymaker! Come on in."

The office door opened, and the burly orderlies strolled inside. Haymaker carried the straitjacket.

Abraham looked at the men from over his shoulder and said, "Is that really necessary?"

"You saw the video," Dr. Jack said. "You're very dangerous. You probably don't remember, but Otis and Haymaker caught a first-hand look at what you can do when you're unfettered." He glanced at Otis's shiner and Haymaker's busted nose. "Otis was an all-American lineman at Alabama. Would have been pro if not for a knee injury. You tossed him through a door like a sack of potatoes. Didn't he, Otis?"

With a scowl on his face, Otis made a quick nod.

Dr. Jack continued. "No, Abraham, a padded room is the safest place for you to be. Now, behave yourself. Me, I have some hunting to do." He gave the orderlies a nod.

The orderlies left the bracelets on and put him back in the straitjacket. They buckled the straps tightly and led him out of the room. Abraham took one last look back through the door at Dr. Jack. The man had turned in his chair and faced the snowy window. Haymaker closed the door. Down the elevator they went, and they gruffly shoved him back into the padded room.

"This is it? I'm back here, just like that. This is crazy! I'm not crazy!"

Otis looked at him with his heavy gaze and said, "Oh, believe me, you're crazy. And where I come from, we put crazy down. That's what I said that they should do to you."

"Come on, do you know who I am? You're an athlete, Otis. I'm Abraham Jenkins. The Jet. I've had rough times, but I've never hurt anyone. This is nuts. Come on, man. You have to help me out. Don't I get a phone call or something?"

"Nope," Otis said.

Haymaker stood behind Otis's shoulder with a syringe and a large vial. He poked the needle into the vial and drew a clear liquid into the syringe.

Abraham backpedaled into the corner. "What is that? What is he doing?"

"It's a sedative. A little something to help you rest and to keep you from hurting yourself. Not that I care," Otis said. "Dr. Jack's orders. Come on now—be still. Let's get this over with nice and easy."

Abraham violently shook his head. "I don't need to be sedated. I don't need it. Look at me! I'm behaving myself."

Otis waved Haymaker forward with a nod of his chin. He held his stun rod and smacked it gently into his hand. "Don't make me use this, Mr. Jenkins. Cooperate. Make it nice and easy."

Abraham cringed in the corner. Fear assailed him as his eyes locked on the man holding the needle. He wasn't sure what was driving his fear, but getting injected, well, it didn't sit well with him. Perhaps he feared a new addiction. "Don't, just don't." He looked up at the camera on the wall of his room and shouted. "I don't need it!"

"You're being difficult. I can't have that." Otis hit him with the stun rod.

Abraham wriggled in his skin and collapsed on the padded floor. Otis held him down. Haymaker stuck him in the neck. The taut muscles in his body eased. His eyelids became heavy. The images of the men towering over him blurred. He let go of his fear. The time had come to go back home. *Titanuus, here I come.*

56

ABRAHAM WIPED THE DROOL FROM HIS MOUTH. HE WAS IN THE SAME padded white room he'd been in before. The red light on the globe-shaped camera stared down on him. He moaned, "Noooo." He rolled over to the wall and propped himself up in the corner. "How long have I been out?" He eyed the camera.

Stop talking to yourself.

The fluorescent lights flickered above him. The steady hum accompanied his nervous thoughts. He'd fully expected to wake up back in Titanuus. Instead, he was trapped in the real world, trapped back home in a world where he wasn't needed. In Titanuus, he was needed. His head sank into his chest.

I have to get back. I have to get back. I know it's real. It has to be real.

Abraham might have had some issues in his life, but being crazy wasn't one of them. Even when he was hooked on painkillers, he'd only committed one desperate act. He learned from it. He got better from it. What Dr. Lassiter was insinuating about him couldn't be more wrong. He wasn't a man prone to violence. Even when he'd lost Jenny, Jake, and Buddy, he didn't have a violent reaction. Instead, he sobbed and cried tremendously.

Be strong, Abraham. Be strong. There has to be an explanation for all of this.

He rehashed the video footage in his mind. His body had been doing the impossible. Even when he was in the best of shape, he could not have done what he witnessed. It was Ruger. He had no explanation, but he and that man had switched places, a bit, temporarily. There was no other way he could have controlled his body like that, not even after all the books he'd read and movies he'd watched. There was no way.

I am in Ruger, and Ruger is in me. That does sound crazy.

He gently bumped his head back against the padded wall.

Think. Think. Think. I can't live like this.

He eyed the camera. He couldn't tell whether it had a recording device or not. He assumed not, but maybe he was wrong. Dr. Jack might have been watching him right then. He had to be careful. He stood up and paced.

Ruger, Ruger, Ruger, if you are a part of this body, I need you to listen to me. He focused on the people in his life, people who could help. Mandi. Luther. *These are people that can help.* He didn't know what to make of Dr. Jack, but the confident psychiatrist might have actually been trying to help. *I don't know about him, but don't hurt anyone.* He envisioned the exits and the stairs out. He ran through the function of the elevator. He focused on anything that he could that might be useful in case Ruger came out again.

This is insane. What am I, Dr. Jekyll and Mr. Hyde?

He paced for minutes that became hours, thinking of everything useful to Ruger that he could. His belly groaned. His wounds ached. The muscles in his body burned as they did the first few days after training camp, but they felt three times as bad. Ruger had pushed him beyond his natural limits.

What is that guy made of, anyway? His will is as hard as iron. I just wish that my body was.

After circling the padded cell until he couldn't walk anymore, he went and stood before the camera. He tossed his arms out and said, "Fine, Dr. Jack. I'm ready to tell you about Titanuus."

He moved to the wall and sat back down. He waited. Another bulb flickered out and went dead. He waited.

His eyelids became heavy. He started to sleep. The door to his cell opened again. Otis and Haymaker came inside, each carrying a stun rod in his meaty grip. With a lazy roll of his neck, Abraham said, "I really hope it's dinner time."

Otis cracked him upside the head with his stun rod.

Abraham's hair curled. The room went black.

57

THE SMELL OF FRIED CHICKEN AND STEAMY MASHED POTATOES lingered in the air. Abraham's eyelids slowly rose. The surrounding light was dim. He hoped he was back in the woodlands of Titanuus.

That wasn't the case. The light came from a brass lamp with a green shade on Dr. Jack's desk. The psychiatrist sat at his desk behind a bucket of chicken. He was sucking his fingers and wearing the same camo suit from before.

Abraham sat up in the same chair he had been sitting in. His head throbbed from the stun rod Otis had stuck him with. "Dinner time?"

Dr. Jack pushed the bucket of chicken his way. "Eat up. Grab some rolls, potatoes, green beans, and fried corn." He waved a chicken leg at Abraham. "Extra crispy. The best. Oh, and sorry for the shock from Otis, but we had to make sure you wouldn't turn wild again."

He didn't have to tell Abraham twice. He reached into the bucket, grabbed a piece of meat, and filled his hands with three rolls. Abraham didn't eat like an animal, but it was close. If he could have, he would have consumed the bone. That was the best food he'd tasted in a long time.

"You might want to wash that down. I'd hate to see you choke yourself." Dr. Jack shoved a huge Styrofoam cup his way. "I hope you like Coca-Cola."

Abraham took the cup in hand and gulped it down to the bottom then let out a long "Aaaaaah!"

"Take it easy, Mean Joe Green."

"I forgot how much I missed that stuff. It feels like it's been forever." He continued eating.

After wiping his hands on a paper napkin, the doctor threw it in the waste bin by his desk and asked, "What do you mean by that?"

After swallowing his last bite, Abraham said, "Because I've been in Titanuus." He grabbed a Styrofoam plate from the desk and scooped out the potatoes and poured on the gravy. "I guess you've heard about it or else you wouldn't be asking me."

"You're prying about Charles Abney. Yes, he did talk about that place. He called it a medieval fantasy world. His descriptions were very vivid. I even had him take a lie detector test. He beat it, but I cured him."

"You cured him?" Abraham loaded in a spoonful of potatoes and spoke with his mouth full. "Was he dangerous?"

"No, not like you. I was young then. I wanted to prove myself. I really wasn't going to buy into *The Road to El Dorado* or this *Stargate* stuff." Dr. Jack grabbed a two-liter of cola and refilled his cup. "So, what do you drink in Titanuus? A lot of ale? Water? Milk?"

"There's nothing processed. It's like going back three hundred years in this world, maybe farther. We ride horses and fight monsters."

Dr. Jack lifted his chin and stroked his neck. He set a small recording device on the table. "I'd like to hear everything, and I want you to start from the beginning."

"Huh," Abraham said as a kind of laugh. "That's going to take a long time because an awful lot has happened."

"Start at the beginning."

"Fine. I hope you don't mind me eating while I talk, but the way my life has been going, I don't know when the next meal is my last one."

"Enjoy. You keep cooperating, and there will be more where that came from. But if you start feeling twitchy"—Dr. Jack held his finger over the button—"I'll be ready."

"Let's hope that doesn't happen." Abraham started at the beginning and recounted the time he'd driven through the sun ring inside the East River Mountain Tunnel and wound up in Titanuus. He talked nonstop for two hours. He ate every crumb of food. "They don't make those little parfait cups anymore, do they?"

"No."

"Man, those were good. I always liked the crumbled-up pie crust in the bottom."

Dr. Jack nodded. "Me too." The inflection in his voice was gone. He seemed listless. He clicked a button on his recorder and said, "Let's take a break."

"Okay. Did something that I said bother you? You seem disturbed."

"I am disturbed, only in a different way than you." Dr. Jack patted the files on his desk. "I've done my homework. Based off of my research, you and Charles Abney never met before, but both of you have described the same world. You have used the same names. Titanuus. Dorcha Territory. Kingsland. Eastern Bolg." He looked at Ruger. "The Spine. My first inclination is that maybe the both of you read the same fantasy books. But I"—he lifted his fingers and made air quotes—"'Googled' it. Nothing of the sort. And based off of my experiences, it's virtually impossible for two people to have the same memories without having been there themselves."

Abraham moved to the end of his chair. "So, you believe me?"

Dr. Jack laughed. "No, no, no, I wouldn't go that far. There is the crazy you know and the crazy you don't know. You usually learn that a few months after the wedding."

Abraham tilted his head.

"That was a joke."

"Oh." He patted his belly. "Sorry, but I haven't had much to laugh about lately. It's been one twisted adventure after the other. And they need me back there."

"You want to go back? In the thick of all of that danger?"

"Yup."

Dr. Jack leaned back in his chair, rubbed his hands together, and said, "I think that I know what is going on here. But please, continue again from where you left off. Try to shorten it, you know, the Cliff's Notes version. You remember Cliff's Notes, don't you?" He started his recorder.

"I do." Abraham refilled his Coke cup and fired out more of the story. He picked up where he'd left off, after he fought Redbeard and met Lewis and King Hector for the first time. He explained about the Henchmen, named them all, and talked about Strong- hold. He did leave out quite a few details intentionally. He never mentioned Eugene Drisk or Solomon Paige by name, but he mentioned the talking troglin. After all, they were all people. He went on about the terra-men and the encounter with the Elder Spawn in the Spine. He went on about the mysterious deaths of the Henchmen that they pinned on Raschel, the assassin from the Brotherhood of the Ravens. He added in the Underlord, Arcayis the Arcane, Lord Hawk, the myrmidons... Abraham got some of the events out of order and had to backtrack from time to time because so much had happened. He could see Dr. Jack scribbling on a notepad. "How are we doing?"

"We can take a break." Dr. Jack looked at his watch. "Whew, that's a doozy of a tale." He lifted his glasses and rubbed his eyes. "You've told me many life-and-death experiences. I mean, one after the other, like an action movie. You know, Indiana Jones stuff."

"More like Conan the Barbarian, but I see your point."

"No, you haven't seen my point, but I'm about to make it." Dr. Jack dropped his glasses on the top of his notes and looked at his notepad. "Do you realize that every time that your life is in imminent danger, something or someone bails you out?"

Uncertainly, he said, "Yeah."

"Don't you get it? Let's see. For example, you are fighting against that Elder Spawn thing, a dragon or giant bat, but your magic sword—"

"Black Bane."

"Yes, Black Bane bails you out. Or your Henchmen—they show up at just the right moment. I mean, everything suddenly works out perfectly. Nothing in real life works out like that. You know that. But in this world you are caught up in, it does. I call it alter-escapism. It's a world that we build in our imagination, and everything turns out the way that we want." Dr. Jack leaned back over his desk. "Abraham, as much as you believe it, Titanuus is not real."

58

DR. JACK'S WORDS WERE LIKE A PUNCH IN THE GUT. ABRAHAM raised his brows and said, "But we were just talking about Charles Abney. You said it wasn't possible that two people could remember the same thing."

"No, I don't believe in the impossible, per se. Just because an event can't be explained at the moment doesn't mean that an explanation can't be found." Dr. Jack clasped his fingers together. "It's cases like this that make my job so interesting. It's fascinating." He took off his glasses and removed a handkerchief from his pocket. He huffed on his octagon-shaped spectacles and cleaned them. "You are in the right place. With my help, we'll see to it that you never go back to Titanuus again. I know that you like it there, but it's for the better."

"You don't have that right to determine what is best for me." Abraham's jaws clenched. "I can live however I choose."

"Not when you are hurting people. That makes you a danger to society. You need to be institutionalized for the time being." Dr.

Jack put his glasses on. "You need to control that animal that is inside of you."

"I'm not an animal, and there isn't one inside of me." He raised his voice. "Do you really think that this is helping me? Is that how your practice works? By telling people that they are crazy?"

"Calm down and lower your voice."

Abraham looked beyond the doctor and at the windows. He wanted to toss Dr. Jack through them. One minute, the man was on his side, and in the next, he was the complete opposite. *Don't let him get to you. You've been through worse than this.* He took a breath. "I'm calm. But wouldn't you be edgy if you were in my situation? You like to point out that incident in the hospital, but I think the matter on your end could have been handled better. Don't you?"

Dr. Jack shrugged. "It was a unique event. But—"

"I don't think it was a unique event now that I think about it. Those guards, well, they were pretty well armed. And there was a lot of them. Have things like this happened before?"

Dr. Jack didn't bat an eye. "This is a secured facility. There are plenty of guards."

"Yes, but why is that? Are there more people like me here? Are there other people that claim to be from Titanuus?" He watched the doctor's eyes and expression widen the slightest bit. One thing was sure—Dr. Jack had a great poker face. If Abraham were to guess, the man lied. He lied a lot. That was his gut feeling. "Are there?"

"Of course not." Dr. Jack cleared the food containers and used napkins from his desk and tossed them in the trash can. "We've been at this a while. I believe it's time to take a break. We can reconvene in a few days."

"A few days? What? No! I'm not going back in that padded room for three more days. That's not right." Abraham got up from his chair. He poked a finger at Dr. Jack. "Quit screwing with my head. I know that is what you are doing."

Dr. Jack hollered, "Otis! Haymaker!" He held his finger above the button linked to the metal bracelets Abraham was wearing. In an easy voice, he said, "Abraham, settle yourself. What I am doing is for your own safety. This is only a precaution. In case the other person in you comes out."

Otis and Haymaker burst through the door with stun rods in their hands. They hustled over and flanked Abraham.

"Easy!" Dr. Jack lifted a hand. "I don't want to have another fight on my hands. Let's all take a breath." He looked at Abraham. "Are you going to cooperate?"

Abraham wanted to say no. The last thing he wanted was to go back into that cell. He would lose his mind in there. *It's no wonder people go crazy. I bet it gets worse after they arrive in places like this.* "I don't have a choice but to cooperate, but why don't you treat me like a man, and give me your word that we will meet tomorrow?"

Dr. Jack gave him an approving look and said, "No, Mister Jenkins, I'm not the kind of man that makes deals with patients. That's a very deadly road to drive down. It's three days, but I could make it four or five. I could use a little extra time in the woods."

"Don't you have any other patients?"

"I do, but right now, I'm losing mine." Dr. Jack gave Abraham a dangerous look. "Don't test me."

Abraham's efforts weren't getting him anywhere. He dropped his arms back by his side. He didn't have a choice. "Okay."

Dr. Jack gave the orderlies a nod.

Otis held the stun rod near Abraham's ribs while Haymaker picked up the straitjacket lying on the floor.

Abraham kept his heavy stare on Dr. Jack, whose index finger lingered beside the button. "You know, when I was playing ball, I used to play poker with the guys for kicks." He glanced at the button. "Most of them thought they were good bluffers, but they weren't."

"Interesting. You are a very observant man, and I agree. I've played my share of poker myself even though I'm more of a blackjack man." Dr. Jack tapped his finger on the desk. "Do you think this button is a placebo?"

"No," he said just as Haymaker started to slide his left arm into the straitjacket. "I think you are." He elbowed Otis in the jaw, lunged for the desk, and grabbed Dr. Jack's hand. He held the man in an iron grip.

Dr. Jack winced, but his eyes filled with fire. "You just made a big mistake," he said through clenched teeth.

"No, you did." Abraham slammed his hand down on the button. The entire room turned bright white as electricity coursed through his body. He screamed.

59

TITANUUS

ABRAHAM SCREAMED AND SAT STRAIGHT UP. HE WAS IN THE WOODS, surrounded by the clamor of battle. Hard voices were crying out in the darkness of the forest. Steel clashed against steel.

Sticks rushed over to him and dropped to her knees, her forehead dripping with sweat. "You're awake. It's about time. Can you fight?"

Abraham blinked his eyes. "I think so."

"Good." She stuffed his sword and scabbard into his gut and said, "Grab Black Bane. We need you!"

Abraham jumped onto his feet and ripped his sword out of the sheath. He didn't know what was going on, but he didn't care. "No more padded rooms for me."

"What?" Sticks asked as she led him through the forest. The overhanging tree leaves were so large that they blocked out the daylight, casting them in smothering dimness.

"I'll tell you later," he said. The farther they ran, the louder the clamor of battle became. "What is going on?"

"We were ambushed. At least, the scouts were." She ducked

underneath some low-hanging branches and leapt a fallen log. "I've been staying back with you. The others are still fighting. It started moments ago. Dominga brought back the warning. Tark had fallen."

"Tark is fallen?" Abraham increased his stride. He passed Sticks, churning toward the sound of battle. In seconds, he arrived on the grisly scene. The Henchmen were down inside a narrow ravine, fighting uphill against a wave of strange attackers. *What are those things?*

Small people covered in long stringy hair rode in pairs on the backs of pony-sized beetles like rhinoceroses. The beetles sped down the hills on eight legs. The little men hurled javelins.

Horace gored a charging beetle through the head on the end of his spear. "Taste the tip of the King's Steel!" he bellowed.

Vern swatted a hurtling javelin aside with his sword and dove away from a charging beetle. It turned at the last second and rammed its strange horn right into him.

Abraham called out, "Vern!" and raced down the hill.

"It's the Captain," Horace roared. His thunderous voice carried down the ravine. "The Captain's awake! Now, put your backs into it, Henchmen! You're fighting like sheep!"

With a tremendous overhead swing, Abraham cleaved a beetle's head off. The hard black shell of its body cracked open like a nut. Green gooey guts spilled. The smallish fur-coated, sharp-toothed men with blood-red eyes jumped off their mounts and bared their sharp teeth. They carried crudely made javelins made from hard wood. They cocked them back over their shoulders.

Solomon emerged from underneath the dangling vines of a willow tree. He grabbed two men by the scruff of their necks and lifted them off their feet then smashed the little men's Cro-

Magnon faces together. "Ugly little idiots!" He flung them aside. "Where have you been, Abe?"

"Long story. I'll fill you in later." Abraham jumped toward the next beetle that charged him. He cut through its mouth and horns. The beetles and little men were everywhere. They were a swarm. He turned Black Bane's wrath loose.

Slice! Chop! Slice! Slice! Slice!

With fresh gore coating him up to the neck, Abraham couldn't have been happier. Black Bane's blade burned red-hot. Its keen edge cut through their attackers like a hot knife through butter.

The ambushed Henchmen rallied. With fierce swings, their weapons sank home. Lewis and Clarice fought back-to-back, battling their hearts out. Leodor cast out shimmering shields of citrine energy that deflected the sting of the little men's javelins. Bearclaw wrought havoc with his double-bladed axe, busting open the husks of the beetles one after the other.

The little men swarmed from all directions. Ruger let Black Bane sing. He pressed the attack and shouted to Solomon, "Did you ever see *Land of the Lost*?"

"No," the troglin said as he swung one little man by the ankles into another. "Is that a movie?"

Abraham gored an attacker in the chest. "A Saturday-morning TV show. There were these cave men. One of them was called Chukka." He decapitated another. "He was nice, but he had two evil brothers. These guys remind me of them." He cut a beetle's horn off. "As for these rhino-beetles, well, they're new to me."

"It's all new." Solomon carried two of the little men in a head lock. He squeezed them in the nooks of his arms. Two sharp cracks of spines snapping followed. He let their dead bodies fall in the ferns of the ravine floor. "I really hated to do that, but these things are merciless."

Shades popped up in front of Abraham. His dagger-filled

hands were stained with new blood. "They are woodlings. Tark and Dominga stumbled upon a nest of them. It's like kicking a hive of bees. They are people indigenous to Hancha." He ducked away and jumped on two woodlings riding a beetle. He knocked both to the ground and killed them. He popped up from the foliage. "Strong, but not the best of fighters."

A foursome of woodlings erupted from the brush and attacked Shades as one. They pushed him down the ravine then vanished among the ferns.

Abraham called out, "Shades!"

60

ABRAHAM LAUNCHED HIMSELF DOWN THE HILLSIDE AND FOUND Shades tussling with the woodlings. They were about the same size as the small man. Their long fingernails tore at his clothing. Abraham clocked a woodling that had wrapped itself around Shades's legs with the butt of his sword. The woodling melted into the bush.

Shades's dagger flashed in the dimness of the ravine and poked a hole in another woodling's throat. It stumbled away, clutching at its throat. Shades squirted free of the last woodling. It gave chase. Abraham stuck it in the middle of the back.

A weird howling carried through the ravine. The woodlings disengaged from the attack. The ones on foot jumped on the backs of beetles. They sped away and disappeared into the woods.

The battered Henchmen gathered. Most of them were bloody from head to toe. Their armor had saved them.

Iris called out from the bowels of the ravine, "Help! I need help."

Abraham hustled down the hillside. Iris was holding Tark in her lap. The lightly bearded black man with light eyes had caught a javelin in the neck.

Cudgel knelt by his brother's side and clutched his hand. "Don't die on me, brother. Don't you die on me."

Tark tried to speak, but he only spat blood.

"I can't do anything for him," Iris said. "I don't have the power. The wound is too grave and delicate. Perhaps Leodor can help. I don't know. It's in the Elders' hands now."

Abraham looked about. "Where's Leodor?" He didn't see Leodor or Lewis among the Henchmen who had gathered. "Find him!"

The Henchmen scattered.

Taking a knee, Abraham put a hand on Tark's thigh and said, "You are going to make it."

Bearclaw erupted through the branches of the low-hanging trees. He had Leodor by the scruff of his neck and shoved the fragile man toward Abraham. "I found him. He was crawling up the hill with Lewis."

Abraham reached up, grabbed Leodor by his robes, pulled him down, and said, "Fix him."

Leodor's clammy face was pasted with sweat. He looked at Tark and said, "That wound is grave. I don't think there is anything I can do for it."

"You're going to try." He pushed Leodor to his knees over Tark. "Do it!"

"I'll need some water, to see the wound better," the mystic said.

Lewis marched down the hill and said, "You can't expect him to perform miracles. He needs to save his energy. What if more of those... er, what are they?"

"Woodlings," Sticks said. She cut away a water skin that was hanging from Lewis's chest. She tossed it to Abraham, looked at Lewis, and said, "Thanks, moron."

"Help me clean the wound," Leodor said to Iris.

Abraham handed Iris the water skin.

"Be strong, brother. Be strong," the bald Cudgel said to his brother. He gave Abraham a desperate look. "He's slipping. He no longer grips my hand."

"So much blood." Leodor's fingers massaged the air. "Very sticky. I hate sticky. I need leaves. Large green ones. Moist. Bring them quick."

Iris pointed into the branches, eyeballed Solomon, and said, "Those."

Solomon reached his great hands up into the branches and gently plucked out several spade-shaped leaves the size of his hands. He passed them down to Sticks, who took them to Iris. The lady mystic cleaned the leaves with water.

"Good, place them here." Leodor pointed at the gaping wound in Tark's neck, which pumped new blood out of it. "Quickly. His flow slows. The Elder of Death comes."

Cudgel gulped aloud. With sweat dripping from his chin, he said, "No, no, no, no..."

Leodor said, "Everyone, keep silent."

The Henchmen clammed up.

The wind stilled the moment Leodor parted his lips and muttered arcane words. He placed his hand and a few of the leaves over the wound. An orange fire emanated from his fingers. The lusty green color of the leaves browned and merged with the ebony warrior's skin.

Tark's eyes popped wide. With his body turning as rigid as a plank, he let out a painful gasp. Then he collapsed back onto the ground, limp and not breathing.

Cudgel bellowed at Leodor, "What did you do? What did you

do? You killed him!" He shook the smaller man by the shoulders. "Murdering mystic!"

Iris wrapped her arms around Cudgel's back and said, "Calm yourself, friend. Your brother breathes. Look at the gentle rise and fall of his chest."

Cudgel released the aghast Leodor. He put his hands in his brother's, and Tark gripped his hand. "He squeezes!" Cudgel made a nervous smile. "He squeezes! Does this mean that he lives?"

"I don't know. I've done all I can." Leodor clutched at the neck of his robes. "Let the spell do its work and keep your paws off of me!" He stood up with an agonized sigh and looked at Abraham. "Happy?"

Abraham guided Leodor aside, threw his arm over the man's narrow shoulders, and said, "Now, that wasn't so bad, was it?"

Giving Abraham an appalled look, Leodor said, "What do you mean?"

"Helping someone. Doesn't that feel good?"

"I've helped plenty of people in my day. This moment is no different." Leodor glanced at Tark with sad eyes. "To be honest, I really don't think he'll make it. Will I get blamed for that?"

"All that matters is that you did your best. Did you?"

Leodor snorted. "My work is always the best." He pulled away from Abraham. "Lewis, will you help me up this hill? I can barely walk."

"What am I, your underling?" Lewis shook his head and walked away.

Solomon stepped in behind Leodor and said, "I'll help you." He showed Leodor an oversized smile.

"I-I-I'll manage," Leodor said while looking up with eyes the size of saucers.

Solomon scooped the man up in his arms and carried him up

the hill, cradled like a baby. "You deserve a break today. I'll carry you."

The remaining cluster of Henchmen chuckled.

Abraham sought out Shades. Once he locked eyes on him, he asked, "Did you say we were in Hancha?"

61

Using Shades for a guide, the Henchmen arrived at a small farm town called Earlin the next day. The farming community was rich with miles of plowed terrain and produce fields. Stone cottages with straw roofs were scattered in the hills and plains. Barns and storehouses were aplenty. The town itself was well equipped for visitors, complete with taverns and stables for travelers.

The majority of the Henchmen set up camp outside Earlin in a clearing near the riverbed. Abraham, Horace, Sticks, and Shades headed into town in the evening, just after the sun set.

With some pep in his step, Shades led the way. His hood was down, and his elbows were swinging. "I have to admit it's good to be back in my country. There is something about the salty air and smell of baking beast that does my essence good."

"Just find us a place to keep a low profile. Not the lowest—just low," Abraham said.

He'd had a lot to mull over the past day. Four days had passed since he'd fallen asleep by the campfire. The Henchmen put him on a stretcher and dragged him over hill and dale into Hancha. He woke in the middle of everyone fighting for their lives against the woodlings. Everyone survived, and Tark was awake. Being back in Titanuus was good. Anything was better than a straitjacket.

The hardworking people walking the streets wore long sleeves and trousers. They moved with hustle and carried cheerful expressions on their grubby faces. Small groups of men and women played music and danced on the street corners. Some men talked quietly on the porches, drinking ales, smoking pipes, and chewing tobacco. Many bellies bulged over their belts. Shades led them up a two-step staircase onto a porch leading into a wooden tavern. The steps and wood-plank porch groaned underneath their feet.

Abraham followed Shades inside the tavern. They took seats at a round table in the back corner of the building. The smell of roasting meat and vegetables lingered strongly in the air. The late dinner crowd had a few drinks in them. They talked with spirited voices. Men and women were there, but the oddest of all were the pale-skinned zillons. Seeing the alienlike people dressed like farmers in overalls and wearing straw hats was strange. A small group sat at a table playing cards. They had long, slender fingers that moved with the skill of a magician's. They quietly chortled with laughter from time to time.

Horace leaned over the table and rested on his elbows. "Strange country. Never been so deep in Hancha. My neck is itching."

"Don't act squirrely," Shades said as he lifted his hand and flagged down a waitress. "You always get edgy around new people. It shows even behind that beard on your face. Just keep quiet and eat something."

"They better not be serving that rat meat. I remember the last time you talked me into that," Horace said.

Sticks chuckled.

"I don't recall the incident. Should I?"

"You were there, but it was a time ago," Sticks said.

A zillon waitress walked up. Unlike the males, who were as bald as pickles, she had a long, flowing black ponytail sprouting from the top of her head. Her large black eyes were pretty, features sharp, with a tiny little nose and small nostrils. She had no ears but ear holes. She was bony but wore a blue blouse that showed off her bosoms. "Would you like to try our house ale? If not, we have several different varieties for your pleasure. Darks, ryes, stouts, fruits, ports, lights."

Horace slung his elbow over his chair and said, "What is a light?"

"An ale to keep husky fellows like you from becoming huskier." She reached down and patted his belly. "But I like a portly man. They make good eaters." She winked at Horace. Her tiny mouth expanded to show her tiny white teeth. "I think you will like the port. It's made by our own brew masters, Edmund and Fitzgerald."

Abraham waved his hand around the table and said, "How about a round of those ports? It sounds like a good start."

In a cheery voice, the zillon waitress winked at him and said, "I'll right back. I'll bring you some appetizers on the house too."

Abraham's jaw could have hit the table. "Did she say 'appetizers'? Is it customary that taverns serve appetizers? And serve light beer?"

"It's not a custom in Kingsland, but it's one of the charms that I like about Hancha. They offer variety," Shades said. A candle sat inside a glass globe in the middle of the table. He rubbed his thumb and finger together over the wick, and the candle started to burn. He made a charming smile. "One of my favorite tricks. I'll tell you what—why don't you let me order? My word that it won't be rat meat, either."

The zillon waitress returned with her ghostly pale fingers wrapped around four mugs of port. "I'll be back to take your order in a moment. But first, I have to help my cohorts honor a guest with a happy birth year song." She skipped away with her ponytail bouncing and hands clapping.

Abraham shook his head, buried his face in his mug, and drank.

62

THE ZILLON WAITRESS BROUGHT SMALL ROASTED HENS FOR appetizers. Chopped salad, meat-and-cheese samplers, and several different pitchers of ale were brought out. Horace was determined to try all of them. Abraham didn't want his company to seem suspicious either. He let them enjoy the local fare, which also included sushi and egg rolls. The tavern served more than the local meat-and-potatoes fare. Their dishes were more sophisticated and just as hearty. The waitress, Anna, dutifully introduced them to the menus, as well as a wine, mixer, and beer list—and a dessert selection. Dishes had fanciful names, after local legends and stories from Hancha. The bustling inn had as many combinations of dishes as a Mexican-American chain restaurant.

Abraham settled for a bowl of Elders' Stew. It was a mishmash of meats from the fields and the sea, with bits of lobsters, red beans, and rice. The stew came in a Jethro-sized cereal bowl that could have served the entire table. Sticks ate a tossed salad with vegetables Abraham had never seen, loaded with crab meat and a sweet-and-sour-smelling celery dressing called the Plate of Ven.

Shades drank many samplers of ale, pushing some aside with a "no" and smiling about the ones he liked with a "yes." Horace drank what the smaller man didn't drink but settled on a fine stout called Red Horse.

Anna, the cute and friendly waitress, advised him to "take it easy on the Red Horse." She winked at the big man. "It will sneak up on you and makes some men crazy."

The tavern became livelier as the evening went on. Excited customers came and went, mostly with warm smiles on their faces. Two large stone fireplaces roared with orange-yellow flames. A lone man sat on a stool in the corner, strumming an eight-stringed guitar and singing. The customers sang along to the dashing singer's campy music: "Sweeet Man-o-Waaahr, buh-buh-buh!"

Abraham dug his stew into a smaller bowl, ate steadily, and drank his ale. The tavern became a medieval version of a local Applebee's. Many twists existed in Titanuus, and this latest stop was a new one. In Pirate Town, they'd had pizza, and this Hancha farm hovel had menu lists as long as a roll of toilet paper. The waitress was an alien straight out of *Close Encounters of the Third Kind*, except she wore clothing and was fetching. He scanned the room. *Maybe I am crazy.*

Horace and Shades were turned in their chairs, engaged in conversations with the locals. Sticks gave Abraham a nudge in the ribs with her elbow and asked, "What is going on in that handsome melon of yours?"

"Nothing," he said dryly.

She gave him the "Do I look like I'm stupid?" look.

"Okay. Fine." He pushed his bowl of stew aside. "Something's bothering me."

"Why don't you tell me about it?" She gave him a pleasant smile, reached over, and held his hand. "You can tell me. I'm all yours."

"Yeh, I bet," he said, thinking of what Shades had told him about her being a prostitute.

"What is that supposed to mean?"

"Nothing."

She squeezed his hand. "Tell me, or I'll pin your hand to this table with one of my daggers."

"I didn't know you used to be a"—he looked at her and away and said—"a whore."

Sticks turned her stare on Shades where he sat beside her with his back turned. She rabbit-punched his ribs.

Shades melted in his chair and fell to the floor. The paling man gazed at her with widened eyes and asked, "What did you do that for?"

"You know what, weasel." She kicked Shades. On his back, he snaked away. She turned her attention back to Abraham. "You knew it from the beginning, though I was glad that *you* didn't know about me. To me, it was a fresh start."

"I guess everyone knew anyway. I really shouldn't judge," he said. "I wasn't braced for it."

"Look, I was young, but when I got my chance to escape with the Henchmen, I took it." She took his hand back in hers. "There isn't anything that you can say to me that will hurt me. You should know that by now. Words don't hurt me. Only steel and fire will."

"I have to admit you and the rest have thick skin. It's refreshing. A lot of people in my world have egos as fragile as snowflakes." He put his free hand over hers. "But I shouldn't have mentioned it. I did like watching you stick it to Shades, though."

"Aside from my whoredom, what really ails you? Is it the sleep?" she asked.

"Where to begin? But yeah, it was the sleep. I dreamed I was back in my world. Actually, I'd swear that I was there, the same as

I'd swear on the brand that I am here. I was locked up in a place where they put crazy people."

"An asylum."

"Yes, an asylum. You have those here?"

"Yes," she said in her expressionless, matter-of-fact manner. "Nothing but horrors in those places. They say it's worse than the Baracha. They place people like you in there. Possessed. Other-worlders. Unless they kill you such as they do in Kingsland."

Abraham winced. "That's hard to hear. Sticks, I have to figure out what is going on. I know this world is as real as the other. It has to be. I can't explain how, but I know it is. So, you know that old Ruger"—he searched her eyes—"the real one... well?"

"Not as well as Horace, Bearclaw, and Vern. But yes. You've asked me this before, but why again?"

"Because I think that he is in my world, trapped in my body."

63

WHILE SHADES MADE HIS ROUNDS THROUGH THE TAVERN, ABRAHAM brought Horace into the conversation. He told them most of the pertinent parts in detail. But mostly, he wanted to get a better understanding about Ruger. He was in the man's body, and he felt as if they shared one mind as well, which was disturbing.

"Would Ruger hurt anyone, say, a defenseless person?" Abraham asked.

"No," Horace said in his bearish voice. "Ruger is a guardian's guardian. He'd never hurt anyone that wasn't trying to harm him. He lived by the highest of standards. That never changed even when he was a Henchman." He combed bread and cheese crumbs out of his beard. "I can't say the same for the rest of us."

"I see. I need to figure out a way to communicate with him. When I go back and forth." Abraham tugged at the scruff on his chin. "Our worlds don't speak the same language, but I understand them both. I need to try to find a way for him to understand what is going on."

Horace exchanged a quick look with Sticks. "Don't underestimate Ruger. He probably knows more than he shows. But maybe a symbol that you can write down will help."

"Like what?" she asked.

"The crown or the Kingsland Crest. He'd know that," Horace blurted out. "Draw him a picture of it."

Abraham envisioned the brand that was a crown with six horns, with a small round tip at the top. That wouldn't be a hard thing for him to draw. The crest of Kingsland, which the guardians wore, might have been a different matter. It was a crowned golden lion's face, with white wings for ears on a royal-blue sea background.

"I don't see why I can't pull that off. At least, without the details." Abraham sighed. "Man, I don't want to go back. Not like that. Shackled in a padded white room is no way to live."

"These are strange mutterings that you share. It awakens the moths in my belly." Horace quaffed a full tankard of ale. "Ale helps."

Abraham offered an uncertain smile. The ale wasn't doing much for him. If anything, it only made matters worse. He sat in a medieval microbrewery, feeling more nuts than ever, as if the world he knew was merging with another. He abhorred the dangerous thought.

"Do you dream?" he asked Sticks.

"Only about you," she said with a winsome smile.

"No, seriously."

"Of course I do," she said. "Not often, but I do dream."

"I dream," Horace added. "I'm hunting a man that I can't catch. He moves like a white stag in the woods. I never even get close. He springs away the moment I see him."

"So, you dream the same dream?"

Horace shrugged. "It's the only one that I remember. The others fade away."

Abraham understood. In the past when he'd had dreams, he didn't remember them shortly after he woke. But the last dreams he had, back home, were as real as the room that he was sitting in. "Keep an eye on me. If I act strange, let me know, in case I drift away."

His friends nodded.

The waitress, Anna, returned. Dipping her ample chest before Abraham's eyes, she asked, "How is your food?"

"Fulfilling," he said. He noticed more of the barmaids, including zillons, sitting in the laps of the hearty patrons. "This is a very nice tavern. Very lively."

"It isn't usually so busy, but this is the date of the Alefest, and many of Hancha's finest soldiers are arriving tomorrow."

He arched a brow and asked, "For the festival?"

"No, silly man." Anna tousled his hair. "The soldiers come to rally the town and raise money for Hancha's noble forces. They raise money to overthrow the evil tyrant King Hector. His wicked treatment of his enslaved citizens must be undone." She gave Abraham a funny look. "Surely you have heard about this? Where are you from, if you don't mind me asking?"

"Tiotan," Abraham said.

"Dorcha," Horace blurted out at the same time.

Sticks jumped into the conversation and coolly said, "We hail from Tiotan but just finished our travels for business in Dorcha. Our guide, well, he's showing us around on our visit to Little Leg. He's a Hanchan, but the area is unfamiliar to us."

"Ah." Anna started picking plates and dishes and loading him on her tray. "I can tell that you are new to the area. Please pardon my intrusion, but I am enjoying getting to know the people." She brushed by Horace as she made her way around the table. "I enjoy a lot of different things."

Horace glanced at the cute zillon and swallowed. "I think I'll get a breath of fresh air."

Anna giggled. "Let me know if any of you need anything." She winked and departed.

Abraham leaned back and watched Anna go. "I wonder if all zillons are so forward."

"You call that forward?" Sticks slipped out of her chair into Abraham's and straddled him. She dropped her hands around his neck. "How is this for *forward*?"

"I'd be lying if I said that I didn't like it." He noticed the passion in her eyes. The strong ale fueled their emotions. He placed his hands on the small of her back and pulled her chest-to-chest with him.

Sticks kissed him.

He crushed her in his arms and kissed her back.

Kissing him fiercely on and off, she said, "I missed you."

Between kisses, he said, "I think it's time we checked into our room."

She nodded and nibbled on his neck.

He picked her up and found Anna looking at him with a lipless frown. He fished out several shards and set them on the table. "I'll need a room for the night as well."

Anna scooped up the coins and grinned. "You will have the best. Take the steps. I'll see you at the top."

With Sticks nuzzling his body, he picked his way through the crowd and made his way to the stairs leading up. Shades appeared in front of the steps, his eyebrows creased. Abraham stopped in his tracks. Shades pointed toward the front door.

Well-armed soldiers entered the tavern. The people and the songs fell silent.

64

THE HANCHAN SOLDIERS WORE OPEN-FACED METAL HELMETS WITH burgundy tunics crested with a black ankh embroidered upside down on the front. Underneath the fine tunics was chain-mail armor. The four sturdy soldiers escorted a towering man who wore a bastard sword strapped to his back. He wore the same gear as the soldiers, but a black riding cloak covered his shoulders. The man's hair was short, and he had gray eyes as hard as stone. A lantern jaw hung half open over his bull neck. His gaze swept the room.

Abraham held Sticks in his arms and leaned against the banister. He averted his gaze from the soldiers scanning the quiet room. Horace stooped down and took a seat in the chair.

Shades melted into the steps behind Abraham. He whispered in Abraham's ear, "Over one hundred Hanchan soldiers rode into town. They've spread out and were asking questions. I got wind of it the moment my toes hit the porch."

"Are they looking for us?" Abraham asked.

"A large company of well-armed travelers," Shades replied as he put his hood up over his head. "A good thing we entered in a small pack."

Across the room, chair legs scraped over the wooden floor. Every head turned and looked. A rickety-limbed farmer with more beard than face lifted up a tankard of ale. He glanced at the soldiers and said, "Long live Hancha. May I buy its finest solders a round?"

The leader of the soldiers stared down on the farmer from across the room, with broad hawkish features. In a rugged voice, he said, "Of course you may." He lifted a fist the size of a mallet and added, "We drink to the conquest of Kingsland! Death to the tyranny of King Hector! Death to his supporters one and all!"

The patrons let out a chorus of wild cries. They stomped their feet and waved their hats. The excited people pounded fists on the tables. The barkeep served the soldiers tankards of ale. The soldiers eagerly took the ale and drank to a chorus of cheers.

The raucous crowd finally quieted. The music started again. The farmer approached the soldiers. He shook the men's hands.

"We need to move on," Abraham said.

"Hold on, Captain." Shades had his eyes on the farmer and the soldiers. "Let me see what they say."

"Are you reading lips?" he asked.

"Shh-shh-shh," Shades said. "Oh, that's interesting."

"What's interesting?"

"The farmer is asking the man with hair as short as my finger what his name is. Oh, that's not good."

Abraham gave Shades an aggravated look.

"Not good at all," Shades continued.

"Will you spit it out?"

"That soldier in the black cloak is Commander Cutter, leader of the king's Black Squadron."

Horace stiffened.

Shades continued, "They are the elite soldiers of Cauldron City. Hancha's finest. Much like the King's Guardians. It's no wonder that crowd froze at their tables when they waltzed in. Their symbol, the black ankh, means death."

"I thought that you were taking us to a place to lay low," Sticks said. "Instead, you brought us right into a viper pit. Idiot!"

The soldiers sauntered into the bar. Commander Cutter remained at the bar, talking with the locals. The farmer moved away and started sharing the name of Commander Cutter to the other patrons. New and excited whispers spread throughout the room.

"Shades, what's going on now?" Abraham asked.

"Commander Cutter is well-known. The leader of the Black Squadron is famous and infamous. He's the best sword in Hancha, with over two hundred kills to his name," Shades said.

As the word spread about the identity of Commander Cutter, the barmaids cozied up to the well-hewn warrior. They posed with him while a local artisan sketched out their picture on parchment.

"You've got to be kidding me," Abraham said. "A medieval selfie? Listen, you two keep our table. Slip out later. Meet us at the camp in the wee hours. Sticks and I will take our room and slip out later. Avoid Captain Cutter and his squad at all costs. We've got a mission to complete."

"Aye, Captain," Horace replied. "We know the drill."

Abraham carried Sticks up the stairs. He took a backward glance. Commander Cutter's penetrating eyes locked on his. He turned away.

"That man looks mean," Sticks said, a slight slur in her speech. "Do you think you can take him?"

"I don't want to find out." He headed down the hallway of the second level.

Anna waited in front of the door at the end of the hall. She opened it. "The best room available. Soft bedding and a fine window view." She stepped aside.

Abraham entered. It was a cozy room with plush quilts, many pillows, and a storage chest at the end of the bed. A small table sat by the window.

"I can bring up breakfast in the morning, and you can watch the sunrise. It's very nice," Anna said. "And if you need anything else at all, let me know. It would be my pleasure." She winked at him and closed the door behind her.

Abraham tossed Sticks on the bed and said, "Hooters, eat your heart out."

Sticks giggled. She took off her bandolier, stripped off her tunic, and tossed the gear to the floor. She nuzzled the pillows between her arms and thighs and said, "What are you waiting for?"

"I don't know if now is the time." He pulled the curtains back and peeked out the window.

Dozens of members of the Black Squadron were patrolling the streets.

"Really not a good time."

Sticks slid onto the floor, glided to the curtains, and closed them. All she wore was a cotton shirt that clung to her fetching figure. She unbuckled his sword belt and dropped it on the floor and said, "I don't take no for an answer."

65

ABRAHAM AND STICKS LEFT THEIR PASSIONS UNFETTERED. THE surrounding element of danger heightened the moment. More than once, they exhausted themselves in one another's arms. After each time, Abraham would check the window. The Black Squadron remained in the streets, posted like watchdogs. Sticks reeled him back into the bed again and again.

With Sticks lying on his chest, he said, "We have to get out of here before dawn breaks. We should have met back at camp hours ago."

Sticks yawned. "I know. But once more. We never know when we'll get this chance again."

"I'm surprised that you, well, let your hair down. Was it the ale or me?"

She kissed his chest. "A healthy mix of both." She ran her hand down beneath the quilt that covered him. "But mostly you."

This is great and weird, being me in another man's body. I don't think I've ever had a night like this. Sticks pressed her face into his neck. Her lips were thin, but her kisses were as soft as rose petals.

He sniffed. "Do you smell smoke?"

She inhaled through her small nose. "I smell smoke." She sat up. "Do you hear that?"

Heavy footsteps ran up and down the halls. Harsh voices called out, "Fire! Fire! Fire!"

Abraham and Sticks jumped out of bed, put on their clothing, and gathered their gear. He opened the door, and smoke poured into the room.

"Holy sheetrock, we have to go!"

They merged with a panicked knot of people crammed into the hallway. The wave of fear-filled faces thundered down the steps. The tavern floor was filled with smoke. Orange flames burned inside the kitchen.

"Fire! Fire! Fire!" several folks called out.

Through the haze, Abraham headed toward the front entrance.

Sticks hooked his arm and pulled him another way. "No, this way." She led him to a window in the back of the room. She picked up a chair and tossed it through. "Let's go!"

They jumped through the window together into a back alley. They raced from it to the barn where the horses were stabled, and Abraham found his horse. Horace's and Shades's were gone. Already saddled, his horse stamped its hooves and whinnied. Slowly, he led the horse out of the barn. He opened the stable gate and led the horse out, and they mounted together.

Down the street, people and soldiers scrambled with buckets of water toward the burning building. They made a chain of buckets scores of people long.

Abraham checked the streets in all directions. The coast was clear. He gently spurred the horse. It trotted down the streets and into the darkness of the night. With the voices fading, he spurred the horse to a gallop and headed back to camp.

———————

"You burned down the tavern? Why would you do that?" Abraham yelled at Shades.

They were back at the camp set up by the river. The Henchmen had broken camp and were on horseback and ready to go.

Perched in his saddle, Shades shrugged and said, "There wasn't much of a choice. The Black Squadron had eyes everywhere. We needed a distraction, and we needed a big one."

Still on horseback, Abraham walked his horse over to Shades, leaned over, and said, "You could have killed innocent people."

"They are Hanchans—far from innocent and enemies of Kingsland. You heard them roaring on about King Hector. If they died, they died."

Abraham punched Shades so hard in the chest that he knocked the man out of the saddle. "We don't do that!"

"Actually, we do," Sticks said in his ear. She'd remained in the saddle with him. "To speak ill against the king means death."

Clutching his chest, Shades climbed back into the saddle and said, "If it's any consolation, I don't think anyone died. Maybe a few, but doubtful."

Abraham searched the faces of his Henchmen. The solemn group averted their eyes except for Vern, Lewis, and Leodor. They held his stare, testing him.

"We don't butcher and burn people." Abraham thought of the waitress, Anna, and wondered if she was safe. "We find a better way."

Sitting proudly in his saddle, Prince Lewis said, "We are at war. No one is innocent in war. We will have casualties, and they will have casualties. The important thing is that they have more of them than we do."

Abraham turned his horse aside, let it walk away, and said, "Shut up, Lewis. Shades, Horace, get us back on the trail."

The Henchmen rode in the darkness of the night. Abraham couldn't help but think about how cavalier the company might have been when led by Ruger. Perhaps they did do devastating things behind enemy lines. Maybe countless innocents were killed. He could have asked but didn't. He'd never been to war before. That wasn't something he fully understood, but at the moment, he was in the middle of a war. So were his men. He had to make sure that he could lead them.

"I don't think what Shades did was bad," Sticks said to him. "Actually, I expected it."

"You did?" he asked, while taking note that the others weren't around.

They were keeping their distance.

"This wouldn't be the first time that we had to create a diversion. I'd thought the same thing myself. I was surprised that you didn't," she said.

"So, Ruger would have done the same thing?"

"Death before failure. Their deaths or ours," she said.

"But those people. They were only enjoying themselves. They were farmers and laymen. I don't want their deaths on my conscience. I have enough on my mind as is."

"Think about it, Abraham. Everywhere we've been outside of Kingsland, haven't people been calling for our heads?"

He nodded, then his back straightened. "But wait, what about the sea captains from Tiotan? We averted them."

"True, and I hate to say it, but that was because of Shades, or else they would have killed us." She nuzzled her chin in his back. "Those soldiers, Commander Cutter and the Black Squadron, do you think they were fools, or do you think they were onto us?"

Abraham saw Commander Cutter's face as clear as crystal. A

warrior knew a warrior. The battle-bred crow's-feet in their eyes gave it away.

"You're right. He knew I was trouble the moment he saw me."

"And a man like that won't forget you either," she said. "He's coming. They'll all be coming."

66

THE HENCHMEN KEPT THEIR HEADS DOWN, RODE HARD LEAGUES away from the east coast, stopped late, and rose early. Two days later, they were on the coastal plains in the Little Leg of Hancha, viewing Cauldron City.

"That's it," Shades said. The man hadn't approached Ruger since they'd last spoken. "The great dogwoods with black bark and white leaves are only found in these valleys."

The petals of the gnarled dogwood trees drifted through the air like snow before landing gently on the ground. They were all over the valley that led to Cauldron City. The plains surrounding the city weren't the same lush green fields of Kingsland. The tall wind-swept grasses were brown and almost gray, giving it a barren look. In the distance, Cauldron City's buildings, made from black stone, could be seen in the morning light. Only the glass-paned windows shone. The city was large, like Burgess, possibly bigger. Travelers and workers moved along the stone-paved streets.

Abraham craned his neck and asked, "If that's Cauldron City, then where is the Cauldron?"

HALLORAN, P CRAIG

Shades pointed above the city. A ridge of mountains in the south was covered in mist. "There, in the bluffs. A one-way road leads up to it."

Lewis and Leodor approached. Lewis yawned and said, "What is that grand plan? Are you going to duck into Cauldron City and burn it down like the last one? I myself wouldn't mind a hot meal and a glass of red wine."

"We aren't going into the city. We're going straight into the Cauldron," Abraham said.

"Now? In broad daylight? How stupid is that?" Lewis said.

Princess Clarice rode up to the group and asked, "What is going on? Are we going into the city?" Her eyes were big and bright. "I've always wanted to visit Hancha. I'm told that they have fabulous wares, festivals, and delicacies."

"Yeah, they probably have a shopping mall and petting zoo too, but this isn't a shopping trip. But," Abraham said, "with a show of hands, who would like to take a tour of the city?"

Lewis, Leodor, Swan, Sticks—back on her own horse—Iris, Shades, Solomon, Clarice, Dominga, and the ailing Tark all raised their hands. Only the grim-faced Horace, Bearclaw, Vern, and Cudgel kept their hands down.

Abraham smiled. "It looks like we have a majority, but this isn't a democracy. I vote no. That means we all vote no. Let's go."

The Henchmen stayed on the outskirts of the city's countryside, using the paths along the hillsides. They continued toward the high hills in the south, where the Cauldron resided. Those black hills bottomed out miles away from the city that the Cauldron overlooked. A light fog lingered at the base.

Abraham gazed upward. The hills were high, the same as the ones that bordered the interstates in the Mountain State. The trees were dark pines, maples, and oaks. A road made of black gravel-

266

like pebbles snaked a pathway up a steep incline and disappeared into the hillside.

He looked at Leodor and asked, "That way?"

"The fog lifts at night, but yes," the older mystic said. "We can't ride up there. Not like this," he said.

"Sure we can. We'll ride up, knock on the gate—there is a gate, isn't there?" He smirked. "And we will ask to see the Underlord. After all, you and Lewis are friends with him."

Leodor scoffed. "That's preposterous."

"Why?" he asked.

"Those hills have eyes. They will know that we are coming," Leodor fired back. "We don't look like members of the Sect. Only members of the Sect may enter."

Gazing up the stark hillside, Abraham said, "Interesting. So, what does a member of the Sect look like? Do they wear special robes, perhaps?"

"Of course they do. In Hancha, they were the burgundy with gold trim," Leodor said. "The leading priests are trimmed in white. They are devoted worshippers of the grand dogwoods."

"Imagine that. So, all we need are some robes. I bet there are a lot of them to be found in the cathedrals inside Cauldron City, right Leodor?"

The froward viceroy said, "That would be a smart place to look."

"Sticks. Shades."

"Way ahead of you, Captain," Sticks said. She rode with Shades back toward Cauldron City.

"Where are they going?" Lewis asked.

"To fetch our robes." Abraham led his horse and the others away from the road leading up to the Cauldron. He eyed Leodor and Lewis. "Come on, you two windbags. We need to chat more about what you know about this place."

The Henchmen found a spot at the base of the hills where the tall treetops and branches concealed them.

Abraham dismounted, looped his reins on a branch, and said to Leodor, "You said the hills have eyes. What did you mean by that?"

Leodor licked his thin lips, looked up into the hills, and said, "The zillon dragon riders. They live in the pinnacles behind the Cauldron. Like hawks, the dragons watch the Cauldron like a nest."

67

"So, are you going to tell me more about where you've been?" Solomon asked Abraham as they were sitting apart from the others, who were on the lookout. "We haven't talked since your *return*."

Nearby, Iris was checking Tark's wounds, but the rangy black fighter had said, "I can ride, so I can fight. We go up, I'm going."

Abraham chewed on a small hunk of dried meat, washed it down with water, and said, "What makes you think that I went anywhere?"

"Come on, I know you dreamed. I'm not stupid."

"I hate to mention it. But if you insist, I woke up in a loony bin. There were more twists and turns too." He watched Solomon's eyes widen. "For example, I think that Ruger's essence is inhabiting my body back home. Does that make any sense to you?"

Solomon scratched the thick hairs on the back of his neck and said, "Unlike you, I'm stuck here, but it's an interesting concept. You aren't pulling my hairy leg, are you?"

"I wish I was, but no. I don't want to go back there. I know that sounds strange, but I'm a nutcase there as opposed to here."

"Actually, you are a nutcase here. Remember how they treat the possessed? They kill them. Man, beast, or troglin."

Solomon dropped a hand to the ground and opened the fingers of his huge paw. He whistled softly. A chipmunk with black-and-brown fur slunk out of some dark-purple ferns right into the palm of his hand. The chipmunk's little nose twitched. It crawled up Solomon's arm and over his shoulders.

"Tell me more," Solomon continued.

With time to burn, Abraham filled in his friend from the home world. "This dream state is really messing with my mind, I have to admit. You said that you came through a portal, didn't you? Or am I remembering that wrong?"

"No, I burst right through a halo of energy, and I've been trying to find that selfsame portal for years." Solomon sighed and glanced up the hill. "Maybe there will be some answers up there."

"Maybe. But I don't think answers are very easy to come by." Abraham finished up his jerky, washed it down with water, and said, "No portals so far. Something isn't right. I know everything is a mess and our lives are upside down, but I believe in my heart that these are two separate worlds and that they are connected. But man, that Dr. Jack really got into my head, telling me it's a dream. No dream can be this real. It can't be."

The chipmunk popped up on top of Solomon's head and started eating an acorn of some sort.

Iris giggled.

Tark managed a smile.

Abraham gave them both an easy look and asked, "So, what's it like for you two to follow a madman?"

"It's fine by me so long as it's a good madman." Tark groaned as he sat up from lying down. With Iris's help, he came back to his feet. "You're doing fine so far, but if I can give you some advice, Captain, don't think about it too much. Let things come to you. And trust your gut. We trust it. So should you."

Iris nodded. With her hand around Tark's side, she led him away.

"Thanks," Abraham said under his breath.

Solomon twisted his head side to side and lifted his eyes upward. "Is he still up there?"

Abraham lay down, propped himself casually on an elbow, and asked, "How do you know it's a he?"

"Ha ha."

The chipmunk scurried right down Solomon's face, jumped away, and dashed into the wood.

"Hey!"

"Looks like you're stuck with me, hippie."

Solomon rubbed his chest where the brand was. "My choice. You know, Abraham, if we are trying to get back to our world, then don't you think that Ruger, for example, is trying to get back to this world?"

Abraham's neck hairs rose. "I hadn't thought about that. I'm not sure that I like that idea either. Is that selfish?"

"Considerably." Solomon arched his back. "I don't think he wanted to leave here, just like I don't think that the people we inhabited wanted to go there. At least you know who you were. Me? I don't know much about the old troglin I became. The troglins don't care much for their elderly. Like lions, they are led by the strongest in the pack."

"Oh man," Abraham said.

"What?"

"I just had a dark thought." He clenched his jaws. The tapping of his heart sped up in his ears. "What if the same thing that is happening to us is happening back home?"

"You mean, our otherworlders are being hunted and killed?"

"Yeah, but maybe locked up. Maybe that was what was going on in that hospital I was in. Perhaps there were more like you and me."

Solomon sat with his fingers locked and rolling his thumbs. "Bizarre. I'm not fond of the idea. It's like coming off of a bad acid trip." He winced. "Oh man, this brain session is giving me a headache."

"Don't say that. I don't want any more headaches."

"Sorry." Solomon lay flat on his back and closed his eyes. "You might want to get some rest."

Abraham sat up. "At this juncture, I think I'll pass."

68

Leaving the horse outside the city, Sticks and Shades slipped into Cauldron City and quickly blended in with the assorted crowd. With night falling, chill winds came down from the high hills, and the citizens were bundled in woolen garb and winter cloaks. Cackling women and carousing men could be heard from open tavern and apartment windows. Eerie music and songs winded through the city blocks' channels. The people, men and women, including a lot of zillons, carried themselves with purpose from building to building, winding down from a day's work. Cauldron City was festive in a dark sort of way.

The black-and-gray stones that made up the buildings and cobblestone streets gave the city a drab atmosphere. The roofs were covered in dark-red clay tiles. Lanterns hung from posts in the streets with the candles shielded by green glass that made for eerier illumination.

Talking quietly, Sticks said to Shades, "You still can't bridle that tongue of yours, can you?"

"Whatever do you mean?"

"You know what I mean. Telling Abraham that I was a whore."

"Ah, so you do have a soft spot for the otherworlder. I knew that you did. I wanted to hear you say it."

Sticks pushed Shades into an alley and shoved him into a wall. She put a dagger against his throat.

"Well, well, well," he said, "I see you are still kinky."

"Shut your mouth hole, or else I'll give you another one. Tell me what game you are playing. I want to know."

"Whatever do you mean? I only want to serve the king."

"Don't feed me that manure. I know better than that. I know you better than anyone."

"I know you do." Shades slipped a hand on her rump and squeezed. "And I know you the same."

She pressed the blade harder on his neck. "Remove your hand."

"You wouldn't kill a man over a little squeeze on the tush, would you?"

"I've killed men for less," she said.

"You won't kill me. But I reluctantly remove my hand from the most delightful part of your body." His Adam's apple rolled against the edge of the blade when he swallowed. "I hope that didn't leave a nick. As for my purposes, I swear they are sincere. And my name's cleared, is it not? I just want to be a Henchman again."

She searched his eyes. Years before, she and Shades had had a strong and passionate relationship. She was naïve and needed a man to lean on. As she grew, she grew away from him. True to his name, Shades was shady. She could never put her finger on it, but he was.

She took her dagger away from his neck, spun it in her hand, and sheathed it back in her bandolier. "I'll figure it out."

Shades rubbed his neck and said, "There's nothing to figure out. Now, if you don't mind, let's go find those cloaks. There are plenty of cathedrals and temples around here. The Hanchans are very fond of their elders." He grabbed her hand. "Come on, dearie."

She jerked her hand away and shoved him forward. "Quit playing games."

With a cheerful step, Shades took the lead. He hopped up on a stone porch front and strutted underneath the tavern and store decks. He weaved his way through the people, nodding politely and offering a greeting from time to time.

Sticks kept on his heels. Whenever she was with him, she felt as though he was a moment away from bolting off. He made her feel like a nervous mother watching over an overactive child. She glanced into some of the windows they passed. Painted strumpets, clad in dark sheer silks, danced shamelessly for the patrons. She didn't miss those days. From what she could see, the assorted life in Hancha was worse. Inky smoke spilled out of the door and windows. The lusty smell of strong perfumes and incense wafted into her nose. She fanned it away.

She caught up with Shades, who'd stretched his lead. "It figures that you are from this place."

He let out a low chuckle and darted across the street into a section of town where the streets were almost barren, aside from the beggars huddled underneath stone benches. He stood in front of a thirty-foot-high portico leading into another section of town.

Sticks stood beside him and looked up at the portico, with three giants within its archway. Every creature and race she'd ever seen or imagined was carved into the stone.

"What is in there?" she asked.

"This is what locals call Elders Alley," he said. "Not really an alley, per se, but a place where the multitudes worship their favored Elders. Come on." He tried to take her by the hand.

She peeled away and headed into the archway on the right. "I'll take it from here."

Sticks didn't have much else to figure out, she realized once she crossed to the other side. Temples and cathedrals of all sorts were everywhere. Finding her way out wouldn't be a problem either.

Just inside the threshold of the giant portico, she said, "That's a lot of temples."

Shades pointed at the biggest one. It had open iron gates leading into a courtyard. "That looks like a place filled with ample contributions."

She led the way. They weren't the only ones wandering through the area. Acolytes aplenty were wandering the streets, murmuring and praying. They were clad in dark robes, some of which were made of the finest materials and others as moth-ridden as paupers'. Shades moved into the courtyard right up the steps of the cathedral. Stealing into the temples wasn't anything new. She and the Henchmen had done it dozens of times. The temples were some of the safest places, considered hallowed ground. She walked right through the great doors, which led directly into the pews facing a stage and altar. Some sort of ceremony was going on. Men and women were gathered on the stage, dancing and singing among the smoke with a glowing paint on their eyes and bodies.

"Can you make out what they are saying?" she asked Shades.

"I never understood their strange tongues," he replied. "I always figured that they made it up. But this appears to be a very popular place. Most seats are filled. I'd imagine they are about to make a sacrifice to the Black Kraken."

Sticks shivered. "I can't stand slimy things. Come on, let's find the cloak room and get out of here."

"You know, the penalty for stealing from a temple carries a

death sentence. That's why they are safe havens," he said with a smile.

"Has that ever stopped us before?"

He shook his head with a grin on his face.

Sticks stole through the darkness of the side aisles. The store-rooms weren't hard to find, nestled away behind the side entrances of the stage in the basement. The temple had many lavish decorations set aside for ceremonies. Bronze candlestands, pewter goblets, silver trays, and bowls loaded with chunks of incense were there. The walls were lined with cloak hooks. Sticks grabbed a dark-gray cloak trimmed with purple satin. Many of them were there.

"These will do. Find a sack or something to put them in," she said as he slipped the cloak on over her body.

Shades had a cotton sack in hand. "Way ahead of you." He stuffed more cloaks into the sack. "The Black Kraken will have our heads for this."

"For what, stealing?" she said. "Who says we are stealing? We are only borrowing them." She rummaged through the variety of sizes of cloaks on the pegs. "Who says that we aren't borrowing them? Besides, we are going right into the heart of the Sect. Right? I have a feeling that we'll be leaving them there."

"I miss your dry wit. It made for grand pillow talk back in the day."

"Keep dreaming." She finished filling her sack and slung it over her shoulder. She tilted her head and looked toward the stairs as the chanting and singing grew louder. "Our timing couldn't be better."

"Agreed." Shades stepped aside. "Lead the way."

She hustled up the steps and stole her way back into the aisle from which they'd come. The petitioners were shaking their hands and arms and singing in a wild frenzy. Something was happening on stage, a living sacrifice perhaps. She dared not look. She didn't want to know. She kept her head down and moved forward. Breaking free of the temple doors, she hurried down the steps and caught her breath.

Sticks, wearing the same robes as she, stood beside her, looked back, and said, "Vile. Simply vile. One of the reasons that I left, and it's only getting worse."

A sharp scream erupted from within the temple.

"I've heard enough." Sticks took off toward the three arches in the portico. Her heart was racing by the time she got through them. She didn't stop as she cut into the alleys. She stopped and caught her breath.

"Is something wrong?" Shades asked as he looked back over his shoulder. "I think we are in the clear."

"Those places. I hate those places." She took a deep breath. "Hate them."

"That's what is coming to Kingsland. An invasion of darkness. Unless we stop them." He shifted his sack from one shoulder to the other. "Lawlessness shall abound. I might be a rogue, but even I see the need for order. Come. I know a shorter way. You tucked us deep in the alleys."

"Go, then," she said as she followed after him.

They avoided the lively crowds building in the streets. Once they broke free of the city's main structures, they took a small road that led back to the horses. A large group of riders came their way. They were well-armed soldiers wearing metal helmets that glimmered dully in the starlight. Sticks and Shades moved aside and kept their hooded heads down. The sound of the approaching horses grew, along with the rattle of armor and gear.

"You, priests," someone called out in a gruff voice.

Sticks knew the voice immediately. It was the harsh tone of Commander Cutter. "Yes, my lord," she replied.

"Tell me, priest, why do you travel away from the city? Is something amiss?"

"No, my lord. We are meeting with our brethren in the woodland to draw strength from the Elder of the Moon," she said. "It is imperative that we work away from the distractions of the festivities."

Commander Cutter's horse snorted near her face.

The commander said, "The Elder of the Moon, aye. Offer him a prayer from Commander Cutter and his men. Tell him we need light shed on the men that we track."

"Certainly," she said, holding out her hand. She stole a glance at Commander Cutter, seeing that the short-haired and iron-jawed man carried himself with a great presence. "I will see to it that your request is heard."

Commander Cutter fished into his purse and dropped two silver shards into her palm. "Make sure that it sticks."

Shades let out a soft giggle and followed it up with gentle coughing.

Sticks slapped him on the back. "Apologies. My fellow layman needs prayers as well. Are there any other services that I can provide, my lord? Anything more specific to pray for?"

"And cost me another round of drinks?" Commander Cutter laughed. "Ha ha. I can't afford the payment. The sack you carried is probably filled with shards as is." He kicked her bag. "What burdens do you carry?"

"Blankets. It will be a chill night, and we've got to set the camp for the ceremony," she said.

"I see. Make sure that you don't forget my prayer, priest. I always follow up with the viceroy of your Sect," Commander Cutter said. "Let's move out, Black Squadron." He waved his hand in a forward motion and marched down the road.

Once the soldiers passed, Sticks and Shades quickly ambled

down the road. She glanced back in time to see the last of the soldiers disappear around the bend. "Sounds like Commander Cutter is on our tail for certain."

"He could be looking for someone else," Shades suggested.

Sticks shook her head. "I don't think so. He's onto us. I know it."

"I agree. Back at the tavern, he was sniffing around but being very subtle about it." Shades took a path into the woodland, where the horses waited. "He wasn't going to let us leave without asking a few questions. He's a clever tracker for certain."

"How do you think he came to be on our trail so quick?" she asked as she mounted up.

"Big Apple. Lord Hawk. Those men might have spread the word. Either that, or the dubious Commander Cutter is looking into the slaughter of the woodlings that we encountered. After all, they are citizens of Hancha. He could be investigating that."

Sticks led her horse back onto the road. "I doubt it." She galloped back to camp.

69

ABRAHAM HELD UP A BLACK KRAKEN ROBE. IT SHOWED THE HEAD, face, and eyes of the great sea monster subtly woven throughout the entire body of the dark robes. "This is nice." He slipped the robes over his armor. "Leodor, what's the protocol? Are we walking or riding?"

"We must go on foot if we don't want to arouse any suspicion," Leodor said as he draped the new set of robes over his frail body. "The walk is long, winding, and steep. I dread it."

"We'll get you there." Abraham donned his hood as the others did the same. "Is everyone ready?"

"Ready, Captain," Horace replied. He was twisting off the tip of his spear that he'd tooled to stay on with a small pin. He put the spear head away and used the shaft like a walking stick.

"If we aren't back in a couple of days, well, come looking for us if you want," he said to Solomon.

The troglin was remaining back with Tark, Shades, and Dominga as lookouts. Sticks had already brought Abraham up to speed in regard to their run-in with Commander Cutter.

"I don't expect you to be a hero," Abraham said. "Lay low. Get word back to the king."

Solomon shook his head and said, "Death before failure. You fail, we will go in, so do me a favor and don't blow it."

"Let's go." Abraham led the Henchmen up the black gravel roadway into the dark and dreary fog. He could only see several feet in front of himself. For all he knew, snakes and dragons could be nestled in the rocks all around them, waiting to strike. Keeping those thoughts in mind, Leodor reassured him that barring an army marching up the path, a small group like this wouldn't draw any suspicion. Any attempt to attack the Cauldron would be suicidal.

The Henchmen trudged up the hill behind him. The fog began to thin. Daylight crept into their eyes.

Abraham shielded his eyes from the bright sun rising over the jagged hills. The road opened into a full view of the Cauldron. It was a great castle carved out of the great hillside, complete with a barbican, a drawbridge, and battlements on the top. It was every bit as long as half a football field and thirty feet of black stone tall. High on its perch, the Cauldron was perfectly fortified like the House of Steel.

"Whoa," Princess Clarice said. "Are those dragons or statues?"

"I'm hoping they are statues," Vern replied with an uneasy gaze.

Stationed along the parapet walls were small towers on the corners and one in the middle that broke the main wall into two sections. On top of those towers were three dragons, similar to the horse-sized ones the zillons had used to attack the king at the House of Steel. The dragons had the rough, bumpy hides of horned toad lizards and burning yellow eyes narrowed into slits. Forked tongues flickered from their mouths.

"Do they breathe fire?" Abraham asked.

Lewis scoffed. "A dragon breathing fire... Who ever heard of such a thing?"

Abraham resumed his march. "All right, everyone, stop gawking. Let's look like we belong. Leodor, get up here."

Panting for breath, Leodor shuffled his way up to Abraham.

"Do the zillons live here as well?" he asked the mystic.

"No, they are in the pinnacles. Look beyond the walls. You will see them."

Beyond the dragons and the wall were pillars of stone stretching toward the sky like great gnarled fingers. Dozens of them towered at least a hundred feet in height above the hills themselves.

"The dragon riders live there?" he asked.

"They are the Keepers of the Dragons that kept eyes on the Cauldron for centuries. It seems we can confirm that they are the Sect's allies now," Leodor said with a glance drifting up. "I've never seen dragons here before."

"Just remember, there is a zillon out there with an assault rifle. And there might be more of them. I know you don't know much about what that is, but if those guards marching behind the battlements had them, they'd be about to pick us off with ease." Abraham increased his stride. "Do they have horses?"

"Much like the House of Steel, the Cauldron is equipped with everything, including a personal army posted throughout the structure." Leodor kept up with Abraham. "I'll do the talking. And please, no one else say anything."

Abraham looked back at the company and said, "You know that plan. Stick to it." He rubbed his chin and kept his eyes ahead.

They had two objectives. Kill Arcayis, and secure the zillons' assault weapon. One would have been a lot easier to do with the other. He crossed the drawbridge, which was lowered over a twenty-yard-long crevice in the hillside. A mist wavered in the depths. "Is this bridge always open?"

"So far as I know," Leodor said.

On the other side of the bridge stood a host of soldiers carrying spears and wearing short swords on their hips, bronze helmets with nose guards and flared spikes on top, and brown leather tunics. They stood at attention and nodded when the company passed by and went into the inner courtyard sanctum of the castle.

The Cauldron's courtyard was rich in gardens and planters with beautiful flowers rich in deep, velvety colors. The dogwoods growing along the walks were small but plenty. Their white petals drifted through the air. All sorts of robed priests and mystics were about, walking with their hands tucked inside their robes. Wearing the Sect robes of all sorts and colors, they strolled down the brick walkways, sat on wrought-iron benches, and gathered in small groups. Scores of men and women were there from all walks of life, whose idle chattering gave life to what otherwise might have been a dreary and depressing place.

In the center of the castle courtyard stood a stone keep, twenty yards tall, with a split-iron fence wrapping around it. At the top of the stark cylindrical structure were the bone-white leaves of a dogwood tree, capped in the middle. A dozen guards were stationed around it.

The Henchmen moseyed through the courtyard, where many of the priests gardened while others prayed, ate, and drank from slender glasses of wine.

"Tell me about that keep," Abraham told Leodor.

"The Tree of the Elders thrives within that stony case. The priests minister to the soil. It grows without the sun or the rain. It is also the location of the Sect leaders' high offices," Leodor said as he looked at the entrance door.

Two men walked out from the dark-red split doors that led into the keep. The burning blue eyes, dark robes, and bald head of one of them were unmistakable. It was Arcayis the Underlord.

70

A ZILLON SOLDIER WITH AN ASSAULT RIFLE HANGING FROM HIS shoulder walked beside the Underlord.

Leodor gasped.

The Underlord's gaze started to drift their direction.

Abraham's fingertips tingled with fire. Ruger's body charged with energy. He pulled his sword out from underneath his robes and charged. "That's them!"

Arcayis's eyes widened. He darted back into the keep, yelling, "Guards! Guards! Stop them!"

The zillon soldier swung the assault rifle around and onto his shoulder. He took aim at Abraham and fired. Muzzle fire flashed.

Bullets ricocheted off Abraham's breast-plate. His stride didn't slow. His swing didn't either. He cut the zillon down with a sword strike that cleaved the zillon's skull.

"For the king!" he yelled. Without breaking stride, he rushed toward the keep's quickly closing door. He jammed his sword through the narrowing slit and put his shoulder against it. The door didn't budge. "Get me some help over here! Sticks, grab that dead zillon's rifle! And his belt!"

Alarm horns sounded in the courtyard. The priests and mystics scrambled to life. Hands holding concealed knives burst out from underneath their sleeves. The soldiers carrying spears charged. Dragons took flight from their perches on the wall.

Horace bulled his way down the path and lowered his shoulder into the door. The red door gave way.

Abraham slipped inside. A dozen men and women in loose-fitting robes scrambled away from the tree that grew in the center. They vanished into the alcoves that lined the keep's inner rim. He caught a glimpse of Arcayis running up a flight of stairs to the second level. Outside the keep's front door, the clamor of battle raged.

"Get everyone inside!" Abraham yelled.

Horace stood inside the doorway, waving his arm in a huge circle and shouting, "Inside, Henchmen! Inside!"

One by one, starting with Leodor, the Henchmen poured into the keep. Bearclaw and Cudgel, led by Sticks, dragged inside the dead zillon carrying the assault rifle.

"I couldn't get the belt off," she said to Abraham.

Horace and Vern shut the door and dropped the locking bar into place.

"Make sure it doesn't open," Abraham said to Iris.

"I will," Iris said. A rosy glow emanated from her fingertips the moment she touched the door. The red-pinkish hue spread over the door.

Abraham knelt down by the dead zillon. A black web belt like the ones the military used was latched around the zillon's waist. He pinched the locked plastic mechanism right before Sticks's eyes and pulled the belt, which included an ammo pouch, free from the body. He gave it to Sticks. "Don't lose this or the rifle."

"How do you use it?" Sticks asked.

"Aim and squeeze the trigger." He clenched his index finger. "I'll show you later." He pointed toward the top balconies overlooking the keep's inner courtyard. "The Underlord went up there, Leodor. What's up there?"

"The Sect's special chambers."

A foursome of robe-wearing, dagger-wielding priests burst out of the alcoves, screaming shrilly at the top of their lungs.

Prince Clarice and Swan dashed into their paths and cut them down in four quick thrusts. Clarice wiped her rapier off on the dead's robes and winked at her brother.

Lewis shook his head. "If you were good, you would have taken all four of them."

A fierce pounding started on the door. Yelling and coarse shouts started from outside.

With all the Henchmen assembled, Abraham headed for the stairs leading to the upper chambers. "Let's go." He took the steps four at a time to the second level.

A ring of arched doorway entrances went all the way around the inner circle. All the Henchmen were gathered on the balconies except for Horace, Iris, and Cudgel, who guarded the door below.

"Leodor, you've been here before," Abraham said. "Any ideas where his special chamber might be?"

"I can't say. They are mostly places for mediation and study," Leodor said. "I've only been in one once before, decades ago. Things can change."

"Spread out," Abraham said. "If anyone sees a creepy bald wizard with blue diamonds for eyes, holler!" He tested the first door handle that he came to—the mechanism was locked. "Dirty donuts."

Sticks knelt down beside him to pick the lock. She gave him a look and nodded.

Abraham shoved the door open. A powerful clawed hand grabbed his arm and yanked him off his feet, pulling him inside. The door slammed shut behind him.

71

ABRAHAM SLAMMED INTO A WALL. A MUSCLE-BOUND MAN WITH A boar's face had him pinned to the wall by the neck. His toes dangled above the floor. He was in a study of some sort, complete with chairs, small tables, and bookshelves. A chandelier of candles illuminated the room. He kicked at the creature that held him fast. The boar-faced man had the jutting bottom fangs of a hog. It sank its nails into Abraham's neck with an iron grip. The inhuman man headbutted Abraham in the face and slung him aside. Black Bane slipped from Abraham's fingers.

"He will be a tasty one, brother!" said another boar man standing by the door. The gruff-voiced boar man dropped an iron bar over it, sealing the three of them inside. "Just as the Underlord said. Today, we dine on the flesh of heroes!"

Abraham rolled up and put his back against the wall. Bright spots filled his eyes. He shook his head. The boar men were bare chested, with bulging muscles popping up underneath the coarse black hair covering their bodies. He saw his sword lying on the floor and dove for it.

The ugly boar man that had grabbed him kicked the sword away with a hoofed foot. "No, no, no," the man said. "That is not how we fight." He balled up his fists.

His brother came and stood behind him, punching a meaty fist into his hand. One of his fangs was broken off. He was shorter, but both of them stood taller than Abraham. "This one wears a shell. Let us crack that shell and dine."

Abraham climbed to his feet. "You two don't look like you've missed any meals. Are you sure that you want to eat me?"

The boar-faced brothers exchanged a look and let out gusty snorts and laughs. "This one jests," the taller one said. "He won't joke soon enough." He raised his fists. "Time to have some fun with the dinner meat first."

"Oh, so you want to box," Abraham said, balling up his fists. "Fair enough." He moved forward and punched the boar man in the face with a right cross. He finished the combo with a punch in the belly. The boar man's hide felt as hard as stone. He unloaded a quick combination of punches to the ribs.

The boar man balled up, winced, and said, "You hit hard for a man. My hide can take it." He started punching back.

Abraham ducked the hard and heavy swings. He blocked a punch and countered with a jab in the ribs.

"Brother, this one fights well," the taller one said. "Help me finish him quickly. I hunger."

"Of course," the shorter one said. He slipped in behind Abraham and unloaded a flurry of punches. "Smash him. Beat him. Eat him!"

Abraham backed into a corner. He forearm blocked their attacks, which rained down on him like sledgehammers. They hit him like heavyweight boxers working him on the ropes. He slipped his head away and blocked. Their hard punches plowed into his breastplate and glanced off his head. He kicked the short one in the gut, and the boar man doubled over. Abraham rammed his knee into its nose. He squirted free of the other and went for his sword.

One foot away from scooping the sword up, he was tackled by the taller boar man. They rolled across the floor in a tangle of limbs. The boar man had the animal strength of a bear. He pinned Abraham down by the neck with his hands. Abraham chopped at his arms.

"You fight well," the boar man said. "When we roast you, we will honor your flesh with a sweet, succulent sauce from the Old Kingdom."

The boar man's fingers dug deeper into his throat. The steel-hardened thews layering his neck saved his throat from collapsing. The boar man squeezed.

"I'm softening him up for you, brother." The shorter one egged him on and kicked at Abraham's ribs, saying, "There's nothing sweeter than the taste of succulent pulverized meat."

The breastplate saved Abraham's ribs from shattering, but painful shockwaves carried through his body. He locked his hands on the bigger boar man's wrist, wrenched, and twisted.

"Ho ho, you will not break my grip. Nothing can. You will die under it."

Abraham's sword lay within reach. He stretched his fingers toward it.

"No, no, no." The brother kicking Abraham hopped to the sword, picked it up, and said, "I have the power. Ha ha ha. Not a fan of the steel, but this would make a fine spit to cook his flesh on. Won't that be fitting? Cooking on your own sword." He tossed it away.

Abraham punched at the ribs of the boar man straddling him. The slavering boar man didn't budge. A thought struck Abraham as he started to lose air and his vision came to blacken. *Use your dagger, idiot.* He'd been so used to using Black Bane he'd completely forgotten about the daggers tucked underneath his cloak. *Bloody Mary, always carry an extra knife.* He squirmed his fingers down by his side, found the hilt of a dagger pressed along his side, and ripped it free. He stabbed the boar man clean through the ribs, piercing the thick hide and hitting the pumping heart.

The boar man arched his back. His pig jaws opened wide. The life in his eyes faded.

Abraham pushed the boar man away and sprang to his feet. He squared off against the other brother, still standing. "You should have searched me, stupid pig."

"Nooo!" The boar man clutched his head and shook it like a bull. "Nooo!" With rage burning in his eyes, he shouted, "You killed my brother! I will kill you!" He scraped his hoof across the floor, snorted loudly, and charged.

In a lightning-quick downward stroke, Abraham stuck the boar man through skull and brain. The boar man died instantly, falling to the carpet underneath their feet.

Abraham retrieved his sword. A loud commotion of battle sounded from the other side of the door. He lifted the bar away and flung the door open.

The Tree of the Elders was burning. The dragons were inside.

72

DRAGONS ROARED INSIDE THE KEEP. ONE DRAGON LAY ON THE FLOOR of the keep by the burning tree, dead. The entire keep was filled with smoky vapors. Crackling flames licked at the bark trunk of the dogwood tree. Skirmishes raged all around.

Abraham cried out across the balcony, "Sticks!" She was on the other side, with Lewis and Leodor, battling two dragons that hemmed them in on the ledge of the balcony. He ran toward them, racing around the outer ring of the keep.

A dragon streaked through the air, crashed through the railing, and blocked his path. Head low, it crept toward him with a hungry growl in its throat. It came at Abraham on the quick, scurrying legs of a lizard.

Black Bane flashed right between the dragon's eyes. The blade sank deep in the dragon's snout.

The dragon recoiled and let out a pain-filled roar. Its breath reeked of rotten flesh and sulfur.

Abraham pressed the attack. He brought the blade up and

down on the horse-sized dragon's snout. Hunks of lizard flesh were hacked away. Teeth were chopped out of its mouth.

It charged.

Abraham braced his feet, lunged forward, and stabbed.

The hulk of the dragon barreled into him, and the balcony railing broke. Man and dragon plummeted to the ground.

Abraham twisted in the air, distancing himself from the dragon. He hit the ground flat on his back, and the wind burst out of his lungs. The dragon landed beside him with Black Bane embedded in its eye socket. It twitched as its tail flapped back and forth, scraping over the ground. Fighting for breath, Abraham crawled over the tail where the dying dragon spasmed. He grabbed the sword hilt, put some weight on it, and jammed it deeper.

The dragon stiffened and lay still.

He pulled his sword free just in time to confront two soldiers rushing him with lowered spears. He knocked one spear aside and spun back into the Cauldron soldier's body and smote the man with an elbow in the face. The man staggered backward. Abraham cut the arms off the second soldier. That soldier lifted up his bleeding stumps for hands and fell over dead. Abraham made quick work of the first soldier he'd attacked. A stab in the heart did the trick. Then he was on the move again.

Horace, Cudgel, and Iris were battling at the keep's front door, slaying new attackers and keeping them at bay. Iris sent fiery rose-pink hornets from her fingertips spraying into the enemy. Cudgel dislodged a soldier's jaw with a fierce hit from his spiked mace. Horace gored man after man on the end of his thick spear. Bodies piled up in bloody heaps around them.

"Horace, do you need help?" Abraham asked as he raced past.

Horace ran two enemy soldiers through at once and said, "No, Captain. Don't spoil our fun. Kill those dragons!"

The rest of the Henchmen were locked up in mortal battle with the dragons on the balcony. Swan and Lewis hacked away at the beasts, keeping them at bay. Through the smoke, Abraham didn't see any more of the dragons as he bounded back up the steps. He raced around the curve of the balcony. Running up on the backside of the dragon attacking Swan, he lopped its tail off with a lethal swing.

The dragon spun around on Abraham.

Swan sliced open the dragon's neck the moment it twisted away from her. "Taste my steel, beast!"

Together, Abraham and Swan carved up the dragon. Its scaly hide was no match for Black Bane and the King's Steel wielded by the guardian maiden. Hunks of flesh flew from the dragon. It thrashed on the balcony with blood spurting from the deep gashes in its body. Its serpentine movement began to slow, and it spread its wings.

"Never!" Swan leapt onto the dragon's back and sliced through both of its wings.

It jumped through the railing, flapping furiously as it nose-dived toward the ground.

"Princess!" Swan called out. She hung from the railing by one hand. Her feet dangled over the edge.

Clarice arrived at the same time Abraham did. The princess wrapped her fingers around Swan's hand. "Hold on!"

Abraham grabbed Swan by the back of the pants and hauled her up. "Next time, let go of your sword in case no one is around."

"Never," Swan replied.

The last dragon lay dead at Lewis's feet. The prince had lizard guts and blood all over him. On the back end of the dragon were Bearclaw and Vern. Their weapons were also drenched with blood.

Abraham surveyed the surroundings. The soldiers were dead, and the tree still burned. Branches were falling from the tree's trunk. He waved at Horace. The bearded warrior waved back. Dozens of soldiers were dead on the balconies and the ground. If any others survived, they were hiding.

"Leodor, are there any other ways out of here?" Abraham asked.

"Only through the roof and through that door. It's a keep. There is only one way in and one way out." Leodor rolled his eyes. "They are designed that way, you know."

"Yeah, thanks, Leodor." Abraham eyed the hole in the roof, which had no access, aside from the tree that burned. "We have to search this place room by room. The Underlord has to be here, somewhere."

"I find that unlikely," Leodor said. "I see no reason why he wouldn't be able to remove himself from the keep with a transportation spell. I'd do the same."

Sticks spun her short swords in her hands and asked, "Wouldn't you need to have one prepared?"

"One can only assume that the Underlord is prepared for everything," Leodor replied.

"I say that we get out of here," Lewis suggested with his eyes locked on the hole in the roof of the keep. "Before more dragons flood through that gap."

"Captain!" Horace shouted from below. "This door won't hold much longer! Magic or no. The wood begins to splinter."

"We're trapped in here. The only way out is against the Cauldron army. No, we're too close. Maybe we caught the Underlord with his pants down." Abraham headed to the next door. "Let's turn this place upside down before time runs out." He knocked on the door. "Room service. It's time to clean your room."

"ARE YOU LOOKING FOR ME?"

Everyone turned. Arcayis the Underlord stood on the other side of the balcony, twelve feet tall with one hand filled with blazing blue bolts of lightning.

73

THE TOWERING FIGURE OF ARCAYIS LOOMED ON THE BALCONY LIKE A great shadow in his black robes. A necklace of bright stones hung around his neck. The stone in the middle burned with blue fire, while the others were white, yellow, orange, and red. His voice filled the room and shook the branches burning on the trees. "I applaud your boldness, Ruger Slade. Ha ha. I didn't expect to see you so soon or at all." He craned his neck. "Ah, I see that you brought my former servants, Lewis and Leodor. Are you ready to come back to the winning side?"

"We didn't come to chat. We came to kill you," Abraham said. He moved down the balcony, where he had a better look at Arcayis. He moved to the right, while Bearclaw and Vern moved left. "You could make it easier on yourself and surrender."

Toying with the necklace draped over his chest, Arcayis asked, "Now, why would I do that? I'm all but invincible. Can't you see that I've already acquired five of the six stones that you seek?"

Abraham shot a look back at Leodor, who shrank inside his robes. "Tell me that you didn't know about this."

"I didn't. I'm as shocked as any," Leodor said. "We are finished."

"Yes, listen to Leodor, Ruger. You are finished. Your quest ends here with me." Arcayis eyed the burning tree. "You really do need to pay for setting fire to the Tree of the Elders. The Sect will frown heavily over that. Someone, most likely you, will suffer eons for it."

"It's just a tree, man," Abraham said. He crept forward and made it one quarter of the balcony ring away from Arcayis. He tingled from the bottom of his spine to the top. "How about we talk about this?"

Arcayis gave him a scornful look and said, "I don't think so. Prepare to watch your Henchmen die."

He flung a bolt of energy at Bearclaw and Vern, who dove as the bolt exploded into the balcony, collapsing it beneath them. The warriors fell to the ground, and the Underlord let out a triumphant laugh.

Abraham charged.

With a flick of his fingers, Arcayis blew away the balcony, leaving a chasm between them. "No, no, no. I want you to stand and watch this."

He hurled bolt after bolt across the deck. The lightning blasted Swan's and Clarice's bodies. The barrage of energy collapsed more of the balcony beneath them. All of them fell to the ground.

"Perfect. It's always easier to kill from a dragon's point of view."

Abraham banged his sword on the railing. "Wake up, Black Bane. I need help."

Arcayis pitched away, flinging bolt after bolt at the bombarded Henchmen.

Bearclaw ran for cover and took a bolt square in the back. His arms flung wide as he sailed into a support column below the crumbling balcony.

Leodor and Lewis hid behind an orange shield of energy. A bolt of energy shattered it.

"You have made my task easy by coming here, Ruger!" Arcayis threw bolt after bolt like a mad god of thunder. "No more elaborate schemes. Instead, a straight-up fight. Once you perish, King Hector will follow. You are the last hope that he has." He laughed like a madman. "Ah ha ha ha ha!"

"Black Bane, wake up!"

The sword was the only thing he could think of that could match the same wroth power that Arcayis wielded. The runes engraved in the blade, which glowed red-hot during moments like this, grew cold.

"Fine! I'm not going to stand here and watch my men get slaughtered." Abraham backed up, sheathed his sword, faced the gap in the balcony, ran, and jumped. He landed with his arms on the rim of the broken ledge.

Arcayis peered down at him with blazing eyes and said, "That was a very stupid thing to do. You are defenseless. Oh well. I'll end this early." He lifted a lightning bolt over his shoulder and drove it down into Abraham's head.

Every nerve ending in Abraham's body exploded with vibrant pain. His sight washed over in blue. He saw himself falling away from Arcayis's leering face. The picture jostled. He was on the ground with his ears ringing and scorched hair stinking. His mouth tasted like the tip of a nine-volt battery. Everything hurt. It all hurt badly.

Above, Arcayis slung his lightning bolt into the fire and smoke. The floor quaked. The keep shook.

Move, Abraham. You have to move! If Abraham was moving, he couldn't tell. *Ruger, get your ass off of the floor and do something!* A body sailed over his eyes. It was Cudgel. His robes were on fire. *No!*

Arcayis continued his barrage of fire with fathomless energy. Bolts appeared in his hands one after the other. Like a hawk's, his eyes locked on a target, then he cocked back and threw.

Rushing blood roared through Abraham's ears. He turned his head. Horace lay on his chest, face down, with the Robes of the Black Kraken on fire and smoldering. As Iris frantically tried to pat out the flames, a blue bolt exploded at her feet. The smoke cleared. She was gone.

74

STICKS POPPED INTO ABRAHAM'S VIEW. HER FACE WAS SKINNED UP and bloody. She grabbed him by the boots and dragged him underneath the balcony. Her lips were moving, but he couldn't make out a word she said. The explosions and sharp ringing in his ears drowned her voice out. He managed to lift a shaking arm.

He waved her away saying, "Go, go, go!"

"Such a delight!" Arcayis's great voice thundered from above. "The King's Henchmen are sheep for the slaughter! Die, Henchmen, die!"

Searing blue bolts of light soared through the keep.

Kra-koom! Kra-koom! Kra-koom!

Sticks held out the assault rifle and waved it in front of Abraham in a frantic motion. Her hands were on the trigger housing. She looked at him and spoke.

Abraham tried to read her lips. He wasn't sure but thought she was asking, "What do I do?" Without full control of his body, all he could manage to do was say, "Pull the trigger." He squeezed his own trigger finger. "Pull the trigger." He couldn't hear or understand his own words.

Sticks tilted her head. Her eyes ran the length of the weapon. Using both hands, she held out the assault rifle. She didn't brace the stock of the weapon against her shoulder but held it straight out in an awkward position. Backpedaling, Sticks slowly walked out from underneath the balcony with the weapon pointed toward the ceiling.

With agonizing pain shooting through his head, Abraham twisted his head around. She didn't know what she was doing. Arcayis would blow her away. He let out another garbled warning, "Nooo!"

Blue lightning lit up the room.

Chunks of debris went flying.

Flaming branches fell from the tree.

The muzzle of the assault weapon flashed.

Arcayis dropped from above and landed hard on his back. A bullet had blown out the back of his head.

Abraham's eyes popped. "Huh?"

Sticks held the assault rifle up, nodded, and smiled. She said something inaudible.

The inner walls of the keep quieted. Only the cracking sound of the burning tree remained.

Abraham managed to fight his way up to his hands and knees. His limbs shook with effort. *How am I not dead? I just took a lightning bolt to the cranium.* He caught Sticks looking at him and said, "Good shot."

Arcayis's giant body shrank back down to normal size.

Sticks slung the rifle over her shoulder. She took the necklace off Arcayis's neck. The burning blue stone had gone cold. She walked over to Abraham and put the necklace around his neck. "Let's go home."

Bearclaw and Vern helped Abraham to his feet.

A limping Lewis used his sword for a cane.

Leodor's robes were in tatters. He swayed with every step.

Swan and Clarice were marred with soot and caked black from head to toe.

Cudgel moved slowly toward the group with a nasty gash on his bald head.

Horace cradled Iris's limp body in his arms. Tears filled his eyes. "She's dead," he sobbed. "He killed her. That fiend killed her!"

Abraham's heart sank.

Everyone's chins dipped.

Horace sobbed loudly. "Curse the Elders and their games!"

Iris placed her hand over Horace's mouth and said, "I'm not dead. Can't you feel that I'm still breathing? I can barely move. The king's armor saved me," she said, glancing at the others with a wobbling neck. "I'd say it saved us all."

"She's alive!" Horace elated. "She's alive!"

The keep's door shook on the hinges. Axes chopped into the wood. Something rammed it from the other side.

Abraham slipped out of the arms of Bearclaw and Vern. His vibrant strength returned to his limbs. He wasn't sure how he'd survived, but based on what Iris had said, he thought the king's breastplate he was wearing had something to do with it. The king's steel, he started to believe, was special. "All right, listen up, there's going to be more soldiers and dragons out there." He glanced up, imagining scores of dragons pouring through the opening of the keep and devouring them whole. "If anyone has any bright ideas, now is the time to share them."

"If I may," Leodor said. His eyes were locked on the bright gemstones dangling from Abraham's neck. "I could harness the necklace's powers and possibly put an end to all of this."

Iris shook her head. "Those are for the king only."

"You know nothing about it," Leodor told her with a cross look.

"I know that you don't deserve it. You might kill us all with it," Iris fired back.

The soldiers outside the keep chopped a large hunk out of the door. Angry stares peered through the gap.

"I'm a Henchman," Leodor said. "I can't use it against the king's will, or I will die."

"Yes, let Leodor have the necklace," Lewis said. "He is the only one that possesses the knowledge to use it," He moved toward Abraham and held out his hand. "My father would approve it. And I am the prince who endorses it. Are Leodor and I not proven?"

"You've pulled your weight," Abraham said, surrounded by doubting eyes. He felt Lewis and Leodor still had a long way to go, despite having gained some favor. As dire as his situation was, he wasn't desperate enough to turn over the necklace. He flicked his fingers. Invisible needles burned all through his body, especially from the elbow up. He clenched his hand. "But not that much weight."

"Don't be a fool!" Lewis pointed at the door. "They'll swarm us the moment they burst through there!"

"We can kill them," Horace said.

The enemy whittled the door down more, bigger chunks at a time.

Bearclaw, Vern, Cudgel, Swan, and Clarice, bearing their weapons, made a fighting line between Abraham and the door.

"This is madness!" Lewis said.

"Indeed," Leodor agreed.

"There's an old saying in my world," Abraham replied. "Sometimes you have to know when to hold them, when to fold them, when to walk away, or run. Now is one of those times."

"What in Titanuus's Crotch does that mean?" Lewis asked.

Abraham smiled. "Horace, I'm going to need your spear. It's time to go Frazetta on them."

"And what, pray tell, is Frazetta?" Lewis asked with a snide look.

Abraham smirked. "You'll see."

75

ABRAHAM DECAPITATED ARCAYIS WITH BLACK BANE AND MOUNTED the Underlord's head on the tip of Horace's spear. Horace hoisted the head up.

"That's Frazetta," Abraham said.

He marched in front of the keep's door with Horace standing on one side and Sticks on the other. Horace held the spear and head upright. Sticks had the assault rifle across her chest. The rest of the Henchmen stood behind them. He watched as the Cauldron soldiers finally burst through the door.

Over a dozen soldiers poured through the busted opening, bearing swords and spears. They came to an abrupt halt. Their battle-hungry gazes hung on the image of the Underlord's decapitated head skewered on a spear.

"Now that I have your attention," Abraham said in a strong authoritative voice, "let me make what is about to happen crystal clear for you. Number one, as you can see, the Underlord is dead. So is everyone else in here, including the dragons. Number two"— he bandied the necklace jewels before their eyes—"I have the

Underlord's power. Number three, we are going to walk out of here without any trouble from you at all. Capisce?"

The soldiers deflated inside their armor, and their hard-eyed stares softened.

Abraham stepped forward as the soldiers cowered back. He marched them back out of the keep. Scores of soldiers and priests were gathered in the courtyard. Several zillon dragon riders were perched on the outer wall. Dozens of the Cauldron's throng gasped at the sight of Arcayis's head.

"Listen up!" Abraham shouted in a harsher tone. "Attack us, and I wipe you out of existence." He shook the necklace at them. "I wipe you out, your wives, your husbands, your children, and baby dragons! I'll kill every last one of them. Do you hear me?"

The crowed murmured in agreement and cleared him a path to the gate.

"I want horses! And I better not see one single cross look!" He looked at a soldier who quickly looked away. He spotted a priest with a lazy eye and poofy hair. "Or any cross-eyed looks!"

The lazy-eyed priest gulped and wormed his way into the crowd.

Abraham continued, "I'll find your cousins, your kin, your house, your fields, and I'll burn it all!"

"Hear, hear," Horace said out of the corner of his mouth.

"Laying it on a little thick, aren't you?" Sticks quietly asked.

"It's my *Unforgiven* moment," he said from the corner of his mouth. "Roll with it."

The Cauldron's enclave made a clear path to the portcullis gate. They brought horses for everyone. Outside the gate, the Henchmen mounted up.

Abraham stared up at the Zillon dragon riders. They showed no expression at all. Saliva dripped from the dragons' fangs. "King Hector lives. All who oppose him die. Pray you don't ever see any us again. We show mercy once, not twice." He turned his horse toward the fog. "Yah! Yah!"

The Henchmen thundered down the road and vanished into the fog.

At the bottom of the massive hill, the Henchmen met up with Solomon, Tark, Dominga, and Shades.

"All of you look like hell, but I see that you brought us a souvenir," Solomon said.

"Nice head," Dominga added.

Shades sniggered. "And to think that you pulled it off without me."

"I wouldn't be overconfident," Leodor said. "They let us escape. They must have."

Abraham shook his head and said, "It's a bluff, old man." He reached across the saddle and grabbed Leodor's narrow shoulders. "You see, sometimes you don't have to fight when you're a man, and it doesn't mean you're weak if you turn that other cheek."

Leodor turned up his nose, slipped from Abraham's grasp, and led his horse away.

With his head turned toward the hills, Solomon said, "What happened up there? I didn't expect you back so soon."

"I guess the element of surprise was on our side." Abraham couldn't help but smile. He'd dodged death again, and all the Henchmen returned intact. "I'll tell you on the ride back. A very interesting story, but we got what we needed and more." He pulled out the necklace from underneath his cloak.

"Are those all of the stones?" Solomon asked with the jewels shining in his eyes.

"All five. Apparently, the Underlord had them. I thought he was going to wipe us out, but Sticks shot him."

"Shot him?" Solomon looked at Sticks. "An assault rifle?"

"And ammo. We ran smack-dab into the zillon that shot at King Hector and Arcayis himself." He chuckled. "They didn't see it coming."

"If you don't mind me saying, you seem a little punch drunk," the old troglin added.

"That's probably because the Underlord jammed a lightning bolt straight through me." He tapped his armor. "This sheet metal kept me together." He lifted an arm. "Horace, Shades, lead us back to the *Sea Talon* with haste." He winked at Solomon. "Don't tell Leodor or Lewis, but I agree—my bluff might not hold, and I don't know how to use this necklace."

"But the dragons... Were there dragons?" Solomon asked.

"More dragons than I have toes and fingers, that I could see. The farther away from them, the better. They are the things to fear most. I'm shocked that the zillons fell for my bluff at all."

"We would have killed them," Horace said as he rode by. "Move out, Henchmen!"

The company moved at a trot and stayed on the back roads. They put the Cauldron's clouded hills far behind them and broke away from the city. Over a mile from the city was a stone bridge over a deep trickling creek.

Horace lifted a fist and stopped at the beginning of the bridge. "Whoa."

Abraham rode alongside Horace and asked, "What's going on?"

Horace pointed at a small army of men gathered on the other side of the bridge. Their burgundy tunics with upside-down black ankhs were a dead giveaway. It was the Black Squadron.

76

"I'LL HANDLE THIS," ABRAHAM SAID. HE LED HIS HORSE OUT ONTO the bridge.

Sticks and Horace followed but kept their distance behind him. The horses' hooves clomped on the wooden bridge. The wind picked up, and the horses nickered.

On the other side of the bridge, three riders approached. The biggest man rode in the middle, the man they'd identified as Commander Cutter in the small-town tavern Shades set on fire. Commander Cutter had a short military-style haircut. The hawkish man had a broad face with strong angular features, great shoulders, and grizzle on his face. A white scar split his chin. He wore a pitch-black cloak over his burgundy tunic. The handle of a bastard sword stuck out behind his back.

He narrowed his eyes at Abraham and spat over the bridge. "I am Commander Cutter. This is the Black Squadron."

"You are in our way, Commander Cutter," Abraham said.

Cutter's hardened stare shifted to the head that Horace carried on his spear. "I'm curious. Where is the body that goes with that head?"

"What business is that of yours?"

"Everything that happens in Hancha is my business," Cutter replied. He dropped his focus back on Abraham. "I'm an important man around here. I don't find favor with people riding the country with heads mounted on spears. But I get the feeling that you and your company aren't from around here, are you?"

"Just passing through. We are taking the head home as a souvenir."

Cutter spat on the bridge. "Let's quit playing games. You were in the tavern the other night, weren't you? The one that burned. I saw you, the big belly and the woman, plus that little fella back there."

"That was us," Abraham replied.

"And you're Ruger Slade, aren't you?"

"Yes and no, but that's a long story."

Cutter rested his corded forearms on the saddle horn. "And the rest of you are King Hector's Henchmen."

Abraham shrugged. "Is there something that I can help you with? You see, we are in a bit of a hurry."

"I imagine that you are. I'd be in a hurry too if I was in enemy territory." Cutter sniggered. "Slade the Blade. The moment I heard about your exploits in Pirate City, I knew I had to find you face-to-face. They say you are the best with a blade. Perhaps the best ever." He spat. "I don't believe it."

"If you were there, you would have." Abraham pushed his fingers back through his hair. "Listen, as you can see, we've had a few tough days, Commander. And yes, I know you're a fine swordsman yourself, and you probably want a piece of me. But before you do something stupid and draw your blade, let me fill you in." He pointed at the decapitated head. "That's the Underlord. The head of the Sect. The prince of the Cauldron. He's dead. Very dead." He gave Sticks a sideways glance. "She shot him with that weapon of mass destruction in her hands. It blew out the back end of his head."

Sticks aimed the weapon at Commander Cutter's face.

Abraham continued. "Not to mention the zillon dragon riders that fell." He dangled the necklace before Cutter. "And I have the Underlord's most precious source of power. Now, I'm going to tell you what I told the others that were smart enough to get out of our way and not die. We'll show mercy once. After that, you die." He tugged his earlobe. "I'll extend the king's same grace to you." He buckled his brows, darkened his tone, and said, "Get out of our way or die."

Commander Cutter's stare swept across the three of them before stopping back on Abraham. "I want sword against sword. Me against you."

"It will have to wait. I'm not in the mood. Step aside, all of you, or my little friend will do the same to you that she did to the Underlord," he replied.

"You are a coward." Cutter spat on the ground and backed his horse away. The other two soldiers did the same. With a wave of his arm, the Black Squadron cleared the road.

Abraham led the Henchmen over the bridge. As he passed Commander Cutter, he said, "I'm not a coward. And you aren't as stupid as you look." He put his heels into the ribs of his horse and galloped away. The Henchmen rode after him, leaving the onlooking Black Squadron eating their dust.

They rode the countryside for miles without stopping. Then Abraham slowed to a walk, allowing the horses to rest.

Horace caught up to him and said, "Captain, I'm not one to question you, but I have to ask, why didn't you fight him?"

"Because," Abraham said, tightening his tingling grip on the reins, "not only can I barely feel my hands, I can hardly lift my arms." The corner of his mouth turned up. "Then again, maybe I have the strength after all. Drop. Your. Sword."

Horace gave him a curious look. "Pardon, Captain?"

Abraham chuckled. "Nothing."

Horace grunted. "Just so you know, we could have killed them."

"I know." He could still smell his singed hair. Painful shards ran up and down his spine. The lightning bolt to the head had some severe lingering effects, and a migraine had come on. "But I had to make sure that we all made it out alive."

77

CHAPTER 77 (EPILOGUE)

The Henchmen reunited with the ship crew at Pirate City. They sailed on *Sea Talon* all the way back to Kingsland without incident. Night had fallen when they ported. A season-changing wintery chill swept through the air. Abraham, Leodor, Lewis, Princess Clarice, and Swan headed straight to the House of Steel that evening. Abraham ordered the rest of the Henchmen back to the Stronghold.

King Hector and Queen Clarann welcomed Princess Clarice with warm hugs and tears in their eyes. Clarice apologized all over herself and shared the demise of the Guardian Maiden Hazel. They had reunited on the king's terrace overlooking the Bay of Elders. Pratt, the commander of the King's Guardians, along with two other Guardians, stood guard on the terrace. The king and queen were quickly brought up to speed on their journey by Clarice.

With a smile of relief, King Hector strolled over to Abraham with his arms swinging by his sides. He practically walked on tiptoe, his eyes glued to the necklace hanging on Abraham's neck. "Surely, those can't be the jewels from the Crown of Stones."

As Abraham opened his mouth, Leodor stepped forward and said with a bow, "Your Majesty, I cannot vouch for the authenticity of the stones myself. Abraham refused to part with them."

"Yes, well, he is the Captain," Hector said, "and wise to keep them in hand." His fingers kneaded the air between them. "So, the Underlord is dead?"

"Dead as stone," Abraham replied. "We killed the would-be assassin too." He reached behind his back, where the assault rifle hung from a strap on his shoulder. He showed it to the king. "This is an assault rifle. An M-16 is what it is called, to be exact. Sticks shot Arcayis in the head with it. It turned his head inside out." He glanced at a round wicker basket sitting in front of Lewis's feet. "It's gruesome, but we brought his head in a fish basket if you want to look."

King Hector looked at his son and nodded.

Lewis squatted down and flipped open the basket's lid.

Queen Clarann walked over at that moment. She and Hector bent their necks over the basket together. She pinched her nose and, with watering eyes, looked away.

Hector's nose twitched, and he said, "Ghastly. And to think that could have been me." His gaze hung on the head. "The entire back of his head is missing, but I know it's him. Those eyes... I'll never forget them." He flipped his hand.

Lewis closed the basket and asked, "What would you have me do with it, Father?"

With his lips pointed toward the sea, he said, "Pitch it over the wall. Let the sea birds dine on it. If memory serves, Arcayis hated birds. It will be a fitting funeral for him."

Without a word, Lewis walked over to the terrace wall and dumped the head out. He tossed the basket after it.

King Hector eyed Abraham, the rifle, and the necklace. He shook his head and, with disbelief in his voice, said, "I am without words, otherworlder. And you have my entire gratitude. To think that I was going to hang you." He dropped a firm hand on Abraham's shoulder. "You have earned the king's gratitude."

"Just me?" he asked.

"All of the Henchmen, but most especially you, Abraham." Hector glanced at Clarann, who was nothing short of a lovely vision. "Not only did you save the love of my life, but my daughter, possibly my kingdom, not to mention my son." He turned his attention to Lewis. "I hope you learned something from this man, Son. Did you?"

"I learned there is nothing that he did that I could not have done," Lewis replied with a heavy crease in his brow. "Besides, it was a united effort. I'm not sure that any of them would have survived without myself and Leodor to pull them through."

"You smug, snotty little liar!" Clarice yelled. Her fists were balled up at her side, and her hot stare could have killed her half brother. "Father, the only thing those two sandbags did was drag us down. The Henchmen are better off without them."

King Hector rubbed his chin, which sagged with age, and asked Abraham, "Is that so?"

His gaze drifted toward Lewis and Leodor. "I think everyone pulled their weight. I can fill you in at length."

The king nodded. "No, I accept your statement. I mean, look at Leodor. He looks like a pauper's dish towel. He must have done something. I can see dirt underneath his fingernails and an ugly bump on his head. We can hash out the details later." He dropped his eyes on the necklace. "May I?"

"Certainly."

318

King Hector waved at Pratt. "Bring the crown over."

Pratt lumbered over to the patio table where the crown sat with bright moonlight twinkling on its metal horns. The big man, who appeared exceptionally huge in his armor, picked the crown up as though holding a baby. He marched over to King Hector and took a knee before him. "Your Majesty," the man said.

King Hector took the crown and said, "Thank you, Pratt. That will be all."

Pratt gave Abraham a heavy look and moved back to his post.

"I guess I won't be needing this anymore." King Hector reached into his pocket and produced the colorful cube. "Your Cube of Rubik. I never solved it." The orange side of the cube had been solved. The other five sides and colors were a jumbled mess. He placed it in Abraham's palm.

"At least you finished one side. That's far better than most that try to solve it." Abraham noticed Leodor staring at them. He turned his broad back to the man, shielding the viceroy's view from the cube. Under his breath, he said to the king, "Hang onto it. Let Leodor still think it's magic."

King Hector took the cube, looked past Abraham at Leodor, and said, "Good idea." He tucked the cube away. Then he handed the crown to Clarann, reached inside his robes, and withdrew his necklace with the emerald jewel set in it. He popped it out of the casing, looked at Clarann, and said, "The moment of truth."

Abraham's throat turned dry. His fingers clutched at his side. With the king and the crown's help, he might be able to go right back home. The problem was, he wasn't so sure that he wanted to. As bad as Titanuus was, he liked it—the people too. The only thing tying him back home was Mandi. He swallowed. *What if this crown opens a portal and sends me back, and I don't want to go? I don't think I'm ready to leave yet. Am I?*

The king set the emerald stone in the front horn's facet. The tiny pronglike claws in the facet locked onto the jewel, which fit inside perfectly. Five more facets were left to fill, two on each side and one in the back. He popped the jewels out of the necklace's golden casing. He began with the blue stone. It clamped perfectly into the facet of the crown's horn in the back. "Marvelous," he said with a warming smile.

The blue stone shone dully in the moonlight.

Leodor moved closer to the king. "It's magnificent, Your Majesty. Gems worthy of a true king."

"I hope you aren't groveling," King Hector said. "I hate groveling." He tried the orange stone next. It didn't twinkle the same as the emerald. The stone wouldn't fit in any of the facets even though it looked as though it would. He turned it upside down. It still wouldn't go.

"Strange," King Hector said.

"Perhaps I can make it fit," Leodor offered.

The king pulled the crown away. He next took the ruby jewel, shaped like a giant teardrop, the same as the others. It wouldn't fit either.

"What is wrong?" Queen Clarann asked.

The entire group formed a circle around the king. All of them watched with bated breath.

King Hector swallowed. He tried the yellow stone next. "I don't know. The crown rejects them." He held the yellow stone up in the moonlight. The shining light reflected dully on the stone. "Clarann, lift the crown into the light."

Clarann's graceful arms pushed the crown into the light. The emerald and blue sapphire stones shone with the glimmer and twinkle of a colorful star. She gasped quietly.

Hector dropped the yellow stone onto the stone patio, where it clacked off the pavement. He lifted his foot and crushed the yellow jewel under his boot heel. A crunch of glass crackled on the rocks as the jewel smashed into several broken chunks of glass.

"What sort of ruse is this?" he asked, anger filling his voice. He smashed all four of the other stones—orange, red, and ice white—the same way. He lifted his voice in anger. "Leodor, explain!"

Stammering, Leodor said, "I am at a loss, Your Majesty. If I only had a moment to inspect them, I would have seen them more clearly." His tired gaze drifted to Abraham. "You could have avoided this embarrassment. I thought that the Underlord fell too easily. This explains very much. Perhaps Arcayis wasn't the Underlord that we seek."

Abraham ground his teeth.

Clarice jumped at Leodor, jabbed her finger in his chest and said, "You saw the Underlord. We all did. He hurled bolts of lightning like javelins. And he stood like a giant. He tried to kill us all. This is not Ruger's fault! Shame on you for implying so!"

Lewis covered his mouth and chuckled underneath his breath.

Leodor shrugged his scrawny shoulders. "With or without the stones, Arcayis would still be one of the world's most formidable mystics. He didn't need all the stones to unleash the potent wrath of his craft. One stone alone would enhance such power."

"At least you have one more stone, Father," Lewis said as he looked at the crown. "Pretty."

"What, then, in the name of the Elders, happened?" King Hector asked.

The sea winds died down, and the group fell silent.

Abraham's heart deflated. At first, he hadn't wanted to go back home. The moment he realized the stones didn't work and he couldn't make it back, he wanted to go. Now, that had changed. Victory had been snatched out of his grip. *How?* He clenched his jaws. An impish face appeared in his mind, and it all came together. They had been set up. He turned and kicked the patio wall and said, "I know what happened."

All eyes fell on him.

"The Big Apple." He turned and faced them all. "That dirty little horned halfling betrayed us."

"But why?" King Hector asked.

"Because he doesn't want to accidentally be sent home, that's why." Abraham smashed his fist into his palm. "But we'll see about that." He walked away from the others and stopped at the farthest end of the patio. He wanted to be alone, but he could hear the anger and disappointment in everyone's voices. They would have to start all over again, and Lewis and Leodor were the unhappiest about all of it.

"Abraham," someone said in a soft voice. It was Clarann, a golden-haired lioness of striking beauty walking in the moonlight. "Can I have a word with you?"

"Sure you can. I deserve it."

"Not about that. I feel you did well. All that you could." She stood shoulder to shoulder beside him with her hip touching his. "Clarice wouldn't boast of your efforts if it wasn't true. She is a very straightforward young woman and full of fire."

"Yes, I can see that. She made mistakes, but she handled herself quite well."

"She gets it honestly from her father."

Abraham nodded and said, "I would have guessed that she gets it from her mother."

Clarann turned and looked at him with eyes searching for something that was lost and said, "No, it comes from her father, the man in my eyes, Ruger Slade."

ABOUT THE AUTHOR

FROM THE AUTHOR/Next Book in the Series

Thanks for reading *The King's Prisoner*! I can't tell you how much fun I am having writing this series. It is my hope that you are enjoying it just as much, and as always, I appreciate the support. Just so you know, I have no idea what is going to happen in the next book. I don't outline. Like Stephen King, I'm a fly-by-the-seat-of-your-pants writer. If I don't know what is coming, then you can't either. That's the fun part. With that said, I hope you will reach out to me if you have any questions. I love talking about my books and hashing it out with you. So, don't be shy, and drop me a note anytime.

Please leave a review. They are a huge help to me! Here is a link.

    *I'd love it if you would subscribe to my mailing list: www.craighalloran.com

    *Follow me on Bookbub at https://www.bookbub.com/authors/craig-halloran

    *On Facebook, you can find me at The Darkslayer Report or Craig Halloran.

    *Twitter, twitter, twitter. I am there, too: www.twitter.com/CraigHalloran

    *And of course, you can always email me at craig@thedarkslayer.com

See my full book list below!

ALSO BY CRAIG HALLORAN

Craig Halloran resides with his family outside his hometown of Charleston, West Virginia. When he isn't entertaining mankind, he is seeking adventure, working out, or watching sports. To learn more about him, go to: www.thedarkslayer.com.

Check out all my great stories ...

Free Books

The Darkslayer: Brutal Beginnings

Nath Dragon—Quest for the Thunderstone

The Henchmen Chronicles

The King's Henchmen

The King's Assassin

The King's Prisoner

The King's Conjurer

The King's Spies

The Odyssey of Nath Dragon Series (New Series) (Prequel to Chronicles of Dragon)

Exiled

Enslaved

Deadly

Hunted

Strife

Boxset 6-10

Collector's Edition 1-10

The Darkslayer Series 1 – (6 books)

Wrath of the Royals (Book 1)

Blades in the Night (Book 2)

Underling Revenge (Book 3)

Danger and the Druid (Book 4)

Outrage in the Outlands (Book 5)

Chaos at the Castle (Book 6)

Boxset 1-3

Boxset 4-6

Omnibus 1-6

The Darkslayer: Bish and Bone, Series 2 (10-book series)

Bish and Bone (Book 1)

Black Blood (Book 2)

Red Death (Book 3)

Lethal Liaisons (Book 4)

Torment and Terror (Book 5)

Brigands and Badlands (Book 6)

War in the Wasteland (Book 7)

Slaughter in the Streets (Book 8)

Hunt of the Beast (Book 9)

The Battle for Bone (Book 10)

Boxset 1-5

Boxset 6-10

Bish and Bone Omnibus (Books 1-10)

CLASH OF HEROES: Nath Dragon Meets the Darkslayer Miniseries

Book 1

Book 2

Book 3

The Gamma Earth Cycle

Escape from the Dominion

Flight from the Dominion

Prison of the Dominion

The Supernatural Bounty Hunter Files (10-book series)

Smoke Rising: Book 1

I Smell Smoke: Book 2

Where There's Smoke: Book 3

Smoke on the Water: Book 4

Smoke and Mirrors: Book 5

Up in Smoke: Book 6

Smoke Signals: Book 7

Holy Smoke: Book 8

Smoke Happens: Book 9

Smoke Out: Book 10

Boxset 1-5

Boxset 6-10

Collector's Edition 1-10

Zombie Impact Series

Zombie Day Care: Book 1

Zombie Rehab: Book 2

Zombie Warfare: Book 3

Boxset: Books 1-3

OTHER WORKS & NOVELLAS

The Scarab's Curse—Sword & Sorcery Novella

The Scarab's Power

The Scarab's Command

The Scarab's Trick

The Scarab's War